DEED OF MURDER

The Burren Mysteries by Cora Harrison

★ *available from Severn House*

DEED OF MURDER

Cora Harrison

This first world edition published 2011
in Great Britain and in the USA by
SEVERN HOUSE PUBLISHERS LTD of
9–15 High Street, Sutton, Surrey, England, SM1 1DF.
Trade paperback edition first published
in Great Britain and the USA 2012 by
SEVERN HOUSE PUBLISHERS LTD.

British Library Cataloguing in Publication Data

Harrison, Cora.
  Deed of murder. – (Burren mystery)
  1. Mara, Brehon of the Burren (Fictitious character) –
  Fiction. 2. Women judges – Ireland – Burren – Fiction.
  3. Burren (Ireland) – History – 16th century – Fiction.
  4. Detective and mystery stories.
  I. Title II. Series
  823.9'2-dc22

ISBN-13: 978-0-7278-8071-0 (cased)
ISBN-13: 978-1-84751-372-4 (trade paper)

All Severn House titles are printed on acid-free paper.

Severn House Publishers support The Forest Stewardship Council [FSC],
the leading international forest certification organisation. All our titles that
are printed on Greenpeace-approved FSC-certified paper carry the FSC logo.

Typeset by Palimpsest Book Production Ltd.,
Falkirk, Stirlingshire, Scotland.
Printed and bound in Great Britain by
MPG Books Ltd., Bodmin, Cornwall.

For my son, William, with much love and thanks for all his assistance while I was writing this book.

Acknowledgements

For an author who writes as many books as I do, this paying tribute to those who have helped can begin to sound repetitive, though hopefully not insincere.

Nevertheless, the debt is there, and must be paid; to family and friends who maintain interest and give encouragement; to my agent Peter Buckman who always manages to spark new ideas in me; to my editor James Nightingale who has to bear the palm among editors for being meticulous, relaxed and appreciative; and, of course, as always, thanks to those such as Professors Daniel Binchy and Fergus Kelly, who translated the Brehon laws from the complexities of medieval Irish.

Prologue

The valley hung high on the mountain slope. On either side reared the silvery heights of bare limestone, but the hollowed area itself was intensely green. Mara dismounted from her horse, handed the reins to twelve-year-old Shane, the youngest scholar at her law school, and looked around her with a smile of pleasure. As Brehon of the Burren, judge and lawgiver in that stony kingdom on the Atlantic fringe of Ireland, she knew and loved every one of its hundred square miles, but coming to the valley of the flax garden always had the thrill of discovering buried treasure.

Completely protected from the four winds, open to the sun and fertilized by a steady drift of limestone dust swept down by the winter rains, this sheltered place had the extra gift of a rich soil which was perfect for growing flax and producing enough linen to clothe all the inhabitants of the kingdom.

Once a year she and her scholars came to the valley. Once a year the ritual of an auction was held; once a year they would go through the ceremony solemnly and once a year, for the nineteen years that Mara had held the position of Brehon, the deed would be signed and the lease of this prosperous business would be granted to Cathal O'Halloran. The small clan of O'Halloran, men, women and children, were all involved in the business, sowing the new flax in the spring, extracting the linen threads from last year's rotted stalks, spinning, weaving and dyeing. And then in August the new crop was ready for reaping – and the cycle began all over again.

Nineteen-year-old Fachtnan and the two sixteen-year-olds, Moylan and Aidan, were busy tying the ponies to the rail by the entrance to the flax gardens. Fourteen-year-old Hugh was chatting easily with the wife of the 'flax king', as Cathal was known. Shane, the youngest scholar in the law school, was explaining everything to fifteen-year-old Fiona who had recently come over from Scotland to attend the school where her own father had studied side by side with Mara. Eamon, a young lawyer, who had come from the neighbouring kingdom of Thomond, across the river Shannon, and who would bring the lease back to be signed, listened with that air of sophisticated amusement which had made him rather disliked by the scholars of the Cahermacnaghten law school during the week that he had spent in the kingdom of the Burren.

'You see, this valley was the marriage portion of the great-great-grandmother of O'Brien of Arra, King Turlough's cousin,' explained Shane. 'In the old days, lots of people used to come to bid for the lease of the valley and they used to have to bid against the candle for the lease of the valley, so O'Brien of Arra keeps up the old custom.'

'All this fuss, just for that one big field!' Eamon, a much-travelled young man, sounded amused.

'Not just the field.' Moylan joined in the conversation. 'It's for everything, the spinning wheels, the weaving looms . . .' he waved a hand at the sheds.

'There's the scutching shed and all the boards . . .'

'And the dyeing vats . . .'

'And the retting ponds . . .'

Mara was amused to see hear how belligerent the boys sounded. Eamon, though full of charm, was not greatly liked by the Cahermacnaghten scholars from the moment when he had arrived, and even after a few weeks this had not changed. He had gone away for a week to the Aran Islands on an errand for O'Brien of Arra, the owner of the flax garden, and the scholars had seemed relieved by his absence.

Fiona, on the other hand, who had only arrived a few weeks ago, also, had been very well liked from the first day. Too well liked, perhaps.

'Everything's ready, Brehon.' Cathal was ushering her into the shed. This yearly ceremony was always pleasant. His wife, Gobnait, was at hand with some mead, his eldest son, Owney, with a candle and pin. Mara solemnly measured one inch from the top with the measure handed to her by Shane and then stuck the pin in.

'Light the candle, Fachtnan,' she said. He had been her eldest scholar for the last two years and she liked to give him some status. He had not been happy ever since Eamon's arrival. There was a great tension between them. She would send Eamon across the river Shannon to Thomond with the lease over to O'Brien of Arra by himself, she determined, as she watched the candle's heat begin to dissolve the wax. Normally she sent her two eldest scholars, but Eamon was a qualified lawyer, twenty-six years of age and well used to travelling. He could do the errand on his own; it would not be a good idea to impose on either the strain of a journey in each other's company.

Eamon was due, unfortunately, to return and spend another week here before moving on to the law school in Galway where he would take up a teaching post for a few years before attempting the final examinations that would admit him to the select band of Brehons. However, the last week of term was always a time when rules were relaxed and humour was good. Hopefully all would pass well in the law school before the departure of the scholars on their Easter holiday.

The shed door was now ceremoniously closed so that the inch of candle would burn steadily and for the allotted time. Mara sipped her mead and made polite conversation with Cathal and his wife. Her seven scholars stood behind her; they also had been given mead and while agreeing with Cathal that it had been a mild winter after the snow last Christmas, Mara kept a sharp eye that they were not signalling for a refill. This mead – too sweet and too tasting of fermented honey for her taste – was strong stuff.

The candle was taking a long time to burn. There had been a pause. The weather had been exhausted as a subject of conversations, polite enquiries about families had been exchanged, the prospects for the flax harvest had been thoroughly aired. Cathal as usual at this stage of the year was gloomy; he had made his usual bid of two ounces of silver and was explaining why this could not be improved. Mara listened, nodding her head in an understanding way. O'Brien of Arra would be happy with that. He had sent a message by Eamon last week saying gloomily that he didn't suppose that any more would be forthcoming and Mara had not pressed Cathal to offer more. It was an uncertain business.

So much depended on the right weather at the right time; a mixture of rain and sun while the plants were growing, then sun as the field burst into blue flower and then some dry days while the plants were pulled by hand from the ground and dried in tent-shaped stooks. And after that a period of wet weather to start the stalk to rot and release their precious fibres.

Surely the candle did not take as long as this to burn in the normal way? Mara peered at it. Yes, her instinct that the time was longer this year than other years had been correct. Now she could see that just below the pin was a hard lump of tallow; the candle burned down on one side, but on the other the pin still held, stuck fast by that small knob.

Cathal shuffled his feet uneasily. Eamon gave an impatient sigh. Moylan yawned noisily and then stared with great interest at his feet when he saw Mara's eyes on him. Cathal's son, Owney, moved to fill Mara's cup with more mead, but she shook her head firmly. His father, however, accepted the refill and swallowed it quickly, his eyes on the piece of vellum lying on the table before them. Neither Cathal nor Gobnait, his wife, could read or write but he would solemnly make his cross, placed in the spot indicated by Mara, and when the signed leaf of vellum came back from O'Brien of Arra, the deed of contract would be carefully locked into the small high cupboard next to the chimney in their house.

At that moment came a diversion. There was a noise of horse's feet on the flagstones outside the shed. A shouted enquiry. The door to the shed opened just as the last stubborn piece of tallow began to melt and the pin began to slope down. This was the moment for the last bid in any auction and as always – almost as though he sat in a roomful of eager bidders, Cathal repeated his earlier bid of two ounces of silver and then looked up.

A man had come in through the door. A low-statured, squat figure. Mara recognized him instantly. He was a farmer from North Baur on the High Burren, directly below the Aillwee Mountain.

'Am I in time . . .?' The words had hardly left his mouth when he instantly summed up the scene: the table; the unsigned deed; the candle; the pin with its head drooping downwards, but still held by one sliver of wax.

'I bid two and a half ounces of silver,' said Muiris O'Hynes. And into the dead silence the pin fell with a small tap on to the wood of the table.

Nothing could be changed from that second onwards – no further bid could be accepted. Muiris O'Hynes – a man without lineage or clan, a successful farmer, but an outsider – this man was now the holder of the lease from the first day in May 1511 until the following year until its eve, the feast of Bealtaine, the following year.

And what would happen to the O'Halloran family, to the O'Halloran clan, wondered Mara as she rode soberly home down the steep road that led to the valley of the flax. Would Muiris continue to employ them? Or would he, as was more likely, employ his own large family, his workers and some casual labour. Muiris was a man whose touch was magic; they said in the kingdom of the Burren that everything he touched turned to gold. He had signed his name to the deed with an air of suppressed excitement, had looked all over the sheds, inspected the spinning wheels and the looms, knelt down to pull a few weeds from the growing crop and then, with a few brief businesslike words to Cathal, he had mounted his horse and rode away.

What would be the consequences of his sudden, impulsive purchase?

One

Dia fis cía is breicheamh I ngach cúis
(To Find Out Who Is A Judge For Every Case).

The law of the land is the responsibility of the king. He may delegate that responsibility to his Brehon, but if the Brehon is unable to swear to the truth of his judgement then the king himself must be the one to hear a case, to allocate blame and to pass sentence.

Fiona MacBetha disappeared just before midnight at the official christening party for Cormac, the baby son of King Turlough Donn O'Brien and his wife Mara. The festivities took place in the large upstairs hall at Ballinalacken Castle, which was a wedding gift from the king to his new wife. It was a perfect place for a festive gathering; a huge room with fireplaces burning tree-sized logs at either end, a minstrels' gallery above and large mullioned windows overlooking the Atlantic Ocean. The guests were a mixture of young and old, mostly Turlough's royal relations: his son and heir, Conor, with his wife Ellice; his daughter, Ragnelt, and her husband, Donán O'Kennedy, or Donán the landless, as he was known. There was also the king's cousin, the Bishop of Kilfenora and some of his allies from other kingdoms. The scholars from Cahermacnaghten law school and some of their friends, young people from the kingdom of the Burren, were there also. And, of course, the godparents of this important child, fifteen-year-old Nuala O'Davoren, the baby's godmother, and Ulick Burke, Lord of Clanricard, Turlough's friend and ally, the godfather.

Up to that moment Fiona had been the focus of all eyes. Every man in the room had wanted to dance with her; every woman had envied her looks. She was fifteen years old and gorgeous – a tiny girl, but with a perfect figure, perfect features, hair like spun gold, gleaming white teeth, eyes as blue as a sapphire and a laugh that rippled like the strings of a zither.

She had been dancing with twelve-year-old Shane, the youngest pupil in the law school, laughing into his face, letting him whirl her around, pulling off the ribbon that braided her hair into one thick plait and allowing her blonde curls to float free.

Mara had smiled tolerantly to herself as she looked on. Fiona was a flirt. She knew quite well that the two eldest from the law school were madly in love with her. Fachtnan and Eamon were, from the time that she had appeared, almost at daggers drawn about her and the position had remained. She had deliberately walked away and chosen Shane who was too young to appreciate the honour done to him. There were times when Mara had half-regretted her decision to admit Fiona, daughter of a renowned Scottish Brehon, and an old school friend of hers. Mara and Robert MacBretha had been amiable rivals for the top place at Cahermacnaghten Law School more than twenty years ago and Fiona had inherited her father's brains. The girl was bright, clever and funny, a good scholar with a keen legal brain; but her spectacular looks caused trouble in a law school full of boys.

'How strange to have a girl law student!' exclaimed the Bishop of Kilfenora, breaking into her thoughts. He looked with disapproval at the wild abandon of Fiona's dance. Now all the young people had gathered in a circle around the two and were beating time with their hands – applauding the performance. Fachtnan, though he had a yearning look in his dark eyes, was laughing at the spectacle of his beloved dancing with a twelve-year-old, but Eamon had turned his back and was busy chatting earnestly with one of the king's friends and allies.

'Not the first for Cahermacnaghten,' Mara reminded Bishop Mauritius with a smile. This man had to be handled carefully. Not only was he bishop of the kingdom, but he was also a member of the ruling royal family, a cousin of her husband, King Turlough O'Brien. He was the cause that her baby son Cormac was having an official christening a good eleven months after his birth. The bishop had departed for Rome just before the child was born and had lingered there during the winter months. Little Cormac, who had a premature and difficult birth, had been hastily baptized by Brigid, Mara's housekeeper, on the traumatic day of his birth, so the official ceremony had waited for the bishop. Mara set herself to entertain him by asking some questions about Rome and about his travels.

And after that she lost sight of Fiona.

If only that silly business with Ulick Burke, Lord of Clanrickard, had not distracted her. Ulick, in full flow, drew every eye to him. Mara found him a tiresome man, quite exasperating at times, but even she could not deny his ability to tell a good story. Now, despite herself, she could not help listening to him as he took his place in front of the huge fireplace, his small slim figure standing out against the more burly stature of the other guests. In any case, he was her husband's greatest friend and she had to be courteous towards him. Turlough O'Brien, King of Thomond, Corcomroe and Burren was never happier than when entertaining friends and relations, but his favourite guest was always Ulick Burke, Lord of Clanrickard with its extensive lands north of Galway, a man famous for having more wives than could be counted!

A large crowd was beginning to gather around them – Ulick was always amusing. But the young people continued dancing, taking new partners now. To Mara's satisfaction she saw that Nuala, a distant relation and a great pet of hers, was being led out by Seamus MacCraith, the poet, the most handsome young man present.

Nuala, from the time that she was quite a young child, had been in love with Fachtnan. He was four years the older, but, even as a ten-year-old, had always been kind to the dark-eyed, intensely intelligent daughter of the physician. Things had not gone well for Nuala in the last year and she now had accepted that Fachtnan's feelings for her were just brotherly. Mara hoped that she would fall in love with Seamus MacCraith, though she feared that the young poet, like the rest of the young men in the room, was smitten by Fiona's extraordinary beauty. Still, Fiona was nowhere to be seen now after her spectacular dance with Shane, so Mara turned a polite face towards Ulick, her husband's best friend and godfather to her son Cormac.

'And there, in the middle of London, there is His Majesty, King Henry, the eighth of that name, and there he is in his great palace at Whitehall, prancing around like a mummer, dressed in silks and velvets and every inch of him hung with gold.' Ulick, though such a small, slim, middle-aged man, lifted his head, expanded his chest and became before their eyes the tall young King of England, roaring out jokes and commands in English and reverting quickly to the Gaelic tongue to paint the scene at Whitehall Palace for his audience, allowing them to picture the arbour of gold on wheels, screened from the audience, and then the dramatic moment when the curtain was drawn back to show the king and his friends with names from old romances, moulded from gold, hanging around their necks.

'And then in comes young O'Donnell, Hugh Dubh, and him bowing and scraping. "*May it please your lordship, certainly Your Majesty, indeed and I will, my lord king.*" That's the way he was going on, whining like a beggar . . .' The mockery was cruel, if funny, and probably untrue, thought Mara; the chances were that young Hugh O'Donnell would have spoken in Gaelic, not in bad English, and have allowed his Brehon to translate for him. It amused the company, though. Donán O'Kennedy, Turlough's son-in-law, was convulsed with laughter, his broad shoulders shaking with mirth.

'Tell us about what happened to the gold, afterwards, Ulick,' he called, looking for approval from his father-in-law, Turlough, who was roaring with laughter. But Ulick was wise enough to know that he had reached the climax of his story with the submission and humiliation of O'Donnell so he ignored Donán and looked around for more wine.

'And he gave up his title of King of Donegal for an English title?' marvelled Turlough.

'*Sure and why wouldn't I?*' whined Ulick, still in character as Hugh O'Donnell. '"*Didn't I get masses of gold and silver and promises of more? And now I am an English knight.*"' He tossed his head in a young man's gesture and so good an actor was he that Mara could almost imagine O'Donnell's long mane of black hair instead of the thinning blonde-grey hair of this middle-aged man.

'We'll show him, won't we?' roared Turlough, his arm around Ulick's shoulders. 'We'll teach O'Donnell what it is to be Irish.

Let him not come anywhere near here with his English soldiers and his English guns. We'll serve him the way that we served the Great Earl last year. Send him back up north with his tail between his legs – a man who could give up being king and leader of his clan in order to get empty titles from the King of England!'

'Fill up your glasses, everyone! Let's drink to King Turlough Donn of Thomond, Corcomroe and Burren,' shouted Ulick, and the servants at the castle scurried around with their flagons.

And the laughter, chatter, music, dancing had gone on until the early hours of the morning.

A good excuse for a party, anyway, thought Mara, looking affectionately across at her husband who was laughing loudly at a joke told by Ulick Burke, godfather to the little prince. This beautiful castle, newly renovated by Turlough for his second wife, was the ideal setting for a gathering such as this. It was good for her scholars, too, to mix with the great men of the three kingdoms. Soon the eldest three would have finished their studies and would be looking for a position as *aigne* – lawyer – in some noble household. So far only Eamon had been making opportunities to talk with these powerful men and women. Fachtnan, Moylan and Aidan had shyly kept their distance and Mara resolved that she must remedy this. Fachtnan, in particular, should be looking for a position as he would, hopefully, pass his final examination in June. Mara looked about for him, but could not see him, and was distracted by Donán, Turlough's son-in-law, who wanted to discuss with her his problems with sore throats.

'You should talk to Nuala about this,' she told him, trying not to be irritated with a young man in the prime of life, who seemed continually concerned with his health. 'Look, she's over there. Even though she has not yet qualified, she's the best physician that I have ever known; she'll tell you all about sore throats and what to do about them.' She had half-thought of suggesting that he talk to Ragnelt, his wife, about it, but the young woman had such a bored, withdrawn look, that she changed her mind.

'Brehon, you must dance with me.' Ulick claimed her and, though she disliked him, she was relieved to get away from

Donán. For once, Ulick did not sharpen his tongue on her, but restricted himself to praising Turlough and commenting on his bravery and his popularity.

'It's no wonder,' he said with what seemed like genuine sincerity, 'that he is such a thorn in the side of those who would make Ireland a vassal of England. You know what the Great Earl said of him, don't you?'

'"*The worst man in the whole of Ireland.*" I think that Turlough took that as a compliment,' said Mara with a smile.

'Goodness only knows what he thinks of him now after the battle last year,' commented Ulick. 'Turlough should be careful. A man like The Great Earl has everything to lose.'

A man that has everything to lose. The words immediately brought back to Mara the scene at the flax garden after the successful bid from Muiris O'Hynes. Cathal, his wife and his family had stood there in such terrible anguish. Owney, the son, had sworn an oath and had slammed his fist on to the wooden table with such force that a crack had appeared. Gobnait had set her lips and looked grimly at Muiris who was now going to rob her family of their livelihood. And Cathal, as white as the bales of linen in the background, had snatched up a knife. It had taken all of the strength that Eamon and Fachtnan possessed, between them, to hang on to his arms and prevent him from hurling it at Muiris. Cathal had everything to lose. The business that he had built up so painstakingly and well over the years was now to be taken from him.

Muiris, in the meantime, had walked away. He was a sensible man and knew when words only made a bad situation worse. Mara wondered whether he now regretted his purchase. That it had been a last minute decision was shown by his late arrival.

I think I'll talk to him before sending Eamon over across the Shannon to O'Brien of Arra; Eamon and I will go over to Poulnabrucky first thing in the morning and see whether he wants to change his mind. I can easily draw up a new deed of contract for the lease if he does so, decided Mara. Meanwhile, she smiled automatically at Ulick's witticisms and her feet nimbly followed the lilting tune of the reel played by the fiddlers, seated high above the crowd in a small balcony that overlooked the great hall at the castle.

I'll talk to Eamon tonight and arrange everything, thought Mara. She knew that the picture of Cathal's stricken face would come between her and sleep if she did not do something before she retired to her rest.

But when she looked for Eamon she could not see him.

Two

Triad 75
There are three qualities to be admired in a woman:
reticence, virtue, industry.
Triad 88
The three glories of a gathering are: a beautiful woman,
a good horse, a swift hound.
Triad 180
The three steadiness of good womanhood are: a steady tongue,
a steady virtue, a steady housewifery.

Two of her scholars missing! And Eamon the lawyer, also! Mara sat up in bed and gazed in bewilderment at Brigid her housekeeper. A quick glance at the window confirmed that it was still early morning. She would have expected that they would all have been still asleep after the late night of dancing – it must have been the early hours of that morning when they eventually went to their beds – the boys to their leather tents set up in the field at the side of the castle and Fiona to a small wall chamber within the castle itself.

'Moylan told me about the two lads,' said Brigid, 'and then I went to find Fiona and discovered that she was missing too.' Her mouth was as tight as the braids of her severely plaited red hair and her eyes were full of fury. Brigid and her husband, Cumhal, felt themselves responsible for the scholars and when at the law school the scholars' houses were directly under their supervision while Mara herself lived in the Brehon's house, a few hundred yards down the road from Cahermacnaghten law school. Here, in a castle crammed with guests and soldiers, supervision was not so easy.

'I'll eat my breakfast and then I'll see Moylan and find out what he knows.' Mara hoped that she sounded calm, but inside she was uneasy. There was something strange about this. The scholars were going to stay the weekend at the castle, join in all the festivities and then on Monday return to their studies at Cahermacnaghten law school – less than a mile away, just over the border between the neighbouring kingdoms of Corcomroe and Burren.

It was nearing the end of the Hilary term. The scholars would return to their homes in a week's time. Moylan and Aidan would ride together towards the south-west of Thomond, Fachtnan and young Shane would go north once Shane's father, the Brehon who served the O'Neill, Earl of Tyrone, had arrived. Fachtnan would ride with them as his home at Oriel was on the way.

Eamon would be the first to leave. This morning he was due to take the deed for the flax garden to be signed by O'Brien of Arra. He would then return to Cahermacnaghten with the signed deed, which would be handed over to Muiris O'Hynes, and after another few days would depart for the MacEgan law school in Galway. The other boys would leave for their holidays soon afterwards, but Fiona would spend Easter with Mara – the journey to Scotland, with the possibility of rough seas, would not be worth the risk for so short a holiday.

'Aidan woke me up and said that Fachtnan had gone, and so was his horse.' Moylan had an amused look on his face.

'And Eamon was missing too,' mused Mara.

'That's right. As soon as I got the sleep out of my eyes, I saw he wasn't there on the other side of the tent. And when we checked the stables we saw that Fiona's pony was gone as well as their horses.'

'Perhaps they've just gone for an early morning ride,' said Mara. But it was no longer that early. And Brigid had confirmed that the trio had not visited the kitchen. They would be hungry now. And why Fachtnan? Surely he would be an unwelcome third if Eamon and Fiona had decided on an early morning ride. While she was pondering over this, Brigid came back. She shook her head as she came in.

'Did she take anything with her?' Mara began to get worried. Surely Fiona, with all the bright future ahead of her as a lawyer, even a Brehon, would not have done something silly like eloping with Eamon? And where did Fachtnan fit into the picture? He was hopelessly in love with Fiona, of course, but she seemed to be just sisterly towards him.

'Not a thing — went in what she stood up in!' said Brigid emphatically.

'Eamon left his clothes, too — but he did take one of his satchels,' said Moylan.

One of his satchels, and no clothes — but why take a satchel? Mara was preoccupied, trying to think back to the evening but could not recollect seeing any of the three after midnight.

'I'm sure that I would have woken up if Eamon came in and Aidan says the same about Fachtnan. I'd say that they went off at midnight,' said Moylan breaking into her thoughts.

'What a stupid thing to do,' scolded Brigid. 'Dangerous, too!'

'They'd have been quite safe riding by night — as bright as day it was. I was saying that to Aidan when we went back to the tents.' Moylan still sounded amused. It was normally Aidan and he who were being scolded for doing stupid things. It was a change for him to have his seniors in trouble. 'Aidan called out to me that Fachtnan had not come back from the castle and when I looked into my tent I could see that Eamon wasn't there either. I was a bit surprised, because I hadn't seen either of them for quite a time — nor Fiona, either.'

Nor did I, thought Mara. She had been concerned about Fiona only because she was a girl, and a beautiful girl, and she was responsible to her father for her welfare. But when she searched back into her mind she realized that she had seen neither of the boys after midnight, either.

But were the three young people from Cahermacnaghten law school, Eamon, Fachtnan and Fiona, present? Mara scanned her memory, hoping that one, at least, of the faces would appear.

Or had they all stolen away by then?

Brigid waited until the boys had gone back out to join some of the men-at-arms at a spot of sword fighting practice before voicing her opinion. She had been Mara's nurse after the death of the small child's mother and she had brought her up, adored her, scolded her, thought she was the cleverest, prettiest girl in the whole of Ireland while relentlessly enforcing good behaviour and hard work. Since Mara had qualified and taken on the whole business of the law school and, later, of the position of Brehon, or lawgiver, law-enforcer, over the whole kingdom of the Burren, Brigid had always been at her side, always working faster than a woman of half her age could do. Mara sometimes wondered what she would have done, how she could have possibly managed all of her affairs without Brigid and her husband Cumhal.

'There's never been a day's peace in Cahermacnaghten since that Eamon arrived,' Brigid was saying. 'It's a pity that you ever said "yes" to him, Brehon. None of our lads like him.'

'Well, they have to get used to new scholars,' pointed out Mara. 'After all, Enda left last summer and I haven't replaced him yet.'

'Scholars are no problem,' said Brigid. 'Even Fiona is not a problem – a bit of a flirt, and she does make the boys silly, but she fits in. She's not a problem in the way that Eamon is a problem.'

'Well, he'll be gone soon,' began Mara, but Brigid interrupted her.

'I think that he was just making use of you, Brehon, mark my words. He's too sure of himself. You should have heard him about that auction up in the flax garden. "I'd have got a better price for it," he says – just as though he knew it all. "I'd have set a new auction going and got the two of them bidding against each other. That's what I would have done and O'Brien of Arra would have rewarded me with a nice piece of silver." And then he turns and tries to give Fiona a squeeze and I could see that Fachtnan was full of black anger. I watched him, Brehon. He had his two fists clenched up as though for two pins he would have hit Eamon in the mouth.'

'I'll keep an eye on them all,' promised Mara. She wished that Brigid had not told her all of this. It deepened her worries.

'So you think that Fachtnan went off because he could not bear the situation between Fiona and Eamon?' The question was out before Mara almost knew that she had formed it. But

she regretted asking it when she saw the worried look on
Brigid's face. It enhanced her own fears.

'I don't know what to think, Brehon. I'll tell you that
without a word of a lie,' said Brigid eventually. 'All I know
is that Eamon makes trouble wherever he goes. One of these
days, mark my words, Fachtnan will not put up with it any
longer. And then Master Eamon had better look out for
himself.'

Three

Exodus 21:24
Thou shalt give life for life, tooth for tooth

Brecha Crólige
(Laws on Bloodletting)

The penalty for a killing is two-fold. There is a fixed fine of forty-two séts, or twenty-one ounces of silver or twenty-one cows. In addition the killer must pay a fine based on the honour-price of the victim – lóg n-enach, (literally, the price of his face).

'Eamon! Dead! He can't be.' Mara, conscious of the stupidity of her words, stared at Cumhal, her farm manager – a man who never opened his mouth before he was sure of his facts.

And yet it did seem impossible that all that liveliness, all that burning ambition, that handsome face, that clever brain, that it all should be dead.

'That's right,' he nodded. 'Muiris Hynes came to fetch me. He was the one that found the body. There it was lying in the flax garden – not a soul near it. And the place full of O'Halloran workers – none of them seeing a thing!'

'Anything with him?' asked Mara.

'Just an empty satchel lying beside the body.'

'Empty!' she echoed. Why had Eamon taken an empty satchel with him?

'It was open,' said Cumhal watching her face. 'Looked like someone might have taken something out of it . . .'

'What about his horse?' she asked.

'Fachtnan is seeing to it, has taken it back to the stable at Cahermacnaghten. The poor beast had broken the skin on his knees.'

'Fachtnan,' echoed Mara. 'But, but where did he come from? Is he back?'

Cumhal looked at her in a surprised way. 'He's been at the law school all day, Brehon. He's been sitting in the schoolhouse studying. I'm not sure when he came back from Ballinalacken, from the castle.'

'I see.' But I don't see, thought Mara. I had imagined that he was with Eamon. 'And Fiona?' she asked. Perhaps a sudden urge to study had come over both of her senior scholars.

'Haven't seen her,' said Cumhal. 'Fachtnan was the only one there.' A man of few words, he didn't question her, just stood waiting for orders.

'Where is the body now?' asked Mara.

'Where it was found, Brehon,' replied Cumhal. 'Up in the flax garden. Muiris said he'd stay with it until I came back. I've got a couple of men waiting with a cart and a litter, but I wanted to tell you first.'

Mara reflected. The less said the better at the moment. Her guests were all on a hunting party up in the Aillwee Mountain. The weather was fine so they would probably spend a few vigorous hours pursuing wolves in the centre of the high Burren before returning for their evening meal to Ballinalacken Castle. She looked around and saw Nessa, Brigid's helper in the kitchen back at the law school and brought here to supplement the efforts of the castle staff for this festive weekend. She beckoned to her.

'Nessa,' she said quietly, 'would you just give a message to Brigid. Ask her to tell my lord, the king, if he returns before I do, that I have to go across to the Burren on important business.'

'Yes, Brehon . . .'

Mara had already begun to turn away when she realized that Nessa was still standing, unmoving, her mouth slightly open and her vacant pale-blue eyes troubled.

'What's the matter, Nessa?' she asked, trying to curb her impatience. Nessa was not too bright and liable to lose the first few wits that she possessed if you rushed her.

'Brigid said to tell you, Brehon, that Fiona is asleep in her chamber.' Nessa looked relieved that she had managed to deliver her message.

'Thank you, Nessa,' said Mara. How strange, she thought.

Three of her scholars were missing this morning – and all three horses were gone as well, but now two of them were back – and presumably their horses, but the third was lying dead in a lonely valley at the side of a mountain in the Burren.

'Well, don't disturb her,' she said aloud. 'But tell my other scholars, Moylan, Aidan, Hugh and Shane, to saddle their horses and to come with me. And Nuala, too.' Nuala was by now a more than competent physician. She would be able to estimate when death had occurred and . . .

'What happened to him?' she asked aloud as Nessa went running back towards the castle kitchen.

'I couldn't tell for sure, Brehon,' said Cumhal in his usual reserved manner. This meant, of course, that he had a good idea, but she didn't press him. Soon enough she would come face to face with the body of Eamon and then she would have to make up her mind. Was it an unfortunate accident – or something more serious?

Nuala was looking well, thought Mara, as she briefly told her the facts. She had always been tall for her age, but now, at only fifteen, she looked at least seventeen. The year at Thomond, where she had been working alongside the royal physician, Donough O'Hickey, a man whose writings were famous even in far-flung places such as Italy, had done Nuala an immense amount of good. Intelligent and knowledgeable she had always been, but now she was poised and confident. She said nothing; but unlike the four boys she did not appear worried or apprehensive, just rode along, busy with her own thoughts.

The air was crisp and cool as they turned to ride up the road that led up towards the flax garden. The road had been carefully made for laden carts as well as horses and it wound a leisurely way around and in between the sharply pointed hills of glittering limestone, the ditches on either side of the road filled with primroses and purple violets. The wind was from the north and it blew strongly, bringing a fine dust of bitter-tasting limestone down from the mountain with it.

They passed the flax workers' settlement of small, circular, stone huts. Smoke drifted from some of these and a few curious elderly women, babies in arms, came out and then returned to their huts. The news had not reached them yet, surmised Mara, as she guided her horse to the centre of the track for the last steep climb.

The small hanging valley was sheltered from the wind. To Mara's surprise only one figure stood near to the body – she had expected a crowd. An unceasing humming noise came from the spinning wheel shed and the rattle of looms from the weaving shed. Several men were dunking large hanks of woven flax into the dye tubs and draping them over a horizontal pole to dry. Others were in the scutching sheds, vigorously banging the plants with wooden mallets and then combing the flax fibres free from the pieces of stem which still clung to them. The O'Halloran clan were wasting no time. Every last ounce of the crop of 1510 had to be turned into linen before May Day – after that date all would belong to Muiris O'Hynes.

'It's here,' said Cumhal.

The large field where the flax grew was completely enclosed by very thin flagstones, each as tall as a man. They had been hewn – perhaps thousands of years ago – from the limestone rock that surrounded the valley. Inside that sheltered space the flax grew tall, protected from the winds and exposed to the sunlight, its rays pouring heat straight down in the midday and in the early morning and late evening bouncing off the dazzling white of the limestone flags.

A pathway, just wide enough for a small cart, lay between the flagstones and the mountainside, and it was there that Eamon lay.

No flax grew here but fine, delicate grasses had sprung up, growing through the limestone. Scattered through the grass were thousands of tiny daffodils, turning their trumpets towards the sun's warmth. Near to the pond the kingcups shone like small brass plates. The grass seemed to have grown inches since she had been here on the day of the auction, less than a week ago, and the tiny valley was like a symphony of green and yellow, the colours blending subtly against the dazzling white of the background.

Mara did not linger to look at the flowers. She and her

companions tied their horses and ponies to the long bar outside
it and then walked forward in silence. Her whole attention
was on the figure stretched out on the hard, stony ground at
the edge of the valley. She knelt beside him filled with a
passionate anger – whatever few foibles and conceits he had,
he did not deserve this.

The four young boys knelt too, awkwardly, overawed by
death in one who, only a few days ago, had laughed and teased,
worked and played alongside them.

Nuala, though, did not kneel. She stood very upright,
looking all around her, at the hill above the pathway, at the
tumbled stones on the ground amongst the grasses. After a
long, appraising glance around, and upwards at the mountainside, she knelt beside the body and touched it with sure,
unfaltering hands.

After a moment she looked up at Cumhal. 'Broken his neck?'
she queried with a lift of her dark eyebrows.

'That's what I thought.' Cumhal nodded and Mara drew in
a breath of relief. This was just a tragic accident. The young
man had probably been thrown from his horse, had tumbled
down the steep slope of the stony hill, had fallen awkwardly
and then broken his neck. Looking upwards she could see the
traces of a narrow pathway high above their heads. She was
about to say something when she noticed Cumhal's eyes were
still resting on Nuala – almost as though he expected her to
say something else.

'Funny bruise on his neck, though. Just here. Almost like a
blow.' She looked at Cumhal. 'What about the horse? Where
was that found?'

'Turned up at Cahermacnaghten – trotted in through the
gates – looking the worse for wear. I'd say it had done quite
a journey.' Cumhal gave the facts quickly, still looking at Nuala
in an enquiring way.

'A journey? How far?' Mara was still wondering how Eamon
had ended up in this place. Was his death then connected with
the flax garden?

'Could have gone over to Thomond, then across the
Shannon, and back, perhaps.' Cumhal had read her mind.

To Thomond. Mara's eyes were on the opened satchel beside

the body before she turned to Muiris who had been standing quietly, well away from the body, just beside the barn where the spinning wheels had been set up.

'Come and join us, Muiris,' she invited. 'You found him?'

'That's right, Brehon. I was just having a wander around – just making plans, you know. Not wanting to get in the way or anything.'

He had the right to evaluate the property that he had leased, but Mara guessed that he would not be a very welcome visitor. She could understand why he hovered on the edge, keeping away from the busy workers, but also noting how the various procedures worked: how the flax went from scutching, heckling and combing in one shed; on to the next shed to be spun; then some of the spun threads to be dyed, but most straight to the next shed to be woven into lengths of stuff, ready to be sewn into the *léinte*, those straight, long-sleeved garments – either knee-length or full-length – that everyone in the kingdom from cradle to deathbed wore every day and night of their lives.

'So you noticed the body,' she said aloud, and he nodded.

'Didn't see it for a while because of all the limestone and his cloak being the same colour . . . I was looking the other way, of course, looking over towards the sheds. But then I noticed him.'

'Was he still warm?' asked Nuala.

'Not warm, but not stiff.' Muiris nodded. 'Not too long dead, I'd say. You see that bit of blood there on his chin – well that hadn't dried too well when I saw him first. It wasn't that black colour then.'

'And how long had you been here when you discovered him?' asked Mara.

'Only a few minutes, I'd say,' replied Muiris looking very directly at her.

Mara looked around. There was something rather strange about the intense lack of interest from the O'Halloran clan. The hum of the spinning wheels and the clank of the looms continued without hesitation. Children scurried from shed to shed carrying and fetching, casting scared glances towards the little group on the edge of the valley, but no adults were to be seen. There was no sign of O'Halloran himself and yet she would have imagined him to be the sort of man who would be continually in evidence, continually exhorting and supervising. She rose to her feet.

'Stay there with the body for the moment, Cumhal,' she said as she walked towards the weaving shed.

After the bright sunlight, it took her eyes a few minutes to get used to the darkness within, but then figures and objects became visible. There were three large flat looms set up within the space; natural, cream-coloured cloth on two of them, the third was a dark red. Cathal O'Halloran was there beside this one, not working a loom, but gazing fixedly at the shuttle as it passed swiftly across from one man to another, carrying the dyed thread over and under the warp thread. He stiffened when he saw Mara and then slowly and reluctantly came across to her.

'You know why I am here, Cathal,' said Mara crisply. She was conscious of feeling angry, but tried to be fair. Yes, every minute would be important to the O'Halloran clan and in the normal way of things nothing could be allowed to distract from the work. But a sudden and violent death was not normal.

'I heard that there had been an accident.' Cathal muttered the words, hardly looking at her.

Mara let that pass. 'Summon all of your workers,' she said with authority, 'and bring them over to where the body lies.'

Not giving him a chance to reply or to raise objections, she turned and went back to the place where poor Eamon lay.

'Stand beside me,' she said to her five scholars when she returned. She took up position with her back to the steeply rising side of the mountain, facing across the valley.

They came slowly from the sheds, dyeing vats and retting ponds. There was something unnatural about the slow pace at which they came, almost as though each person hung back and hoped another would go ahead. There was something very strange, also, about the lack of sound. The noise from the sheds had ceased, but the workers did not fill the silence with questions or exclamations. They came up and stood in a long line with their backs to the tall slabs that enclosed the precious flax crop.

And they looked at her and the scholars.

No one seemed to look at the body on the ground.

Or at Muiris O'Hynes, the man who had found Eamon.

If he had not been there to raise the alarm would the body have been tipped into one of those deep holes that were to be found everywhere on this stony mountain?

Four

Cáin Lánamma
(The Laws of Marriage)

If the divorce takes place while the flax is still growing the wife is only entitled to a cup of linseed oil. If the stalks of the flax have been pulled and bound into sheaves, the wife is entitled to a ninth share. When the sheaves are dry and the flax beaten, the wife is entitled to a sixth share. If they have been scutched, then half goes to the wife. If they have been woven, the wife takes half of the cloth.

The sheds now appeared empty. All the workers had arrived and stood ranged up before her. About twenty adults and numerous children, thought Mara. They were a toil-worn set of people, hands roughened by the hard work. Some had hands stained red from the red dye made from the roots of the madder plants, others had pieces of fibre and seeds still stuck to their clothing; many hunched from long hours spent over a loom or a spinning wheel.

The last to come out was Gobnait, Cathal's wife. Mara observed a quick look flashed between husband and wife, but then Gobnait cast down her eyes. Puzzling, thought Mara. Why the constraint and the feeling of awkwardness? However, there had been a death, perhaps a violent death, and death was always disturbing.

The people of the Burren, especially the four main clans, the O'Lochlainns, the O'Briens, the MacNamaras and the O'Connors, had confidence in Mara. They knew her well, had listened to her judgements, brought their legal affairs and their problems to her, but these people, the O'Hallorans, were not a Burren clan; they came from an isolated place beyond Kinvarra, a semi-island, accessible only at low tide, in the sea of Galway Bay. They spent the winter there and then every spring, in carts, on donkeys or on foot, they moved from that barren, salt-encrusted patch of land into this rich mountain valley on the Burren, grew the flax and turned it into linen.

What was now going to happen to them and to the children that they bore in such numbers?

'I've asked Cathal to give me a few minutes of your time,' began Mara, eyeing the way the O'Halloran clan seemed to squeeze back against the tall flagstones, almost as though they feared the body of the young man lying so still there on the opposite side of the pathway.

'I would just like to ask if any one of you, this morning,' she continued, 'saw this young man, Eamon the lawyer, this man who has been killed? Did anyone see him come into the flax garden or ride along the mountain pass?' The easy question first, she thought.

Heads were shaken as she looked from face from face, but no one spoke, not even Cathal.

Mara's face hardened. Surely someone must have noticed Eamon if he came along the road to the valley. He would have been conspicuous on his horse in this lonely place.

'And no one heard anything?'

Again the heads were shaken.

'And what about the children?' Now she spoke directly to the dozens of children grouped in front of their parents. They stared back at her. Was there a look of apprehension in those dark eyes? Or were they, perhaps, just shy?

'None of us know anything, Brehon.' Now Cathal spoke out, his tone loud and confident as always, but his eyes were watchful. 'We're all so busy, trying to get two months' work into two weeks,' he continued. 'So if . . .'

His meaning was obvious and Mara gave a resigned nod. Why should she have any suspicion of them? What good would it do any of them to be involved in the death of a young lawyer without any real connections to the Burren? There was only one person on the Burren – to her knowledge – who might have wished for Eamon to disappear.

Where was Fachtnan? Surely he could not still be attending to the horse. One of the farm workers could have done that task. Surely he would realize that she would go straight to the scene of the death. Even if he had gone over to Ballinalacken Castle first, he would have found that she was missing and would have guessed where she had gone. Surely he would have arrived at the flax garden by now.

She gave one last look around.

'You can take the body back to the law school now,' she said to Cumhal. 'Send a messenger to Blár and ask him to make a coffin.' She lowered her voice. 'I think we will have to bury him here at Noughaval – it's pointless sending the body back across the Shannon to the law school at Redwood. He has no living near relations; I know that.'

'I'll go back with Cumhal and have a proper look at him then before he is coffined,' said Nuala unemotionally. 'You'll probably want to have a look around, Mara, so I won't wait for you.' She nodded a dark head towards the path. 'And what about this satchel?' She picked up the leather bag, opened it widely, looked into it and then closed it again. 'Nothing in it,' she said.

'I'll take that,' said Mara. She, also, glanced inside, but there was no scroll of vellum, no deed of contract. So she closed it and placed it inside one of the bags that hung from beside her saddle.

And then they waited while Cumhal and Danann lifted the body into the cart. When it was settled Cumhal and Nuala mounted on their horses and the sad procession made its slow way down the mountainside.

'I'll come back in a couple of days,' said Mara to her scholars when the cart had lumbered beyond their sight. 'By then some people may have recollected noticing something. Or perhaps one of the children may be sensible enough to tell their parents whether they saw Eamon the lawyer during the afternoon.'

She nodded to Moylan to fetch her horse and took leave of Cathal and his wife, watching the relief in both sets of eyes as the preparations for departure were completed. She mounted her horse, waited until the others were on the backs of their ponies and then moved off at a stately pace, lingering by the entrance to the flax garden until all of the O'Halloran clan had returned to their work. Muiris, she noticed, remained – a low, squat, watchful figure.

'We'll search the road coming up for signs that Eamon
and his horse rode up this way,' she told her scholars and
waited until they were all busy arguing over the age of horse
droppings before beckoning to Shane, the smallest and most
unobtrusive of her boys.

'Just go up to that path up there and see whether you can
find any signs of Eamon having come from the opposite side,
from the Galway side, Shane,' she said quietly and watched
while he tied his horse to a bush and climbed in catlike fashion
to the small path that ran above their heads.

He was back very quickly and he had something in his hand,
something so unmistakeable that all of the others immediately
stopped looking around and came across to look.

It was a circle of pink linen ribbon tied in a neat bow.

Mara took it from him. She knew that bow as well as she
knew her own fingers. Every deed drawn up by her, once it
was signed and witnessed, was tied with a piece of linen ribbon.
From the time that she had been a small girl her indulgent
father had allowed her to do this part of the ceremony, and
even acceded to her request that the linen tape should be pink,
rather than a grubby white.

So Eamon had left Ballinalacken Castle last night – probably
at midnight. It looked as if he had taken advantage of the
splendid moon to begin his journey to Thomond, carrying
the deed for the new lease of the flax garden in the Aillwee
Mountain.

But why had he ended up eighteen hours later in the middle
of the Burren? It was not on his route. There had been no
reason for him to go there.

'Looks like he had a deed with him,' said Moylan after a
minute. 'Was it the deed for the lease of the flax garden,
Brehon, do you think? He was due to take it to Thomond
today, wasn't he?'

'That's right,' said Mara. 'I wondered about that as soon as
I saw the satchel.'

'Strange though . . .' Moylan looked at her in a puzzled way.
'I thought . . .'

Mara did not reply. She, like he, had thought that it had
been an amorous adventure; that Eamon and Fiona had gone

for a midnight ride, and that, perhaps, Fachtnan had followed them. Now it looked as if Eamon, fired by wine and excitement, and the restlessness which was so much part of his nature, had decided to get the ride to Thomond over during the hours of the night. If he had taken the usual route south, crossed O'Briensbridge and turned north, then he would have been with O'Brien of Arra at breakfast time. He could have got his signature to the deed, and been back to the Burren by mid-afternoon.

But why take such a strange way – go north instead of returning the way he had come? Would there be any sense in taking a journey through difficult riding conditions, mountainous most of the way? And why take a journey that would bring him through hostile land?

What had happened to Fiona? And to Fachtnan? Both of these had seemed to have left the castle at the same midnight hour.

'He couldn't have come straight from O'Brien of Arra, though, could he?' asked Shane shrewdly. 'I've just been thinking about the route. He would have had to come through the Kelly kingdom at Ui Maine, wouldn't he? He'd never have done that. Kelly is in the pocket of the Great Earl. I've heard King Turlough say that again and again.'

'You're right, Shane,' said Mara. 'I was just thinking of that myself. But perhaps he went south of the Kellys' land, perhaps he just came through the mountains . . .' It didn't make sense, though, to her, either. Why should Eamon ride through the mountains – she wasn't sure that there was even a path – why go that way, close to enemy land instead of the usual lowland route that he would know so well? She had sent him often with messages to Turlough, to Thomond across the Shannon, and every time he had taken the same route across O'Briensbridge. There was something very puzzling here. She stayed very still for a minute, conscious of the noise of hunters in the background. Soon they might be interrupted.

'Listen,' said Hugh, 'I heard the horn. Listen! They've found a wolf!'

A pack of wolfhounds swept past them, all panting heavily,

tails whipping the air, eyes blazing with excitement. Even Bran, Mara's devoted dog, passed with just a quick lick and a wag of the tail for his beloved mistress.

'Perhaps Eamon heard the hunt and he came up the mountain to see it,' said Aidan, looking pleased with his own brilliance.

'Perhaps,' began Mara dubiously. Unlikely, she thought. It would have made more sense to have delivered the signed deed to her and then concentrated on enjoying himself. Surely, in any case, even someone with the energetic nature of Eamon would have wanted a sleep after his midnight ride. She wished that she was back in the law school, sitting quietly and allowing her brain to sift through the various possibilities. However, there was no chance of peace at the moment. Turlough, his cousins, his son and his son-in-law, his allies and his friends, all came into sight, waving sticks, shouting encouragement to the dogs, their heavy leather boots sliding on the loose scree of the limestone.

'My dear Brehon,' said Ulick Burke. 'You are everywhere. What brings you up here? Have you by any chance conveyed a meal and refreshments to the hungry hunters?'

'You'll have to wait until you return to Ballinalacken for that,' said Mara. She was quite surprised to see Ulick had joined the hunting party. He wasn't much a man for this sort of exercise, normally, especially as Turlough always insisted on hunting these mountains on foot.

'We've had a splendid morning – killed two wolves already,' said Turlough. He spoke absent-mindedly though, and did not appear to find the sudden appearance of his wife on the side of the Aillwee Mountain to be in any way surprising. His eyes and ears were following the wolfhounds' progress. The four scholars gazed after the dogs, also, with a mixture of envy and longing; Mara was sorry for them, but unrepentant. Turlough would have taken the boys if she had asked, but it was nice for him to spend the day with his friends and relations without having schoolboys listening in to every incautious word.

'They've found!' yelled Donán O'Kennedy and Turlough patted his son-in-law heartily on the back. Mara was glad to see that gesture of friendliness. For the sake of Ragnelt, Turlough's daughter, she had often wished that Turlough did not so openly show his contempt for Donán.

And then five of the six men departed, slipping and sliding, steadying themselves with their sticks, but going down the mountain at breakneck speed, leaving Ulick Burke gazing at his hostess with an expression of interest.

'So what really brings you here then, my dear Brehon?' And without waiting for a reply he moved over to the edge of the path and peered down the mountainside, not looking towards the hunting party, but following the rough roadway as it snaked its gradual way down to the flat land of the high Burren.

'Ah,' he said with satisfaction after a minute. 'That looks like your faithful servant Cumhal. And why the cart? Was there an accident? But why send for the Brehon for an ordinary accident?'

'I think I hear my lord the king calling your name, Ulick,' said Mara mildly.

The lie did not convince Ulick. He flashed her a quick grin and bowed. 'I shall leave you to your investigations, Brehon,' he said and moved off after a keen glance towards the figure of Muiris, still standing impassively by the stone fence in the flax garden.

'I'm sure that's why Eamon came over this way,' said Aidan as Ulick moved lightly down the steep side of the mountain. 'He must have heard the hunters and decided to come and see the sport.'

'Perhaps,' said Mara absent-mindedly. Another matter had occurred to her and she looked speculatively at Muiris O'Hynes.

There had been a deed that gave Muiris the lease of the valley and all its equipment, crop and furnishings from May Day 1511 to the eve of May Day 1512. The deed had been drawn up by her and signed neatly by Muiris, who, to her surprise, had turned out to be literate. The deed had been sent to O'Brien of Arra for his signature. Whether or not he had signed, the position now was probably that no deed had survived.

The auction would have to be held again.

And this time, Cathal O'Halloran might get in the last and, ultimately, successful bid.

Five

Oi Ascuð Chor
(On the Binding of Deeds of Contracts)

There are some circumstances which can make a contract be declared invalid:
1. *A contract made under duress.*
2. *A contract made by fear.*
3. *A contract made while drunk (except in the case of co-ploughing agreements which are valid even if one, or all of the parties, are drunk at the time of signing).*
4. *If a contract contains a fault which cannot be reasonably detected by the disadvantaged party, that contract has to be rescinded or adjusted.*

No contract is valid unless the document can be produced and the signatures verified.

Nothing could make Fiona look plain. In her normal good spirits she sparkled, every blonde curl alive, blue eyes shining, cheeks pink with health. This morning she was pale and subdued, but had the fragile beauty of the snow-white windflowers that illuminated the little wood beside Mara's house.

Mara seated the girl on one side of the fire and took her place on the other side. The hunting party had not yet returned but she had no wish to have her interview with Fiona interrupted or overheard so had asked Brigid to bring the girl to her own bedroom.

'Had a good sleep?' she asked.

Fiona nodded, but the purple shadows under her eyes belied the acquiescence.

'Will you tell me what happened last night?' asked Mara gently.

Fiona nodded again, but seemed to find it hard to start the

story. Mara looked at her compassionately. Perhaps the Bishop of Kilfenora was right. Perhaps it was not wise to mix young girls with youths at this vulnerable age. She herself had made a disastrous marriage with an idle scholar at her father's law school and had bitterly repented it soon afterwards. Her father had died soon after she had qualified as *ollamh* – professor – so she had to cope with the law school, her baby daughter and a husband who had given up the law and spent all of his time in alehouses. A lucky chance had given her an excuse to divorce him, but the experience had been unpleasant.

'Eamon persuaded you to ride with him to Thomond, to bring the deed for the flax garden to O'Brien of Arra, was that it?' she asked.

Fiona coloured. 'I just thought it would be fun,' she said. 'We thought that we'd be back before we were missed. Eamon said that everyone would be sleeping late and no one would look for us before midday.'

'I see,' said Mara. 'Just tell me everything that happened.' It probably would have been fun, she thought understandingly. To steal away from the party, find their cloaks, mount their horses and ride along with the intense white light of the moon illuminating their path and the stars pricking the darkness overhead.

'Which way did you go?' she asked when Fiona did not reply.

'Along the high road.' Fiona seemed relieved by the simplicity of the question and added, 'We could see the sea and we could see some lights from Aran. We thought that they must be having a party over there, also. We didn't meet a person until we came to Kilfenora – and that just turned out to be a stray cow.' Fiona smiled slightly at the memory.

'And then through Kilfenora and over towards Thomond and you crossed the Shannon . . .'

'At O'Briensbridge,' confirmed Fiona.

Mara mused on the route. It was as she would have expected. So what had brought Eamon so far out of his way?

'You enjoyed the journey?' She expected an instant affirmative, but Fiona seemed hesitant.

'I suppose so – well, in the beginning at least.'

Mara turned an enquiring glance towards her and after a moment, with a sudden rush, Fiona said, 'I kept thinking that someone was following us. I kept looking behind me. There was a sound, but not horse hoofs, not on the road, anyway. But it must have been a horse because we were going quickly and it kept the same distance behind us all the time.'

'Strange,' said Mara. A horse on the road would have been unmistakable. The roads of the Burren were stone – that stone which lay everywhere in the kingdom with only a few inches of earth covering it. Unlike other places there was no need to build roads with load upon load of gravel and broken stone. On the Burren all that needed to be done was scrape away the soil and keep it clear.

How odd for someone on horseback not to choose to ride on those excellent roads.

Fiona, however, was not a nervous or fanciful girl so the chances were that she was right in her suspicions. It would be easy for a third person to ride unseen through the roadside fields, well hidden by the stone walls that surrounded them.

'Go on,' she said. 'What about when you had passed through Kilfenora? When you were in Thomond? Did you hear anything then?'

'A few times, but we were talking and then we started singing so I suppose I forgot about it. That is until we reached O'Briensbridge. We went racing across it – the horses' hoofs made a great din on the timbers and then when we were well past and had turned towards Arra, I was sure that I heard another horse cross over – not racing, just walking, but walking on those timbers is like beating a drum.'

'It would be dawn by then, I suppose,' said Mara.

'Oh, yes, the sun had risen by the time we reached the castle at Arra. They got a bit of a surprise when they saw us. We had to wait for a while – they gave us wine and bread straight from the oven. We were there for ages, eating the bread and drinking the wine.'

On top of what they already had at the party at Ballinalacken, thought Mara. Eamon was not a young man to deny himself. She could imagine him, quaffing goblet after goblet as they waited, still talking brilliantly, but probably getting wilder and more reckless as the time wore on.

'And then the O'Brien himself came. He got a shock when he saw me and I said that I was one of your scholars.' Fiona giggled, a little colour coming back into her cheeks. Mara smiled. Fiona, like she herself as a girl, enjoyed the shock caused by being a female law student.

'He asked me all sorts of questions; he seemed to be angry with Eamon for bringing me. He kept looking at Eamon and frowning, and then Eamon began to hiccup – he'd had too much to drink and the O'Brien rang a bell and got his house-keeper to take me out and show me to one of the chambers where I could rest while he and Eamon did the business together. He just shooed me away as though I had been a hen.' Fiona sounded so indignant that Mara had to smile before asking,

'So you didn't actually see the deed being signed?'

Fiona shook her head. 'No, but Eamon told me that it had been signed and witnessed by the O'Brien's steward.'

'And then you started on your return journey.' Mara sat back and waited. Something had gone wrong, obviously, and this was going to be the moment that Fiona had to decide whether to trust her, or whether to tell some story. The hesitancy was in the girl's eyes before she lowered them, nudging a small piece of turf with the side of her foot. Mara bent down and picked it up, tossed it on the fire and then added some bigger pieces from the basket, carefully arranging them so that the flames blazed up between the brick-like shapes. She loved the smell of turf – a wood fire was brighter and hotter, but nothing compared to the pungent aromatic smell of the peat.

'I suppose you and Eamon had a row,' she said eventually, looking casually over her shoulder at Fiona. The sapphire-blue eyes snapped open and the girl's cheeks turned red.

'How do you know?' she asked.

'I know what boys are like when they have had too much to drink,' said Mara dryly.

'Well, the first thing that happened was that he started galloping quite quickly down the road and I shouted after him that he was going the wrong way. He wouldn't stop so I was forced to go after him.'

'And when you caught up with him?'

'He refused to turn back, he kept on teasing me and saying that I didn't know the right way and then when I stopped and said I wasn't going any further, he grabbed my pony's reins and started to lead it. The pony didn't like it. She was snorting and plunging. I was afraid I would fall off. I screamed at him. I managed to pull the pony up to a stop and then I got off and said that I was going no further until he told me what he was doing. I thought he must be drunk. I was saying to him "Look, Eamon, this lake goes on for miles and miles; we have to go back and cross the Shannon at O'Briensbridge. It's the only place where we can cross unless we go right up to Ui Maine."'

Mara bit her lip with annoyance. This girl should have been more carefully supervised. If any harm had come to her it would have been hard to explain to Robert Macbetha how his only child came to be alone with a drunk young man in the middle of the night twenty miles away from the law school where he had carefully deposited her less than a month ago. Still, she thought, the girl, if she is to work as a lawyer, will have to learn to deal with these matters sooner rather than later and read the reflection of her own thoughts in Fiona's eyes.

'I wasn't afraid of him,' she said with a toss of her head. 'I've always been with boys in my father's law school and I know how to keep them under control. I shouldn't have allowed him to drink so much, though, because he was quite wild, going on about us getting married and him having a bagful of silver and the two of us opening up a law school together – all sorts of silly talk like that. He knew well that even if we wanted to get married that we both had to finish our law school terms and pass our examinations. And then we would each have to get a position with some great lord or king. I told him that he would have to have saved up plenty of silver before he could think of marriage – and that I had other plans.'

'So what did he say?' Mara was reassured by Fiona's resolute manner.

'Oh, he just went on about how much he loved me and that he would find a way, so I just told him that I didn't love him enough to get married and that I was going back and he could follow if he wished to ride with me or else he could keep going up to the north and beyond if he wished. Then I offered to take the deed back to you if he was going to go on to Galway.'

'So he wanted you to go to Galway,' mused Mara. 'Was that what he said? Didn't he know that he would have to go through the Kelly territory to get there?'

'I told him,' said Fiona with another toss of her bright gold curls. 'I told him it all and then he grabbed me and tried to kiss me. I kicked him hard and screamed. I told him that someone was coming and he just jumped on his horse and rode away.'

'And you came home – alone? Why didn't you ask O'Brien of Arra to give you an escort? That was a stupid thing to do, Fiona. I'm surprised at you.'

'I thought that Eamon would come after me,' confessed Fiona. 'I thought that he would apologize and behave himself. I kept thinking that I heard him following me. I didn't look back because I didn't want to encourage him, but I was sure that he was only a little bit behind me the whole way back until we came to Corcomroe. I was so tired then that I just stopped thinking about him. As soon as I reached the castle I went straight to bed.' She looked up at Mara and said, 'Don't look so worried, he'll be home soon. He was just in a bad mood, but he won't fail to bring you back the deed.'

Mara looked at the girl closely. She had known her for over six months now and had always found her to be honest and straightforward. There was nothing about her to suggest that she was lying or hiding the truth in any way. The story was a plausible one.

'I'm afraid, Fiona,' she said gently, 'you'll have to prepare yourself for a shock. Eamon will not be coming home.'

'Why? What's wrong? Have you had a message? Where is he?'

Mara contemplated the girl carefully. Could she be sure that the ingenious face presented to her was as innocent as it appeared to be? She wasn't certain. Fiona was very bright, very clever; she could not be positive that the demure face before her did not conceal some knowledge of Eamon's demise. Nevertheless, she proceeded in a calm, straightforward manner.

'Eamon's body was found at the valley of the flax about noon today. It was discovered by Muiris O'Hynes – you may remember him as the successful bidder for the lease.'

'Eamon – dead? Dead, today? I can't believe it.' She stared wide-eyed at Mara and then began to cry hysterically, tears pouring down, her face white and shocked. The broken words would be just what you might expect from any girl when appraised of the death of a young man who, less than twelve hours ago, had rode with her, proposed marriage to her, quarrelled with her and disappeared from her vision.

But did she know more than she had related? Was the puzzling death of Eamon, and the disappearance of the deed, countersigned by O'Brien of Arra, cousin to King Turlough Donn O'Brien himself, was this death anything to do with the wide-eyed, beautiful girl opposite.

'You seem surprised,' said Mara, purposefully brutal and then waited for the sobs to subside. Fiona said no more, just cried helplessly. Mara longed to comfort her, but the truth of that night had to be ascertained. It could be that Fiona had left Eamon at Arra and had returned by O'Briensbridge and the southerly route to the Burren. But it could also be that she had gone north with him and that the quarrel had begun on the mountain pass. She was a small girl, but sturdy; a healthy girl who loved the outdoors and happily played hurling with the boys – perhaps one strong push from her would have been enough to have overbalanced Eamon.

'No one is saying this is murder – as yet.' Mara waited for a reaction, but none came. Fiona was making a strong effort to control herself now, but Mara's words seemed to be unheeded by her.

'It may have been an unfortunate accident; a quarrel. One person pushes another, he overbalances, strikes his head on a rock, tumbles down, is killed.' I must talk to Nuala, thought Mara. I'm not even completely sure how Eamon died. At the same time as these thoughts raced through her head, she watched Fiona narrowly. The girl lifted her blue eyes, now reddened and filled with tears, and shook her head wordlessly. She had understood the implication of Mara's words but that did not necessarily condemn her. Fiona was an intelligent girl who would instantly realize the implications of Eamon's death.

'Was I the last one to see him?' She choked slightly over the words, but now she had herself under control.

'That's not possible for me to answer,' said Mara. 'It depends . . .' Purposely she did not finish the sentence.

Fiona nodded. 'It depends on whether he fell or was pushed.'

'Who did you think was the secret follower of you both?' asked Mara, wondering whether this was just a piece of imagination, or even a tale told to cloak the real killer. In fact, for a moment she thought she saw a hint of puzzlement in Fiona's eyes – almost as though the girl did not know what she was talking about.

'Who was the rider who had followed you both from the Great Hall of Ballinalacken Castle? Who followed you both through the lands of the Burren, the lands of Corcomroe through Thomond, and right across the mighty width of the river Shannon itself, that's what you told me . . . Isn't that right?' added Mara as Fiona said nothing, just looked straight ahead of her.

'I don't know,' said Fiona slowly, but her eyes told a different story.

Something had just occurred to her.

Six

Brecha Déin Chécht
(The laws of Déin Chécht)

There are twelve doors of the soul, twelve places where a blow may kill a man:
1. *Top of the head,*
2. *Occipital fossa, (back of the skull)*
3. *Temporal fossa, (above the ear)*
4. *Thyroid cartilage, (base of the neck)*
5. *Suprasternal notch,*
6. *Axilla, (armpit)*
7. *Sternum, (breastbone)*
8. *Umbilicus, (navel)*
9. *Anticubital fossa, (cavity near elbow)*
10. *Popliteal fossa, (cavity between legs)*
11. *Femoral triangle, (inside of thigh)*
12. *Sole of the foot.*

The houses at Cahermacnaghten law school were built within the immensely thick walls of an ancient enclosure. Up to recently there had been just four small, oblong, lime-washed and stone-built cottages: a kitchen house, a scholars' house, a schoolhouse and a farm manager's house. To these buildings, Mara had recently added a roundhouse for female scholars and hoped that soon she would have another girl to join Fiona. At the present time she herself was the only woman Brehon in Ireland, but there was no reason why there should not be more. In fact, Mara secretly thought that a woman, more than a man, possessed the skills necessary for administering a law which was not enforced by imprisonment or by savage punishments such as whipping, branding and hanging, but by the consensus of the people of the kingdom. The law needed qualities of tact, understanding and a willingness to listen – very much women's qualities, thought Mara, and she dreamed that her school would produce a line of women Brehons, all as successful at maintaining law and order in the kingdom as she had been.

Throughout almost twenty years as Brehon of the Burren, she thought proudly, she had experienced only two cases where the culprit refused to pay the fine and had escaped into an alien territory. Neither of these men could be permitted ever to show their faces in the kingdom of the Burren until justice was done and the penalty paid. All other cases had been settled, the fine paid and the culprit restored to a life of usefulness to the family and to the community. A Brehon was a valuable profession, and she hoped that this latest case could be solved quickly and the peace be once more restored.

Cumhal came forward when Mara's horse turned in at the gate and stood beside her, holding the reins while she dismounted. 'Nuala is in there with him, and Brigid, too, in the roundhouse,' he said indicating the new cottage.

The roundhouse had been built in the style of the monastic huts on the smallest of the Aran Islands. It had a large room facing the door, with four small bedchambers, screened by leather curtains, beyond it. A big iron brazier, filled with logs, stood against the wall near to the doorway and in the centre of this room was a sturdy wooden table and some stools. Even on a winter's night this was a cosy place to sit and study and the walls were so thick that the heat was retained even when the fire went out.

Today, there was no fire and on the table there were no books or writing materials – just the body of the young man stretched out to the length of it. Brigid, Cumhal's wife, had washed and dressed the corpse and he lay there, his eyes weighted shut, wrapped in his white cloak, his face looking younger than Mara had ever seen it. Mara swallowed hard. Young men died; that was a fact of life. They died in battles, they drowned in stormy seas; they died because they were reckless and they did dangerous things. Fortunately this particular young man, unlike others, had left no one behind to mourn him. Both father and mother were dead; there were neither brothers nor sisters, or, as far as she knew, any near or dear relation.

But why did this young man die? This was a question that she had to solve.

'What do you think?' she asked, looking directly at Nuala.

Nuala made no reply to this; she just undid the fastening on the white cloak and parted it so that Eamon's neck was visible. Mara leaned over the body. The injury had been hidden by the cloak, but now it was unmistakable – the purple bruise on the base of the young man's neck showed as shockingly obvious.

'The small bones here have been smashed,' said Nuala.

'In falling?'

Nuala hesitated. 'Of course, there were cuts and bruises on the face, and one bruise here, but . . .' She did not finish, and, in front of Brigid, Mara did not question her. Brigid was very dear to Mara, had been her nurse, had been everything to a motherless small girl. These days she managed the two households, looked after the scholars, cooking for them, cleaning, washing clothes, mothering them, also. Often, Mara wondered how she could possibly manage without Brigid and Cumhal to support her. However, this death was a matter for the law now and Brigid never interfered in any legal matter. She walked towards the door, obviously wanting to leave them alone together to discuss this untimely death.

'Cumhal has been to the priest, Brehon,' she said with her hand on the latch. 'Father O'Connor will bury him tomorrow morning. He wanted to know if there would be a wake and I said that I thought not, but that we would let him know.'

'No,' said Mara. 'No wake. He hasn't been here long. Very few people will know him.' Wakes were tedious and distressful affairs, she always thought, where newly bereaved and grieving members of the dead person's family were subjected to a night-long procession of friends and neighbours arriving with condolences and staying to eat and drink the hours away.

'Thank you, Brigid,' she said affectionately. 'You've done wonders. We'll coffin the poor lad as soon as Blár, the wheelwright, arrives. I'll bring the others to say a prayer for him in the church, I think. Is Fachtnan with Cumhal?'

'No,' said Brigid with surprise. 'He rode off at least an hour ago. Almost as soon as the body arrived. I thought he had gone over to Ballinalacken Castle. Didn't you see him, Brehon? You saw him go, didn't you, Nuala?'

'I must have missed him,' said Mara hastily. She didn't like to see the hurt, proud look on Nuala's face. She would have been upset to see Fachtnan leave as soon as she arrived. What a tangle it had been for the last few months, she thought with a sigh. Nuala in love with Fachtnan; Fachtnan in love with Fiona; Eamon in love with Fiona . . . And Fiona? Just in love with life, probably, thought Mara. 'Ask Cumhal if he could spare someone to ride over to Ballinalacken and tell the scholars to come here,' she said aloud. She followed Brigid to the door. 'Do you know Cathal O'Halloran, Brigid?' she asked. She need say no more. Brigid would understand that her thoughts had turned towards the inhabitants of the flax garden and to surmises about how the death of the man who had borne the deed for the new lease could perhaps be connected with the O'Halloran clan.

'Don't know him, Cathal, very well,' admitted Brigid. 'But I know Gobnait, of course. She was an O'Connor from Corcomroe before her marriage.'

'Really,' said Mara. 'I didn't know that.'

That was enough for Brigid. She herself and her husband Cumhal belonged to the O'Connor clan and would know it, seed, breed and generation, as she put it herself. She was a woman who loved to impart knowledge, to pass on gossip and, above all, she liked to be asked to have a hand in the law business of the kingdom.

'Why would you?' she said immediately. 'Gobnait would be a good ten years older than you. You wouldn't have been interested.'

'Gobnait,' mused Mara, 'it's an unusual name. I haven't heard of it before in these regions, but there was a Gobnait once, way back, a thousand years or so. She was an abbess, with a convent full of nuns, this Gobnait. Anyway, an army was approaching and coming very near to these holy nuns, so what did Gobnait, the abbess, do? Well, she released swarm after swarm of bees, a hundred thousand of them, the story tells, and they flew, straight as an arrow, towards the army and the soldiers could not stand up to them and they fled and the noise of their shrieks of pain filled the plain of Ireland. That's how the story goes.'

'Sounds like this Gobnait,' said Brigid smiling. 'A tough woman. I can just imagine her sending a swarm of bees after you if you annoyed her. I knew her mother well and she was a tough woman, also. Gobnait is the living image of her. She was well trained by her mother in spinning and weaving and they say that she was the one that pushed Cathal into making the offer for the flax garden and she was the one that made a success of it. Wouldn't be easily robbed of that place, Brehon, that's what I say.'

Brigid looked meaningfully at Mara and then, as if she feared she was saying too much, she backed away and went out of the small house.

'I wanted to talk to you about this injury,' said Nuala as soon Brigid had gone out and shut the door behind her. 'It's a bit difficult to explain –' she frowned thoughtfully – 'it's not something that I have been taught exactly but I noticed it first a few years ago when father was called to a farm to attend to a man who had been gored by a bull, though he was dead by the time that we arrived. The wife of the farmer had sent someone for Malachy and I went along with him. I suppose I was only about twelve at the time,' said fifteen-year-old Nuala and Mara smiled briefly, remembering the long-legged, dark-eyed child lugging around the heavy leather medical bag belonging to her grandfather.

'The bull was still in the field and the farm workers could not get it away from the body for quite a while. I saw the animal toss the poor man again and again, until eventually they managed to drive it away and lock it up. But – and this is the strange thing – although the man had been gored again and again, there were gouged out places all over his body, but only one of these holes seemed to have bled much. I remember asking father whether blood didn't gush out after someone is dead – he said he didn't know – that's what he usually said to me. But from then on I kept an eye on dead bodies and I even did a little experiment with one by cutting a vein when no one was around and that proved to me that, after death, blood doesn't really flow. And I also found out that the longer after death the cut occurs, the less blood there is.'

Mara looked at her attentively. Nuala was a true professional. She had a huge admiration for the girl patiently experimenting with no help given to her by her strange father, Malachy O'Davoren.

'Why I'm telling you this is because I know you have to find out what happened to Eamon,' continued Nuala. 'I think that someone killed him.' Once again she pulled down the cloak and showed the terrible bruise at the base of the neck. 'This injury killed him, I think. The thyroid cartilage here is one of the spots that is most vulnerable. Someone pressed their thumbs in here and strangled him.'

Not Fiona, then. Mara breathed a sigh of relief. Surely a girl as small as Fiona would not have the strength to do that to a young man like Eamon. 'Would it be difficult to do this?' she asked.

'Not terribly,' said Nuala indifferently. 'You'd have to know what you were doing, of course. Or else be lucky enough to find the right spot instantly. He would have lost consciousness almost immediately. But,' she said emphatically, 'this is the interesting bit. He fell down the mountainside, as we know. He bounced from rock to rock, you can see the marks. And look, here on the scalp, you can see the fall has actually smashed the skull at this point. Come around here to the head.' Nuala parted the dark hair and showed the depression.

'But you don't think that was what killed him?'

'No, not at all. I'm certain of that. In fact, I think that he was dead before he fell down the mountainside.'

'What!'

'That's right. You see if he hadn't been dead for a while when this happened the scalp would have poured blood. Scalp wounds bleed more than any other injuries. You've probably seen that for yourself if any of the boys got a scalp cut from a hurley or something.'

Mara nodded. 'They even frighten themselves the first time they see all that blood.' Her mind went back to Eamon. 'So you don't think that he was killed at that spot just beside the flax garden then? So how did he fall and why was that done?'

Nuala shrugged her thin shoulders. 'I'd say that someone did not want the body to be found where he had been killed. Probably wanted to pretend that it was just an accident.' She went across the room, picked up her medical bag, checked its contents, looked around the room and then went to the door.

'I'll leave you now,' she said. 'I want to have a look at my property in Rathborney. Ardal has put a man in there to manage it for me. I'm hoping that when I qualify as a physician next year I will be allowed to live there, even if I can't find a husband for myself by then. I suppose you haven't managed to find one for me yet, have you?'

With a dry laugh she went out without waiting for a reply. Mara would not have known what to say, in any case. There was only one man that Nuala wanted – had always wanted – and that was Fachtnan, the nineteen-year-old scholar at Cahermacnaghten law school.

Fachtnan had failed his final examination last year. Mara hoped that he would pass it this year, but Fachtnan had serious memory problems and it was hard to predict how he might react in an examination situation. If he passed then he could earn a living as a lawyer, but if he failed once more, he had another possibility in front of him. If he married Nuala, it would be 'union of man on a woman's property', but he would lack for nothing. Nuala had been left a rich estate at Rathborney and in addition she would have her work as a physician. Even as a young girl the people of the Burren had trusted her more than they trusted her father, Malachy, and had sought her advice and used her medicines with confidence.

But Fachtnan was deeply in love with Fiona. Nuala knew that, and it was probably the reason why she had not stayed to see the arrival of the scholars. She could not bear to see Fachtnan and Fiona together, especially now that Eamon had been removed as an obstacle.

I must talk to Fachtnan, thought Mara. Tell him the truth. Tell him that Fiona has no real interest in him. Try to probe, delicately, his feelings for Nuala. He had been fond of her for years. She would play the matchmaker; a dangerous game, perhaps, but she was sure that Nuala and Fachtnan would be happy together.

But when the scholars arrived, there was no sign of Fachtnan. Mara had gone to the gate of Cahermacnaghten to welcome them, had heard their voices calling greetings to some farmer from a long way off. There they were, Moylan and Aidan in the front, then Hugh and Shane, and Fiona riding rather soberly behind them.

'Where is Fachtnan?' she asked as they came close and they looked at each other with raised eyebrows.

'I thought he was here, Brehon,' said Moylan.

'Not at Ballinalacken,' said Aidan. 'Not unless he's in the eagle's nest. Did you know that there's a golden eagle nesting just above the castle, Brehon?'

'Shut up,' muttered Moylan.

'Oh, I forgot.' Aidan crimsoned with embarrassment and the two younger boys blushed in sympathy with him. It would be all quite unreal to them that one of their own who had eaten and slept beside them for the last couple of weeks was now lying dead.

'I'd like you all to leave your horses and ponies here for the moment and go across to the fields and gather some flowers – there are tons of early orchids out and I think it would be nice to put them in the coffin,' said Mara. Her quick ear had caught the sound of a heavy cart coming trundling up the road. That would be Blár with the coffin. She had not reckoned on Fiona's presence, thinking that she would have been too upset to come. She did not want the girl to see Eamon, who had loved her, lying dead on the table in her house.

'Make sure that you get a very big bunch. I'll call you when Eamon has been coffined and then we'll walk with the coffin down to the church. Father O'Connor will receive the body and he will be buried tomorrow morning.'

The walk down to Noughaval Church had been a silent affair. The scholars had prayed with sincerity in the church, joining in the priest's prayers for eternal rest to be granted to the young man whom they had known so well for a short time.

When they emerged from the church Fiona was shivering and the two younger boys looked pale. Mara looked at them with understanding. It was an age when they felt eternal and now they had had a shock when one of their companions had been killed.

'One thing that we can do for Eamon, now, is to find out who killed him and make that person pay,' she said, making her voice as matter-of-fact as she could. Beside her, she heard Fiona take in a deep breath, but no more was said until they returned to the law school.

Somehow everything was better then. This was the place where legal questions were debated and the familiarity of the well-worn desks, the wooden press full of law books and scrolls, the board on the wall, regularly whitewashed by Cumhal, with its ledge beneath for the charcoal sticks and the damp sponge – all of these familiar objects seemed to settle the scholars into a steady, though sombre, frame of mind.

'Nuala feels that Eamon was dead, perhaps for as long as an hour, before his body was hurled over the side of the cliff below the flax garden,' began Mara and she outlined Nuala's reasoning to them, watching the heads nod with comprehension. The Cahermacnaghten scholars knew Nuala well and respected her learning.

'Why did you leave him, Fiona?' asked Shane curiously.

Fiona hesitated for a moment, colour rushing into her pale face, and then she said uncertainly, 'He started to . . . I . . .'

'Anything to do with Heptad forty-seven?' asked Moylan delicately, assuming the airs of a man of the world, while Aidan blushed for his friend.

'Heptad forty-seven? What's that?' murmured Hugh to Shane, who rapidly licked his finger, looked directly ahead at Mara in an attentive manner while writing RAPE in damp letters on to his desk.

'Nothing like that,' assured Fiona with the ghost of a smile.

'You should read *Bretha Nemed toisech*, my lad,' said Moylan to Hugh in an undertone. 'Essential reading for a boy of your age! Would make your hair stand on end. Full honour price penalty if a woman is kissed against her will! Read *Cáin Adomnain*, too. Ten ounces of silver for touching . . .'

'That's enough, Moylan,' said Mara, but she was grateful to him for lightening the atmosphere. Fiona was laughing in a natural manner and she began to explain to the boys about Eamon going north and how she turned back and left him.

'And the deed had definitely been signed by then?' asked Aidan.

'Definitely,' said Fiona. 'I asked him and he took it out and showed it to me.'

'Did he unroll it?' asked Shane sharply and then before Fiona could reply, he said quickly, 'Think, Fiona, do it step by step. He opened his satchel . . .'

'He opened his satchel,' repeated Fiona obediently, 'and he unrolled it and—'

'But wasn't it tied?' interrupted Shane. 'Did he untie it, or did he slide it out of the loop?'

'Yes, you're right; it was tied.' Fiona shut her eyes and sucked in her lips with concentration. 'He slid the tape off it,' she said suddenly and opened her eyes and blinked at Shane's air of triumph. 'Is that important?' she asked in a puzzled way.

'Shane found the linen ribbon,' said Hugh. 'It was on the path above the flax garden.'

'The path coming from the north,' supplemented Aidan.

'Still tied in a loop,' said Shane.

'So,' said Moylan slowly, 'the murderer, be it a he, or a she . . .'

'You needn't look at me,' said Fiona tartly. 'I was nowhere near the flax garden today. In any case, if I went around murdering everyone who tried to kiss me, the place would be littered with dead bodies.' She looked meaningfully at Moylan, who blushed a bright scarlet.

'Never mind all that, now,' said Mara taking pity on him. 'Shane has uncovered an interesting point. If Eamon definitely had the deed in his satchel when Fiona parted from him, then the deed was either lost or stolen.'

'Why steal the deed?' asked Hugh in a puzzled voice.

'Because now there is no deed! The auction has to be held again.' Shane sounded triumphant and Mara looked at him with respect. He was only twelve, but with his sharp brain and excellent memory he might be one of her top scholars by the time that he was seventeen or eighteen. 'This puts Cathal the flax manager as a prime suspect, doesn't it, Brehon?'

'May I write on the board, Brehon?' Hugh looked pleading and Mara nodded. Hugh had excellent handwriting, was a hard-working, well-behaved boy, but he was a problem, nevertheless. His mother had died two years ago of the sweating sickness, and for a while she had thought this might be the problem with his work. But now she was beginning to worry as to whether he had the brains to qualify in five years' time. And if not, would it be kinder to inform his father, the silversmith, at the end of this year and allow the boy to follow his father's trade? However, that was a matter which could wait. In the meantime, this murder had to be solved, so she turned her mind back to the problem of Eamon and the missing deed.

'Put up the headings, Hugh,' called out Aidan. 'Reasons to murder . . .'

'Fear, anger, gain, revenge,' said Shane.

'Remember Heptad forty-seven,' murmured Moylan.

'That would be covered by "anger",' said Shane placidly and Fiona laughed.

'Or revenge,' said Hugh wisely. 'That's if he managed . . .'

'Can't think of anyone for "fear". That's usually when someone is being blackmailed. Did Eamon know any terrible secrets?' asked Aidan.

'Doubt it,' said Moylan. 'He was such a . . . well, I think if he did know any secrets he would not have been able to stop himself from hinting at it. Anyway he hasn't been here for very long.'

'But if the deed is missing and the auction has to be held again, then Cathal's name will have to go next to "gain". Does everyone agree?' Shane looked around at his fellow scholars.

'I think that if you are being fair you should put my name beside "anger",' said Fiona. 'I was very angry with him.' Her eyes filled with tears for a moment and the others looked away.

'And Fachtnan,' said Hugh innocently. 'He might have been very angry if he saw you leave with Eamon.' The other three boys looked at each other uneasily and then surreptitiously at Fiona. Hugh wrote up FACHTNAN beside FIONA and then turned back to look at his fellow scholars.

'And Owney, Cathal's son,' said Moylan hurriedly. 'He's supposed to be getting married this summer. Do you remember that girl that he was with last Halloween? The daughter of the woman who sells linen at the fairs, do you remember her? He might not have been able to afford it. Marriage is expensive . . .' He trailed off, looking uneasily at Fiona who was staring at the desk.

'Do we know anything much about Eamon's past life, Brehon?' asked Shane. 'I was wondering why he was so anxious to go over to Arra in the middle of the night. He didn't stop anywhere on the way, did he, Fiona?'

'No,' said Fiona, 'but I think that he went in the middle of the night because he had been drinking and he thought it would be fun to just go – and he persuaded me into it. If I had said no, perhaps he would have waited for the morning. The puzzle is why he didn't come back with me. He must have had some reason to go north instead of going back across O'Briensbridge. I think that if we knew that, we might find the solution to the problem.'

'I've thought of a reason,' said Shane suddenly. 'Eamon was very keen on money. What was it that he said to you, Fiona, about getting a bagful of silver? Perhaps he went north because he decided to go to the flax garden – after all that was where he was found – to go and talk to Cathal . . .'

'And give him the chance to steal the deed before it was delivered to Muiris.' Moylan shouted the words in his excitement, but Mara said nothing. She loved to see her scholars' minds working quickly.

'*For a bag of silver, you can knock me over and take the deed from my bag, Cathal,*' supplemented Aidan.

'Or Owney,' said Shane wisely. 'He's a great hurler. He'd be strong enough to kill someone. Perhaps he didn't mean to; perhaps he just knocked him down.'

'Nuala thinks that Eamon was killed, not by being thrown down the mountainside, but by being hit in the exact, dangerous spot at the base of the throat,' said Mara.

'*Bretha Déin Chécht,* number four,' exclaimed Shane. 'The windows to the soul. The thyroid cartilage is one of them.'

'So someone grabbed Eamon by the throat and squeezed,

or punched him right on the thyroid spot, and then threw the body down the mountain,' said Aidan.

'Depend on it,' said Moylan, 'the secret lies in the flax garden. After all, that's the only possible reason for Eamon to go north after O'Brien of Arra had signed the deed.'

'Did he put the ribbon back, Fiona?' asked Hugh and Mara nodded approval to him. That was a good question.

Fiona shut her eyes, obviously concentrating hard. 'Yes, he did,' she said, opening them quite suddenly and fixing their blue light on Hugh, who blinked and blushed. 'Yes, he did. I'm certain of that. I remember that when he rolled it up it wouldn't quite slip through again and so he had to untie it and retie it.'

Mara reached into her pouch and took out the pink tape, still tied in a loop, still with the neat bow on top of it. She examined it carefully. 'I didn't make that bow,' she said. 'I loop it differently, but that doesn't get us a lot further. Remember that either Eamon or the O'Brien will have undone it before signing and then retied it. Still it's a valuable point that you made, Hugh, because it might suggest that the murderer of Eamon checked the deed before taking it away. That would explain why the tied loop was found just in the place where Eamon was probably killed.'

'Perhaps we could hunt through all the belongings of the suspects to see whether we could find the deed,' suggested Aidan.

Mara's eyes went to the lengthening shadow of the apple tree outside the window. She could tell the time so accurately by that shadow; for more than thirty years she had watched it from the schoolhouse window. 'Well, I must be getting back to Ballinalacken – the hunters will have returned,' she said. 'What would you boys like to do? I'm going to suggest to Brigid and Cumhal that they stay here. After Mass at Kilfenora cathedral tomorrow at noon, my visitors will go home. Do you want to stay here at Cahermacnaghten or come back to Ballinalacken with me?'

She looked at her scholars and saw signs of doubt on their faces. Fachtnan was not here – he would normally have given the lead. Eventually Moylan said tactfully, 'You have enough

to do without having us to look after, Brehon. Shall we stay
here?'

'Just go and have a word with Brigid about this, will you,
and if it is all right by her, then you can stay here tonight.'
She understood. They were tired of the splendours of
Ballinalacken castle and wanted to be back with their muddy
field, their balls and hurling games, thought Mara. 'I will see
you all at Eamon's burial service at Noughaval tomorrow,' she
added. Turlough would understand that she would not be able
to accompany him to the cathedral tomorrow.

'I've thought of something, Brehon,' said Moylan tentatively.
'You'll be busy tomorrow with your guests and everything,
but would you trust us to make a search of the mountain area
around the flax garden and see whether we can find the deed?
After all, it might have just slipped out and fallen into a hole
somewhere.'

'That would be good,' said Aidan enthusiastically. 'We could
divide the area between us. Danann could come too; he'd
enjoy that.'

'I'll have a word with Cumhal and see whether he can spare
Danann,' promised Mara. Better still, perhaps Cumhal might
go, also, and keep an eye on all. She did not normally fuss
about her scholars, thinking that they needed to gain habits of
self-reliance under her care, but now she suddenly felt vulnerable. Would the girl sitting opposite her now be dead if she
had accompanied Eamon, or was her mind moving in quite
the wrong direction?

Was the murder of the young lawyer the result of
anger, rather than of greed? Thoughtfully, she wiped the
entries on the board clean with her damp sponge and
waited until she heard the boys' voices talking to Brigid at
the door of the kitchen house before turning to her remaining
scholar.

Fiona had not followed the boys out but sat and waited
demurely to speak until Mara had looked at her. 'You'd prefer
me to go back with you, is that it?' she asked.

'That's it,' said Mara firmly. 'I feel worried about you. And
I'd like you to promise me that you will not go off with anyone
again without asking my permission.'

'I'm not likely to,' said Fiona sadly. 'I've learned my lesson, I suppose.'

But what was the lesson? wondered Mara as they both rode in silence across to Ballinalacken Castle.

Not to arise jealousy in the minds of young men. Was that it?

Could the murder of Eamon have been the result of a young man's anger?

Or was it a matter of retaining a profitable business?

Or could there have been some other motive?

Seven

Brecha Nemed
(Laws for Professional People)

There are three skills that give status to a fili (poet):
The knowledge that lights up the world
The ability to chant in rhyme
To be able to tell the future

The hunting party had brought back immense appetites and very loud voices. Mara sat at the end of the table and watched the face of her husband at the top of the table. He had had a very good day. The sport had been excellent and he had spent the lovely sunny April day out in the fresh air on the stony mountain in the company of his nearest relations, allies and friends. He smiled down at his wife and lifted a glass in salute and Mara lifted her glass in return to him – one of the precious set of glasses that her father, the first Brehon of the Burren, the first *ollamh* of the law school of Cahermacnaghten, had brought home from his trip to Rome.

'Seamus, a poem,' he called impetuously to the young poet. Mara had placed Seamus MacCraith between Nuala and Fiona and hoped that the three young guests would amuse each other. Seamus would make a possible husband for Nuala, she thought. He was quite a gifted young man and had written some extraordinarily beautiful poetry about Mullaghmore Mountain on the Burren when he had come there on a winter's afternoon, some months ago. Nuala was so brilliantly intelligent that it would be a pity for her to marry a husband too far beneath her in brains.

However, the morning's hunt had not inspired him – or else he was too interested in his conversation with Fiona.

'Not yet, my lord, these matters need time. I have to sow

the seed and wait for the flower,' he called out, his beautiful voice making a song out of the simple sentences.

Ulick Burke eyed him severely. 'What is it the law says, my boy? My dear Brehon, you will put me right if I err: *"There are three things which do not profit the world by anything they do, whatever their fame for wisdom, art, and piety: a grasping miser; an arrogant poet; and a kept priest."* Methinks that such arrogance is unbecoming in such a young man. If the king asks for a poem, then as a good workman you should produce the poem.'

Seamus MacCraith looked at him furiously. 'I do not claim for myself the status of a workman, my lord; that would be very wrong. I am merely the channel through which the words of God flow in praise of the kingdom that He has created. You know what the great Fithail says: *"There are three duties of one who is Fili: to teach their people to live fearless in strength; to teach their people how to avoid the attention of the Mighty Ones and to teach their people the Laws of Nature."*'

Mara looked at Ulick with amusement. How would he answer that?

'And what about Triad two hundred and forty-eight?' demanded Fiona with a triumphant glance at Ulick. 'I don't suppose that you have heard of that, have you? We at the law school learn all of these.'

Ulick smiled gently at her. 'I think I remember it, dear girl. How does it go? *"There are three improprieties of one who is a Fili: to claim as their own work, what the Gods have done through them; to demand gain or pleasure as a servant of the Mighty Ones; to allow themselves to be kept by labour that is not their own."* Yes, no man should claim that God is working through him, just in order to allow themselves to be kept by a labour that is not their own, you would agree, my lord bishop,' he said to Turlough's cousin, who was busy asking a servant for more wine, but who had caught the word 'God' and nodded gravely at Ulick.

'He agrees,' said Ulick enthusiastically. 'How wonderful to be on good terms with the church! I had been afraid that the little affair of having five wives had earned me the disapproval of Rome.'

'I meant,' said Fiona flushing slightly, 'that Seamus is right in wishing to wait for inspiration – from God, perhaps.'

'My dear child,' said Ulick smiling at her benignly, 'I know full well what you meant, and don't think that I am unsympathetic. I remember well how it felt to be young . . .'

'"*There are three qualifications for poetry*",' interrupted Fiona. '"*These are: endowment of genius; judgement from experience; happiness of mind.*" That's from Triad four hundred and seventy-eight.'

That's not correct, thought Mara, that's the wrong Triad; but she said nothing. Nuala had asked Seamus MacCraith a question about the years of study for qualification as a poet and Mara decided to keep Ulick's attention on herself. There was something that she was curious about, in any case.

'You know a lot of law, Ulick, don't you?' she asked, taking a sip from her glass and eyeing him over the top of it. 'How does that come about?'

'I'm a magpie, my dear Brehon,' he replied. 'A mere magpie, picking up little nuggets of shining bright knowledge here and there.' He tasted his wine, taking one fastidious sip, then drank the whole glass down and turned to look for a servant to refill it.

'And yet, you remember, even more correctly than my scholars usually do, the exact number of an obscure triad. I feel that you must have studied the law at some stage in your life.' She made the comment looking very straight at him.

He had been stirring his food with a fork and had just speared a piece of meat, but at her words he dropped the fork and allowed it to remain on the floor. He bore the look of a man who is thinking hard, turning various answers over in his head.

'Study the law, I?' he prevaricated.

'That's what it seems like,' she said firmly, making a signal to a servant to pick up the fork. These forks were very precious to her. They had been brought from Rome by her father many years ago and Turlough had told her that in the whole of Ireland he had never seen such things – not even the Great Earl used forks.

Ulick gave a light laugh. 'Well, I did think of studying law, took quite an interest in it, but that was before my two brothers died and the clan decided that I would make a good *tánaiste* – heir to the chiefdom of Clanrickard,' he said lightly.

'So you probably know a lot about the law – the law of contracts – you would have studied that and known that unless the document can be produced, a deed is invalid.' Mara wondered whether she was wise in saying this, but she was interested to see his reaction. For the moment, she decided to reserve the knowledge that the blow to Eamon's throat, on the exact vulnerable spot where the thyroid was located, appeared to show either medical or legal knowledge.

She saw no reaction, though; he was busy calling out to Turlough. 'My lord, a toast,' he called, and now he was on his feet. 'A toast for the wolf – may he long provide good sport for kings – and warm cloaks for the king's followers!'

There was a great laugh at that. Turlough's face was alight with fun and good humour. Ulick was a great friend as well as companion of arms. Mara turned towards Donán, Turlough's rather unprepossessing son-in-law. He was always a man to take offence easily so she racked her brains for a pleasant subject of conversation. There were so many things that one could not mention to him. Certainly not his castle at Nenagh, which had been seized several years ago by the Great Earl and, because of that occurrence, had forced Donán to rely on his father-in-law's charity. Mara thought about asking about his children, but then decided that might remind him how his sons' inheritance was lost. That subject of conversation would not be wise, so eventually she decided to choose a neutral subject and so she discoursed on hunting dogs. That, however, only made Donán observe in a disagreeable manner that he, personally, could not afford to keep a wolfhound. Mara looked in despair at Nuala, on his other side. Seamus MacCraith was now wholly occupied with Fiona so Nuala responded bravely by talking to Donán. He turned out to suffer from rheumatism and he had tried every remedy that Nuala could suggest.

'Well, I'm going to attempt to make a new medicine for rheumatism, and I'll try it out on you,' said Nuala good-humouredly. She went on to describe some herbal remedy in

her grandfather's medical notes, which she had now discovered
grew up beside the flax garden.

'I've never seen it anywhere before,' she said enthusiastically.
'It's called bogbean plant. Grandfather had drawn a picture
of it. I thought I might have to go to a bog for it, but I
found it up in the flax garden, just by the pond that they
use for rotting the flax fibres.'

Donán, surprisingly, was quite enthusiastic about this plant.
It appeared that he suffered a lot from his rheumatism, which
he attributed to playing too much hurling in his youth. He
knew the spot that she mentioned and even offered to accompany her on an expedition some time to dig up some of the
roots.

'The children would enjoy it,' he said. 'I would like my
youngest boy to be interested in becoming a physician. Perhaps
when he is a little older you might take him on as a pupil –
he is only six now. Perhaps I myself would have been happier
with a profession like that. I hear that you are going to start
a school for medicine at Rathborney when you qualify next
year. That would be just right for him as he will be seven by
then and seven is the best age, I've heard, for starting on a
profession.'

'What about your wife? Would she mind parting with her
youngest boy?' Nuala gave a glance at Ragnelt, that silent,
colourless woman who sat beside the Bishop of Kilfenora. Mara
was surprised that Nuala even knew where to look. Ragnelt
O'Kennedy, the daughter of the king, was one of the most
self-effacing women that Mara had ever known. She always
took the seat furthest from the fire, always spoke in a shy
undertone, always kept her eyes fixed on the floor, or on her
plate, or on the sewing, with which she was eternally occupied.
Mara sometimes wondered whether her big, burly husband,
with his hurling player frame and his loud voice was unkind
to Ragnelt, but Turlough thought that they got on quite well
together. He himself was usually a little impatient with this
silent, shy girl and preferred his other two daughters, though
he saw less of them as their marriages were with Scottish
chieftains.

Now another round of dishes was being brought in and

placed on the table. It was a splendid feast and it looked as though it would go on forever. More wine was carried in. Fiona, Mara was glad to see, had placed a delicate hand over her glass when Seamus MacCraith had tried to add some more from a brimming flagon. Nuala drank water only and was deep in conversation about her proposed medical school with Donán.

'You're neglecting me, my dear Brehon,' complained Ulick.

Mara turned to him with a smile. She was not fond of the man, but Turlough was, and for his sake she made an effort to be friendly.

'Nuala seems to have got her first pupil for her medical school,' she said. 'Donán is talking about sending his youngest son to her when she qualifies and takes possession of her property at Rathborney.'

'She was a lucky girl to get that wonderful piece of property left to her,' said Ulick, his eyes resting thoughtfully on Nuala. 'A very rich girl, indeed, isn't she, once she gets possession of that magnificent house and all the lands at Rathborney? I presume that will happen as soon as she takes a husband. Do you agree with me, my dear Brehon, that an older husband is a very good thing for a young girl in possession of a large estate like Rathborney?'

'I doubt her guardian, Ardal O'Lochlainn, would give his permission for Nuala to be your sixth wife, if that's what you are planning, Ulick,' said Mara in her firmest manner. 'And even if you did succeed in winning his consent, I don't think that you would get Nuala to agree.'

'Well, one feels that she is wasting her time with that arrogant young poet. And as for your scholar Fachtnan, well, that's a waste of time, also. Where is the boy, by the way? I haven't seen him since last night. Now, my dear Brehon, tell me all about the other young man, what was his name? The young lawyer. It was he that was killed in the flax garden, wasn't it?'

'You will excuse me, Ulick,' said Mara. 'My lord does not know of this yet, so I don't want to discuss it now. I will be obliged if you don't mention it until I get a chance to talk with him.'

But perhaps Turlough did know. Ulick chattered continuously. It would be unlike him to keep the news of a dead body on the side of the mountain to himself. And yet, Mara consoled herself, the pace of the men stumbling after the fleet-footed wolfhounds would have been too fast to allow for the sort of leisurely gossip that Ulick indulged in. Turlough would have talked of nothing but the sport and his cousin Teige would have been the same.

As soon as the meal was over she would have to take Turlough aside and tell him about the untimely death of Eamon, scholar of Cahermacnaghten law school, eldest son of the late Brehon of Cloyne, a man destined for the highest echelons of the lawyer's profession. And also that a deed for the lease of the flax garden, drawn up by his wife, Mara, Brehon of the Burren, was, as far as she could tell, now missing, and if not found would be null and void.

But that could wait. Now, she decided, was the time to gain information about one of the key players in the tragedy that occurred on this sunny morning in April.

'I can never remember,' said Mara, during one of those sudden silences into which even the most convivial of dinner parties were liable to fall, 'what exact relationship the O'Brien of Arra bears to you, my lord.' She addressed her question to Turlough and sat back to listen to his answer.

As she had guessed there was a huge pile of genealogical material poured out, supplemented with Teige O'Brien's memories, contradicted and argued with, not just by Turlough and Conor, but also Turlough's son-in-law, Donán O' Kennedy, whose family had, up to about twenty years ago, lived within ten miles of O'Brien of Arra's territory and who was distantly related to the man himself. A few scurrilous stories were resurrected and laughed over, but nothing that gave her a picture of the man. He was well connected and he was rich, owning vast tracts of land ranging from estates south of the river Shannon, in the county of Limerick, to others deep into Ui Maine and even including the little gem, the flax garden, in the centre of the Burren.

Mara gave up listening. There was no help for it. She would have to go to see Brian Ruadh, the O'Brien of Arra himself. Moylan and Aidan were too young and not responsible enough to send them across the Shannon. In any case, she would not be sure of their judgement. This was a task that she could have entrusted to Fachtnan if she had not feared that he was already involved.

And where was Fachtnan? Mara was used to boys and their moods, but Fachtnan had now been missing for nearly twenty-four hours. Her eyes went to Fiona. Seamus MacCraith was reciting one of his poems to her – something that sounded rather wonderful about a woodland scene in the early dawn. However, Fiona was not looking at him, but listening intently to the conversation about O'Brien of Arra. Perhaps the visit to Arra last night had engaged her interest. Mara turned back to her neighbour.

'What sort of man is he, really?' That was one advantage of having Ulick Burke on her right-hand side. One could always rely on his love of gossip for a quick sketch of any personality.

'O'Brien of Arra? Harmless!' he said with a laugh. 'Poor fellow! No confidence in himself. Turlough doesn't like him, but there's no harm in the man. Just finds it hard to take a joke.'

'Why doesn't Turlough like him?' queried Mara. 'She had noticed that O'Brien of Arra was not on the list of guests invited for this late ceremonial christening of their son, but she had not thought to enquire. There were so many O'Briens, so many complications of relationships. She had never fathomed them all. It was interesting, she thought, how little time she and Turlough had to talk to each other, although they had been married for eighteen months.

Of course, it was not surprising that they had so little time. Turlough was Lord of three kingdoms. As well as his normal duties, he had been at war, on and off, during the recent years, with the Earl of Kildare who was backed by the might of England and had been made Lord Deputy of Ireland by the new young king of that country, young Henry VIII. She was Brehon of the Burren, responsible for all the legal affairs of that kingdom, teacher to a school of law students, farm owner, mistress of two households, and mother of an enchanting eleven-month-old boy, son of a king. When their busy lives allowed them to come together they met as lovers, as parents,

or even as King and Brehon. There seemed little time for idle
gossip. Even now she was anxiously looking forward to getting
him on his own and consulting him about their baby son,
Cormac. Cliona's desire to get back to her own house and her
own farm was understandable, but how would Cormac fare
without her? Physically he had done very well after his premature birth and his bad start to life. He and little Art, Cliona's
son, were inseparable – almost like two puppies in a litter as
they rolled on the floor together. Still, this was a decision to
be postponed until the murder of the young lawyer was solved.

'Donán doesn't seem to like O'Brien of Arra much either,'
she said idly, noting the sour expression on Turlough's
son-in-law's face as he listened to the gossip. 'Why is that?'

'Well, Donán, poor fellow, is always like that – always got
something to complain about. I suppose he doesn't like O'Brien
of Arra because when there was the attack on the castle at
Nenagh, the Kennedys felt that Arra should have come to the
rescue.'

'He must have been only a child then,' said Mara, watching
the sullen face of her husband's son-in-law.

'These things go deep,' said Ulick shaking his head. 'You'd
be surprised how long these matters remain. Look at my own
family. Clanwilliam are the bitter enemies of Clanrickard and
yet we all stemmed from the same father originally – two
brothers, Richard and William. They went their separate ways
and never since have the two branches had a civil word for
each other. I could tell you some stories . . .'

Please don't, thought Mara, I've probably heard them all
before, but there was no stopping Ulick when he was in full
flow so she half listened and half pondered on her problems.
What was she going to do about her baby? She disliked the
idea of allowing him to be fostered. Turlough's daughter,
Ragnelt, had not the look of a happy woman; neither had her
sister-in-law Ellice, the wife of Turlough's eldest son and heir.
Both women bore a discontented, bored look. Both had a
family of children, both had all their children placed in foster
homes, as was the custom in the family. Turlough himself had
been fostered. He and his cousin Teige O'Brien had been
brought up together and they were as close, or even closer

than brothers. Both of them were happy men, she decided, amiable men, happy in their lives. Fosterage had done them no harm. It might be good for the children, but bad for their mothers, thought Mara, her mind still on her own problems, and she was startled to hear them echoed by Ulick.

'Of course, Donán Kennedy was fostered by Ormond, which just goes to show how these English-born earls have no honour. Ormond did nothing to stop the Great Earl, his own brother-in-law, from attacking the Kennedy stronghold at Nenagh Castle! But I think that O'Brien of Arra was the one that the Kennedys resented. They didn't really expect Ormond to quarrel with the Great Earl.'

'What about Turlough? Turlough must have been king, then. Does he resent Turlough for not coming to his aid?' Mara gave Ulick her full attention.

'Oh, no, he wouldn't do that. Why should he have married Turlough's daughter if he felt like that?'

Because it was a very good match for a man who had been dispossessed of much of his estates, thought Mara, but she said nothing. Her husband had a grown family when they married, and even before marriage she had decided that she had no responsibility towards these young men and women – unless any breach of the law occurred in the kingdom of the Burren, of course.

'No, no, no, Donán wouldn't bear Turlough a grudge. Good fellow, Donán,' Ulick assured her. 'Devoted to Turlough.' He turned away from her and leaned across the table, silencing Conor who was just explaining about his treatment for the wasting sickness that he had suffered from a year ago.

'Turlough,' he called, 'don't let this pleasant company dissolve. What about your annual visit to Aran? Why don't we make up a party now and take off in the middle of the week? The weather is good. We'll have a calm crossing. What do you say, Donán? I know that you have been telling me how much you hate sea journeys and how much you dislike Aran, but I don't think that I believe you. A fine young man like yourself. You should enjoy these expeditions. You'll come, won't you?'

'Well, I don't mind being cold, I don't mind being wet, I don't mind being sick, I don't mind being in danger of my

life. It's just all these things coming together that put me off
going to Aran,' returned Donán.

That's rather witty from Donán, thought Mara, feeling
amused. It was more like something she'd expect from Ulick
than from that gloomy and rather sullen young man.

'Count me out,' said Teige bluntly. 'I've no love for Aran
and who knows when a storm might blow up and we would
be stuck there for a week before we could chance the return
journey. Worst sea in the world; a Spanish sailor told me that.'

Most of the rest of the company hastily excused themselves
at that.

'Well, I suppose I'll come. A man's got to die some time,'
said Donán with false bravado. He tossed back a glass of wine
and looked towards his wife, but Ragnelt had her eyes on her
plate and did not attempt to dissuade her husband. She would
probably be glad to be rid of him for a few days!

'What about inviting O'Brien of Arra, my lord?' asked Mara,
a brainwave suddenly dawning on her. She would like to talk
to the man, but to ride over there with her scholars might
antagonize him and worsen the relations between himself and
Turlough. She could not think what he might contribute
about the death of Eamon, but she had learned long ago the
value of meticulous and thorough investigation of everything
and everyone connected to a crime. In any case, the matter
of the missing deed would have to be settled.

'Good idea! I'll send a messenger for him first thing
tomorrow. No, he can go now. The moon will be full. Fergal
–' Turlough turned to his bodyguard standing behind him –
'Fergal, find some young fellow who would enjoy the ride.
He can sleep at Arra tomorrow and then come back with
Brian Ruadh. The man won't refuse. He can't refuse. He owes
me service and hospitality and it's a long time since I called
upon him for anything. That's a good idea of yours, Ulick.
We'll make a festive few days of it.'

Mara returned Ulick's satisfied smile. No doubt, Turlough
would enjoy Ulick's company, the flow of wit and fun from
the Lord of Clanrickard would make up for the surly Donán
and the possibly disgruntled Lord of Arra.

'Will you grace us with your presence, Brehon?' asked Ulick.

'Alas, no, I have so much to do that I could not possibly spare the time,' said Mara.

She had an impression that Ulick was relieved at her words. He would probably find that her presence put rather a damper on the proceedings. He left her with a quick assurance that it was probably no journey for a woman and went over to Conor, bending over the young man and whispering urgently into his ear. After a minute he straightened up with a beaming smile and announced, 'My lord, your son Conor will come also. We will make a wonderful few days of it. Brian, the Spaniard, will open his best barrels of wine and we will feed on lobsters and oysters and steaks of sea shark. Five merry young bachelors, that's what we will be for five days and then back to wives and families again.'

Eight

Óire
(Text on Honour Prices)

Every person in the kingdom has an honour price. This honour price is a measure of status in the kingdom. Women without a trade or a profession take the honour price of their husband or father. Children under the age of seventeen have the honour price of their father. A Brehon has to know the honour prices of all. No judgement can be given, no fine imposed without this knowledge as the first part of the fine is the honour price.

List of Fines:
1. *The honour price of a king is: forty-two séts, or twenty-one milch cows, or twenty-one ounces of silver.*
2. *The honour price of a Brehon is: sixteen séts, or eight milch cows, or eight ounces of silver.*
3. *The honour price of a* taoiseach *(chieftain) is: ten séts, or five ounces of silver, or five milch cows.*
4. *The honour price of a physician is: seven séts, or four milch cows, or three and a half ounces of silver.*
5. *The honour price of a blacksmith is: seven séts, or four milch cows, or three and a half ounces of silver.*
6. *The honour price of a goldsmith is: seven séts, or four milch cows, or three and a half ounces of silver.*
7. *The honour price of a silversmith is: seven séts, or four milch cows, or three and a half ounces of silver, or four cows.*
8. *The honour price of a wheelwright is: seven séts, or four milch cows, or three and a half ounces of silver.*
9. *The honour price of a boaire (strong farmer) is: three séts, or two milch cows, or one and a half ounces of silver.*
10. *The honour price of an ocaire (small farmer) is: one sét, or one heifer, or half an ounce of silver.*

The church at Noughaval was unexpectedly full when Mara arrived followed by five of her six scholars. The Burren was full of churches, the O'Davoren family traditionally attended Noughaval, but Kilcorney and Rathborney were almost as near to the law school. Each church had its own set of patrons and there were seldom any surprises at the Sunday Mass ritual.

Today, however, the church was full of strangers, standing at the bottom of the church, leaning against the side walls, huddled together with the air of people who felt they were trespassing. It was only when Mara noticed the huge frame and wide shoulders of Cathal's son, Owney, that she realized the O'Halloran clan had forsaken their own nearest church of Ballyalban and had come to Noughaval to attend the burial mass of the young lawyer whom they had known for a brief half-hour before losing everything they had worked so hard for over the last twenty years.

Mara glanced along the line of her scholars. All were serious, but tears flowed only from Fiona. How much had Eamon meant to her? Perhaps it may have been more serious than Mara had realized, or was Fiona feeling guilty?

Guilty. That word was going to come up again and again until this murder was solved, but it was the first time that she had associated it with Fiona. As she stood, sat, knelt, gave out responses in a clear tone, Mara pondered over the girl at the end of the bench. Nothing in life had ever seemed serious to Fiona before now. Even examination papers were signed off with a flourished '*Salutations!*' Her quick wits made learning easy for her and she joked and laughed her way through lessons. All the boys, except perhaps Shane, were in love with her. Hugh and Aidan were reduced to a tongue-tied series of blushes until they got used to her presence; Moylan to a would-be-man-of-the-world, excruciatingly gallant; and Fachtnan to a state of awestricken adoration.

Eamon, of course, had been more sophisticated and ever since he had arrived Fachtnan had retreated further and further into his shell. Where is Fachtnan? thought Mara, turning an attentive face towards the priest as she composed herself on the seat, ready to listen to the sermon.

But there was no use speculating. Fachtnan was nineteen

years old, a man, he could be anywhere. He might have decided to go home early, though that was very unlike the courteous, well-behaved Fachtnan that she had known for over fourteen years. Still, love could do strange things to a young man. Mara turned her thoughts back to Fiona.

Fiona had left Ballinalacken at midnight, had ridden across O'Briensbridge, gone to the O'Brien castle at Arra, left there, still in the early morning, quarrelled with Eamon and returned back the way that she came. That was her story.

But what if that was not true. What if she had done Eamon's bidding, rode north with him, and then for some reason had quarrelled with him, picked up a stone and flung it at him, stunned him, then perhaps squeezed his throat and killed him.

If that were the case it could have been an accident. An accident, where she would have been completely blameless if the young lawyer had attempted rape.

But if that were the case, why had Fiona not admitted to the deed and said that was an accident?

But what if it was not an accident? An unlucky chance, Nuala had said. *Only someone with a physician's training would have known that a blow on that particular part of the neck would result in death.* These had been her words.

But, of course, it was not just physicians who possessed that knowledge.

The law scholars chanted the words, day in and day out, from the laws of Déin Chécht: *There are twelve doors of the soul: 1. Top of the head, 2. Occipital fossa, 3. Temporal fossa, 4. Thyroid cartilage, 5. Suprasternal notch, 6. Axilla, 7. Sternum, 8. Umbilicus, 9. Anticubital fossa, 10. Popliteal fossa, 11. Femoral triangle, 12. Sole of the foot.*

And two scholars from her school were suspects in this murder.

'That was kind of you to come to the burial, Cathal, and all of your family, also.' Mara made a point of going rapidly to the back of the church and standing beside the O'Halloran clan while the coffin was being carried down the aisle of the church.

'Terrible thing to happen.' Cathal was ill at ease, looking at her and then looking away quickly.

'Terrible,' echoed Mara. This was not the time, nor the place, to do any questioning, but she was interested to see the glances from the O'Halloran clan that seemed to flicker between looking at Cathal and then at her. Almost as though they expected some sort of announcement from her. But how could they know of the loss of the deed?

Well, they would have to wait, thought Mara. She would first of all have to see O'Brien of Arra, check that the deed had been signed, check that it was not lying somewhere among the rocks and fissures on the mountainside.

Only then would she be able to tell the O'Halloran clan that no deed existed and that another auction would have to be held.

'Excuse me,' she said to Cathal, and took her place behind the coffin as it was carried out into the little graveyard on the south side of the church. She stood at the side of the grave, listened to the prayers, made the responses, watched the coffin being lowered down into the hole and then took a small, symbolic handful of clay from the pile beside their feet and threw it down.

'*Requiescat in pace,*' she said. She hoped that Eamon would rest in peace. She had seen his body committed to the grave, would commission a stone marker to commemorate him with an inscription. There was only one thing more to do now, and that was to find his killer.

'Brehon,' said Moylan, 'what is the honour price of a flax master?'

Mara looked at him with surprise. She and her scholars had been standing at the gate to the churchyard for what felt like ages, greeting neighbours, thanking them for coming to take part in the burial service, accepting their condolences and fielding questions about Eamon's untimely death.

Now they were alone, the boys preparing to walk back to Cahermacnaghten where Brigid would have a large meal ready for them and Mara, accompanied by Fiona, about to mount her horse and ride back to Ballinalacken and entertain her husband's guests, when Moylan's question made her stop to consider her answer. She noted to her amusement that he had waited until they were completely alone before speaking. Moylan was growing up and becoming responsible.

'As far as I can remember, Moylan,' she said carefully, 'there is nothing about flax in the laws, except in so far as it forms part of a settlement in the case of a divorce. As in so many other cases in law we have to draw an analogy. Flax in this case has to be taken as a crop. Cathal pays a rent; something which covers not just the use of the land, but also the use of the equipment such as the looms, the spinning wheels, the scutching shed and the dyeing vats. We'll have to look up *Cáin Sóerraith* tomorrow, but, for these three reasons – use of land, use of equipment and payment of an annual rent – I would be inclined to classify him just as a free client. So the answer to your question is probably that he does not have an honour price, but he is a free man.'

'I see,' said Moylan nodding his head wisely.

'What made you ask the question?' Shane sounded curious. 'After all, Cathal O'Halloran wasn't the one who was murdered. We'd only be thinking about his honour price if an offence had been committed against him.'

'It's always good to consider every aspect of the case,' said Mara, though she herself was curious about why Moylan had wondered about the honour price of the flax master.

'In any case, *Cáin Sóerraith* might come up in the summer examinations,' said Aidan wisely.

'Muiris asked you that question, didn't he, Moylan? I saw you talking to him,' said Hugh innocently.

'It's an interesting question, and I'm very glad that you brought it up,' said Mara hastily, noting the angry glance that Moylan cast towards Hugh.

'Why did Muiris ask Moylan that?' wondered Shane.

'I've been trying to decide that myself,' confessed Moylan. 'He came up to me and asked how I was getting on with my studies and when would I qualify as a lawyer and what would be my honour price.'

'He was trying to find out if you are a fit husband for Cait,' said Aidan with a loud guffaw.

The other boys laughed heartily at that. Cait, Muiris's daughter, was a very pretty girl with two thick flaxen braids and a pair of gorgeous, harebell-blue eyes. Even Fiona smiled a little at this.

'I think, perhaps, that Muiris is interested in honour prices because of rising from being an ocaire to a bóaire two years ago. Do you remember that?' asked Mara tactfully and Moylan neatly overbalanced Aidan with a quick push.

'So he asked you about your own honour price first and then he went on to ask about Cathal's,' said Fiona shrewdly. 'That sounds to me as though he was trying to disguise his real question – which was about Cathal's honour price.'

'Wondering whether it would be worth his while to murder him and then take over the flax garden.' Aidan picked himself up from the ground and kicked Moylan on the leg.

'But the fine for murder is twenty-one ounces of silver and double that for a secret and unlawful killing,' said Hugh. 'It doesn't make sense for him to worry about whether Cathal's honour is one or two ounces of silver, or even nothing.'

'That's very true,' said Mara with an approving nod at him. 'I think you boys should go back now; Fiona and I will join you tomorrow morning and we'll talk it all through. A visit to the flax garden might be useful.'

'Tell me about Muiris,' said Fiona as they rode together, side by side, down the stone road towards the west.

'Why do you want to know more about Muiris?' Fiona was beginning to look better, thought Mara. She would be better still once she was back in the law school atmosphere where sharp wits rubbed up against each other and the day was punctuated with jokes and roars of laughter.

'I noticed that you stiffened a bit when you heard that it was he who wanted to know about the honour price of a flax manager.'

Mara looked at the girl with respect. 'You're right,' she said, 'but I can't give you any particular reason why I reacted like that. It just struck me as strange, and you know I'm a bit like Bran here.' She looked down at the huge, grey wolfhound loping tirelessly beside the horse. 'My hackles go up and I start sniffing around when anything strikes me as strange while I am investigating a secret crime.'

'Could it just be idle gossip?'

Mara shook her head. 'Muiris is not that kind of man,' she said firmly.

'That's why I said tell me about him,' said Fiona.

Mara smiled but did not reply for a moment, sifting through all the facts that she knew about Muiris. There were the facts that everyone knew, a few that not many people knew and one about how he killed his brutal father that was told to her in great confidence and which she would have to keep locked away in her mind from everyone else.

'Muiris had a poor start in life,' she said eventually. 'He worked for the O'Lochlainn, the father of Ardal O'Lochlainn – Nuala's uncle. He was a very good worker and when he was a teenage boy he saved the life of a cow and her calf and the O'Lochlainn gave him a present of the two animals, saying that the stockman had given up all hope and without Muiris they both would have died. And when Muiris was about sixteen he gave him a few acres of land – nothing worth much.'

'And that was the beginning of his good fortune.' Fiona nodded thoughtfully.

'That's right. No one is sure how Muiris managed to do it, but everything went right for him. He bought more and more land. Built himself a house with the labour of his own hands – well, you've seen the house.'

'And now he is a bóaire.' Mara knew from Fiona's thoughtful face that she was visualizing the large house, made from well-cut blocks of stone thatched with durable reeds, the cow cabins in the well-scrubbed yard whitewashed inside and out, the emerald-green fields around the house, grazed by fat contented cows and enclosed by well-built walls.

'Everything he touches turns to gold, that's what Cumhal says, and you know what a good farmer Cumhal, himself, is.'

'And now Muiris wants to be a flax manager.'

'That's right – but I can't for the life of me think why he

asked that question about an honour price,' said Mara. She always liked to be completely honest with her scholars. She turned to the girl at her side, reining in her lively mare who was trying to get ahead of Fiona's pony. 'Who do you think killed Eamon?' she asked and then when she got no reply, added after a long minute, 'Do you fear that it might have been Fachtnan?'

Now it was out in the open. Fiona gave a startled gasp and her pony shied, causing Mara's high-bred Arabian mare to dance on her back legs for a moment. Bran moved neatly into the hedge to avoid both horses and after a minute all was under control again.

However, the words had been spoken and Mara waited for a reply. What would the girl say? Deny? Prevaricate? Feign innocence?

'I think he might have,' said Fiona in a low voice.

'You think it was he that followed you?'

Fiona's silence gave a good answer to that question. Mara looked back over her shoulder and saw her look ahead with a troubled expression on her face.

'Why did he do it?' she said eventually, and then added quickly, 'I don't mean why did he kill Eamon. I mean why did he follow us?'

Mara thought about this question, but decided not to answer it. The path was narrow and she had to ride ahead of Fiona. She would postpone this conversation, she decided.

'There's Ballinalacken,' she said. 'Let's get in and stable our horses, then we can talk in peace. The visitors won't be back from Kilfenora Cathedral for an hour or so. The bishop has promised them some refreshments after the service.'

A light wind was blowing as they scaled the steep path that wound up to the castle, which had been a wedding present to Mara from her husband King Turlough Donn. Ballinalacken Castle was built on a high crag, a dramatic shadow against the western sky on the road to Corcomroe, a place so high that you almost felt you could touch the stars from its turrets. Originally there had only been a dark, gloomy tower house, but a new extension had been added on shortly before their marriage. This had provided plenty

of bedchambers and a great hall whose broad mullioned
windows faced the sea.

And what a sea! It stretched out in front of them, sapphire
blue, the waves streaked across its ruffled surface like cream
whipped to rough peaks. The colour was so intense that the
sky itself paled before it and the limestone rocks were black
and mirror-like against the continuously moving water. Far
out towards the Aran Island two boats, white sails filled with
the north-easterly wind, slid across its polished surface.

'Fetch baby Cormac from Cliona for me, Fiona, would you?
Bring him up to the hall. There will be no one there but
ourselves and he loves to have all that space to crawl on.'

Unwillingly she admitted to herself that she did not wish
to face Cliona alone, for a while. Not until she had time to
talk the whole matter through with Turlough and make up
her mind what to do.

However, when Fiona pushed open the door of the great
hall with one shoulder, Mara saw that she had two children
in her arms, not one.

They were so unlike one another, these two little boys. Mara
never saw them together without a slight pang. Art, Cliona's
son, was so sturdy, a brown-haired, solid child with his mother's
dark eyes. Although he was only six weeks older than little
Cormac he was so very much bigger that he seemed to be
double in size.

Cormac is perfectly healthy, Mara said to herself, taking the
slim, blue-eyed, fair-skinned little boy from Fiona's arms and
holding him close for a moment before putting him down on
the floor.

'I had to bring Art as well,' said Fiona apologetically. 'He
screamed when I took Cormac to the door and then Cormac
screamed as well when he realized that Art was going to be
left behind.'

'Much better to have the two,' Mara assured her. 'They will
amuse each other.' To herself she said silently, *how can I ever
separate them?*

The two little boys were off immediately crawling rapidly
down the flagstone floor. Cliona had made a little pair of
breeches for each so that their knees didn't get skinned by the

hard floors, and they progressed with great rapidity to the far
end of the room, turning around when they reached the
chest there and coming back again like a pair of spirited
racehorses.

Mara carefully erected a barrier of chairs and stools in front
of the fire and then went to sit on the window seat. Fiona,
she noticed, had taken a seat at some distance from her. She
waited though, looking casually out of the window towards
the sea. The two carracks were getting nearer to Aran and for
a moment she wondered about them. They looked too large
for sailing boats. Probably something to do with Brian the
Spaniard, Turlough's cousin, she thought. Guests arriving;
traders from foreign parts, perhaps.

'Cormac will be able to walk sooner than Art,' said Fiona
from across the room.

'Don't encourage me to be competitive,' said Mara carelessly,
but she watched with pleasure as the smaller, lighter boy pulled
himself up and moved carefully along the line of chairs until
he came to where Fiona was sitting. He placed a fervent wet
kiss on her knee. Then he glimpsed his foster-brother moving
back down the hall and in an instant he was after him, like
a hound after a hare. Bran walked anxiously behind, keeping
an eye on both babies. Fiona laughed and Mara was glad to
hear the merry sound and even more glad when Fiona, of
her own accord, came across the floor and seated herself
beside Mara.

'You're a very popular young lady, you know,' Mara said,
scrubbing with a handkerchief at the wet stain on Fiona's gown.
'All the boys love you – even Cormac. I think that Fachtnan,
if he did follow you the night before last, did it because he
was fond of you and worried about you.'

'A knight in armour,' mused Fiona. She looked touched,
but thoughtful.

'It makes sense, doesn't it? After all, whoever followed you
did no harm to you. He rode behind you the whole way there.
But did he return with you? That is the question.'

'I thought I might have heard something for the first few
miles, but I'm not sure,' said Fiona. 'I was a bit upset at Eamon
behaving like that. I was crying.'

'And then?' asked Mara.

'And then, once I was over the bridge, I started to gallop as hard as I could possibly go. My pony just went hurtling down the road. All I could hear was the noise of her hoofs against the stone.'

Mara sighed. The large ponies, bred on the barren hills of Connemara, were incredibly hardy with an immense amount of stamina – fast, heavily built animals. She kept a collection for the use of any of the law school scholars who did not have their own horses. Cumhal made sure that they were well fed and well shod. She could just imagine that if Fiona had given the pony its head, that she would hear nothing above the noise of drumming hoofs.

'Fachtnan was in the schoolhouse this morning, according to Cumhal. He found him studying.' Mara watched Fiona's face carefully.

'So it wasn't him,' she said, 'but if it wasn't him, who else followed us and followed me back over the bridge?'

'It still could have been Fachtnan. The fact that he was in the schoolhouse this morning does not mean that he slept the night at Cahermacnaghten. Moylan and Aidan seem fairly sure that neither Eamon nor Fachtnan slept at Ballinalacken on Friday night.'

Art and Cormac caused a diversion then by bumping heads with each other and simultaneously setting up a loud roaring sound where each seemed to compete to make the most noise. Mara picked up Art, who was nearest to her and Fiona picked up Cormac. When both were kissed and comforted with a sweetmeat from a silver jar on the table, they set off on their race course again, with Bran, this time, moving in between them as if he wanted to keep them apart.

'Before you parted from Eamon, while you were still on friendly terms with each other, did he say anything about when he planned to leave Cahermacnaghten to go to the MacEgan law school. Was he going to come back and leave at the end of the week or had he planned to do something else?'

'He didn't actually say anything about when he was going to leave,' said Fiona. 'But he did say that Muiris – is that the name of the man who had made the last bid for the flax garden? Well, he said that man had asked him to do some law work for him when he returned from Arra.'

Nine

Crích Gablach
(Ranks in Society)

An aire déso (high lord) is a man who is related to royalty. He has an honour price of fifteen séts, or seven and a half ounces of silver or eight milch cows.

He would normally have twenty clients, has a retinue of nine persons, has a wife of equal rank to his own and eight horses including a saddle horse with a silver bridle. His house should have twelve bed-cubicles.

Brian Ruadh O'Brien, Lord of Arra, was a man of about the same age as his second cousin, King Turlough Donn. Not a tall man, but immensely broad of shoulder with long arms and huge hands. His hair and square-cut beard were of that particular shade of iron grey which showed that in his youth he had been very dark-haired. But his eyes were blue – intensely blue – dark as the ocean.

'Brehon, it's lovely to meet you again,' he said holding out his hand to Mara as she came to greet him.

'And a great pleasure to me, also,' returned Mara. She had no memory of encountering him before, but supposed that they must have met at some ceremony in Turlough's castle in Thomond.

'And I want to thank you very much for doing my legal business for me, year after year,' he went on, still holding her hand as if it were something very precious.

'Ah, the flax garden. Well, we must talk about that; perhaps I might trouble you on this matter before bringing you to meet the other guests.' Mara managed to detach her hand and waited while he surveyed the landscape.

'I had not imagined you so near to the sea,' he said.

'You are fond of the sea.' There was a look on the man's

face that turned her observation from a question into a statement.

'I love it,' said Brian Ruadh softly. 'I was fostered on Aran, you know. The man there was a true father to me and his wife was a mother.'

'That would be the father and mother of Brian the Spaniard, would it?' Mara made the query mechanically. Her mind was very much on fosterage. *Closer than brothers,* where had she read that?

'That's right, we were brought up together, the two of us. The two Brians, they used to call us. His mother is a wonderful woman. She took us on walks, told us stories about mermen and magic seals. I spoke Spanish more than Irish in my early days.' His eyes shone as they gazed hungrily at the restless ocean, sparkling in the April sunshine.

'Well you will enjoy the trip to Aran, then,' said Mara. She hoped that she had time to discuss the affair of Eamon's death before bringing him indoors, but Turlough's eldest son, Conor, had appeared at the door. She searched for words to turn the conversation, but found herself warming to this man. She did not care for many of the O'Briens. With the exception of Turlough and perhaps of his cousin and foster-brother Teige, the clan seemed to her to be very vainglorious and self-seeking, obsessed with their inheritance from Brian Boru who had been dead for five hundred years. Perhaps this Brian Ruadh might be of a more sensitive mould. There was a dark, yearning look on his face as he gazed out to sea. The look of someone who sees his dream and hopes that it is about to come true.

'Conor's looking better,' said Brian Ruadh after a few moments. He glanced up at the young man. 'A bit more meat on him! There was a time that I thought he would never make old bones and that the hope of the clan would rest on his brother Murrough. Where is Murrough now?'

'I'm not sure,' said Mara briefly. She hoped that Brian Ruadh was not going to bring up the subject of Murrough with Turlough. It was a source of such great sorrow to the king that his second son spent much of his time in London, dancing attendance on the Great Earl and paying court to King Henry

VIII at Whitehall. It would spoil the planned excursion to Aran if this was harped upon.

'I must ask you something before you go in,' she said. 'It concerns the young lawyer that I sent to you with the deed for the flax garden.'

Brian Ruadh gave an amused look. 'Did you know that he brought a young lady with him – from your law school, also, I gather?'

'I didn't know at the time, nor that they set off at midnight,' said Mara frankly. 'Just a silly escapade. I suppose we have all done ridiculous things in our youth.'

'I must say that I was shocked. Still, no harm done, I suppose. He seemed a nice lad, son of the old Brehon of Cloyne, in Cork, I believe. Between ourselves, not a very admirable character, his father. Great man to take bribes, so they said. Meddled in politics, too. No one trusted him. Still, I mustn't speak ill of the dead. And this lad seemed a good fellow. I don't think he goes back to Cork often. Seemed happily settled at the law school at Redwood. Alone in the world, now, I understand, neither mother nor father, not even an uncle, he was telling me.'

'I'm afraid that he met with a tragic accident on the way back,' said Mara.

'No!' The shock on the man's face was huge. 'What happened?' he asked urgently.

'He met his death on the side of the mountain in the centre of the Burren,' said Mara gravely.

'An accident? On the way back from Arra? Why?' He thought for a moment, looking puzzled. She had nodded at his first two exclamations, but had not offered a comment on the third. 'But why was he climbing a mountain? You'd think that he'd be exhausted. Did he deliver the signed deed back to you?'

Conor was lingering in the distance, hesitating on the threshold of the castle door. A sensitive young man, thought Mara. So different from his brother Murrough. Was he of kingship material, though, she wondered in the back of her mind, while simultaneously watching the man in front of her. And yet Turlough had been such a successful king, far better than either of his two dominating uncles.

'No,' she said aloud after allowing a few moments to pass. 'No, he didn't come back here first. He went north from Arra and then crossed the mountain pass, and came down by Aillwee and the flax garden.' It was not quite an answer but it would do him for the moment.

He looked puzzled, didn't know the land west of his own possessions very well, she thought. Never once, during her almost twenty years of office, had she known him to visit the flax garden.

'But what about the girl?' he asked suddenly. 'Did she go with him? Surely she was with him.' A shade of anger passed over his face. He must be quite strait-laced, she reflected in an amused fashion. The thought of Fiona had brought a look of hot indignation to his blue eyes.

'No,' she replied, 'they quarrelled. They parted and Eamon rode north, while Fiona went south by the route of O'Briensbridge and through Thomond west and Corcomroe.'

'I see,' he said. Oddly, he seemed relieved about that. Perhaps his notions of propriety were such that he felt it was better for a girl to ride alone at night rather than with a young man who had lived in the same law school and worked side by side with her for the last few months.

'I scolded Fiona for doing this,' continued Mara. 'I told her that you would have given her an escort.'

'I certainly would have been very happy to do that.' He said the words with great sincerity and Mara had no doubt that he was telling the truth.

'There is another problem,' she continued. 'You signed the deed and gave it back to Eamon −' she waited for his nod before continuing − 'but unfortunately when the body was discovered, his satchel, which he would have worn strung across his body, was lying in a different place. It had been opened and it was empty.'

'The deed had been stolen!' The shock in his voice was almost as great as when he had heard the news that the young man had been killed.

'Yes,' said Mara briefly. She had said what she had planned to say and had observed his reactions. Shocked and horrified, was probably how she would have characterized them.

Whatever mystery there was about Eamon's death, it certainly
had come as a surprise to this man. Of course, she reminded
herself, her judgement was not infallible. Brian Ruadh could
be just a good actor. It would have been easy for a man of
his power to send a trusted man-of-arms after the young
lawyer. Perhaps his surprise was about the location of the
murder and the news that Fiona and Eamon had parted. And
yet, why should Eamon be of interest to him? Even if he did
dislike Eamon's father, why harm the son? She thought about
her colleague, Fergus MacClancy, Brehon of the kingdom of
Corcomroe, a man thirty years older than she. He would
know all the gossip about the Brehon of Cloyne. She resolved
to have a word with him as soon as possible. Perhaps on the
day that the party set out for Aran she would ride with them
to the coast and call into the MacClancy law school on the
way back.

'And since the deed is missing and therefore no longer valid,'
she continued smoothly, 'I was wondering whether we should
take advantage of your presence and hold the auction again
tomorrow, if you could spare the time to ride with me up to
the flax garden in the afternoon.'

There was something hesitant about the way in which he
promised. She handed him over to Conor and went back to
her room for a few minutes before facing the dinner party
again. She felt tired and discouraged and torn into too many
pieces. This murder, if it was a murder and not just an unfortunate accident, was proving puzzling and she felt that she
wasn't tackling it systematically.

Perhaps, thought Mara, she was really not able to cope
with anything extra outside her daily routine. Perhaps she
should not have insisted on keeping on the law school and
her appointment as Brehon of the Burren when she got
married. Perhaps it was all getting too much for her – and
then there was Cormac. If only she could be like one of the
women in the farms around, going about her daily duties
with a baby tucked snugly into a sling on her back. If only
she could spare the time to be with him more often. Brigid
had reported proudly that Cormac had said his first word – it
was only a two-letter word – a loud and explosive 'No'

apparently, but it felt sad that his mother had not been there to hear it.

'So, had the O'Brien of Arra anything of interest to say about the death of your young lawyer?' enquired Ulick, coming to join Mara as she stood watching the servants scurry to and fro, spreading the dinner feast on the huge table in the hall. This would be the last ceremonial meal for most of the guests; only Ulick, Donán, Conor and Brian Ruadh would be left behind to escort Turlough on his annual visit to Aran. The rest would depart for Thomond after a quick breakfast.

'Not much,' said Mara briefly. The wretched little man had probably been looking out of his window and observed all of her conversation with the Lord of Arra.

'That's his trouble, poor man,' said Ulick with a sigh. 'He never does have much of interest to say. It makes him a very boring person. No friends, you know. Watch Teige trying to get away from him!'

'I thought him charming! So sincere!' retorted Mara. 'It makes quite a change for me.'

'Dear Brehon. So sharp.' He smiled at her benignly before adding, 'It's a wonderful thing, this legal training, is it not? Sharpens the wits – and the tongue.'

'Allows a man to talk his way into and out of every situation, wouldn't you say, Ulick?' said Mara sweetly and added, 'Remind me, Ulick, which was the law school where you studied?'

'Not me, Brehon. I just pick up pieces of knowledge here and there from acquaintances and friends; just a crumb from the medical profession, another crumb from the lawyers. Used to haunt the house of my father's Brehon at one stage; got quite a few crumbs from him.' Ulick put his head to one side, observing her from one eye, looking quite like a little bird himself. 'But let's not talk of me, Brehon,' he went on, 'let's talk of you and your new scholar. How charming it is to see the female sex taking over the profession.' Ulick's eyes went across the room to where Fiona was merrily shaking her curls as Seamus the poet read from a manuscript.

'I thought it was Nuala you were interested in last night,' said Mara. She spoke more sadly than she intended. Nuala was a great favourite of hers. Mór, Nuala's mother, had been a great friend of hers and the poor girl had died when her daughter was only nine years old. Mara had promised to watch over the child. She had seen her grow tall in body and strong in mind. Straight as an arrow, through and through, thought Mara. A girl of huge intelligence, great determination, hard-working, sincere and compassionate – but alone in the world, with few to care for her. This young poet, Seamus MacCraith, was talented, highly educated and would have been a good husband for her, but it looked as though his interest was focussed on Fiona. Mara glanced back at Ulick, half wishing that he would praise Nuala, would admire her new-found poise and the improvement in her looks, but he only said lightly, 'It's just a matter of business, my dear Brehon, a matter of business – the older I get, the more I realize that everything comes down to business. One girl is prettier than the other, but that can't blind me to the fact that the other girl is possessed of a good fortune.'

'Ulick,' said Mara throwing caution to the winds in a fit of exasperation. 'You have three living wives, two dead wives, two mistresses to my certain knowledge. Just leave Nuala alone and allow her to choose a young man of her age and whom she loves.'

'She seems to be taking her time over it,' sighed Ulick. 'Let's hope that the bloom doesn't disappear while she is choosing. Still, she's dark-skinned and dark-haired like you, and look how you have kept your looks, Brehon, so let's hope that the same good fortune attends little Nuala.'

'I think we can all take our seats now,' said Mara. 'You sit here, Ulick. Seamus, I'll put you here – and Nuala between you both. Fiona, bring down my Lord of Arra and we will entertain him between us.'

Adroitly she went around the table seating friends together, keeping enemies apart. Ciara O'Brien, Teige's friendly and talkative wife, would keep Turlough in good humour. The silent Ragnelt, well away from her surly husband, Donán, but placed beside the bishop who would make conversation enough for two. The Limerick O'Briens well separated from the O'Briens of Clondelaw.

The soup was taken in comparative peace with neighbours murmuring to each other, but then someone brought up a battle of a hundred years ago and immediately hackles began to rise. Mara decided to intervene swiftly. Let the last meal end in peace.

'My lord,' she said in the clear, carrying voice which she used at public meetings. 'I wonder whether our guests have heard the full story of the unfortunate death of the young lawyer, Eamon, who dined with you all at this very table two nights ago.'

'So sad, such a handsome young man,' said Ciara in a comfortable tone of voice. She had obviously heard the news from Teige.

'Where did it happen?' The O'Brien of Clonderaw addressed his question to Donán and Mara waited while her husband's son-in-law took a long draught of wine.

'On the mountain.' It wasn't a very full answer, but that was Donán, who appeared to bear a permanent grudge and who offered words with the hesitancy of one who was giving away pieces of silver.

'Yes,' confirmed Mara, 'on the Aillwee Mountain, the very place where you all hunted on Saturday morning.'

'Ulick got us all out of bed early,' chuckled Teige O'Brien, cousin and foster-brother to the king, and then looked serious when his wife gave him a reproachful look. 'Terrible, terrible thing to happen, a young man like that,' he muttered.

'I wondered whether anyone might have seen something. Might have noticed him fall . . .' I'll leave it at that, she thought. The word 'murder' might make everyone clam up.

As it was, the questions came quickly. Everyone was intrigued.

'Where was he coming from?' Mara fielded that neatly, referring to Brian Ruadh to corroborate the hour when Eamon had left. There were few surprised remarks about the route that the young man took, but people were busy asking each other whether they remembered seeing someone on the mountain pass.

'What was he wearing, Brehon?' asked Teige.

'He was wrapped in an undyed *brat*,' said Mara with a sigh.

If only Eamon had worn his blue cloak there might have been
some chance of him being seen, but the other, with its untreated
rough, cream-coloured wool, had probably been warmer for
the midnight ride.

'And he was riding a white Connemara pony,' she added.

'Difficult to see against the limestone,' said Ulick. 'In fact,
I avoided looking at the stone with the sun glittering on it. I
must get you to look into my eyes, my dear young physician,'
he said to Nuala. 'I fear that I have injured them. Light always
hurts them.'

Mara gave him an exasperated glance, but decided that Nuala
could easily handle Ulick.

'What could you see from the side of Aillwee?' She threw
the question out, looking around the table. 'This would have
been an hour or so before I met you. I think that you had
already killed the first two wolves and the third had been
scented by the dogs. You all came towards the flax garden.'

And then she sat back and allowed the broken sentences,
the contradictions, the assertions to flow into her brain. Fiona,
she was pleased to note, had stopped looking across the table
at Seamus MacCraith, the poet, and had an eager face turned
towards the other guests and seemed to be thinking hard about
their recollections of the wolf hunt.

'What do you think of your little godson?' asked Mara. After
the meal had finished, she, Nuala and Fiona walked down the
stairs to the babies' nursery on the floor beneath the great hall.
Nuala had asked to see Cormac, to have a proper look at him
and Fiona had joined in. Mara was glad of both of their
company.

The room was a lovely one. When she and Turlough had
planned the new extension to the ancient tower house of
Ballinalacken, she had envisaged the possibility of bearing a
king's son. Designed by Mara down to the last detail, this was
a room that should be every child's dream. It was a large room,
full of small alcoves, little nooks and secret corners, a place full
of light and playthings, a place for a very special child to grow
to maturity. A large window, barred for safety, overlooking the
Atlantic Ocean, with a view on to the Aran Islands, had a low,

cosily cushioned wide window seat in front of it, providing a place for her child to sit and dream or read some of the books that Mara had carefully preserved from her own childhood; a wooden horse that rocked when a child sat on it was in one corner and in the other a splendid model of a miniature tower house peopled with tiny warriors.

'Doing well.' Nuala picked up Cormac and weighed him in her arms and then put him down on the floor, watching him crawl rapidly across and grab triumphantly at the cloth that lay on top of the table. In a moment he had pulled it down and Cliona laughed. 'You little villain,' she crooned, picking up Cormac and nuzzling into him, causing him to dissolve in a fit of giggles and then replacing him on the floor. She had no sooner put back the tablecloth when her son, little Art, pulled on the cloth. At the top of his voice, Cormac shouted, 'No!' Cliona laughed, beaming on them proudly.

'The son of a king,' said Nuala with an ironic smile. 'All must obey him. They're both lovely, Cliona. You must take such care of them.'

'I wish Cormac was a little fatter – but he gets all that he can take.' Cliona shot a quick glance at Mara and then back at Nuala.

'He's a different build to Art,' said Nuala knowledgeably. 'I've been doing a bit of training with children in Thomond and it's surprising how they differ. They all have their own ways of progressing. Cormac looks very healthy to me.'

'That's good,' said Cliona. 'I'll take Art away now and let you have time on your own with Cormac.'

'No, leave him,' said Mara. 'You go. We'll look after both. You deserve a little rest and the two amuse each other.' As soon as the door closed behind Cliona, she turned away from the little boys and asked the two girls, 'What did you make of all the recollections of Saturday morning's hunting that we've just heard?'

'That story of the row going on in the flax garden. That was interesting,' said Nuala.

'I didn't hear that.' Mara was annoyed with herself. She frowned and then smiled when she saw Cormac look at her alertly. Clever little fellow, he can already read expressions, she thought proudly.

'You were probably listening to Conor, who was speaking at the same time,' said Fiona. 'I found what he said to be the most interesting. Do you think that he really saw someone on the mountain pass with a white pony?'

'It was probably Eamon leading the pony,' said Nuala.

'No, I don't think so.' Fiona was so quick to contradict that Mara wondered whether there was a slight rivalry between the two girls. 'Eamon was wearing a white cloak – and the *bánín* was just the same colour as the pony's coat. He wouldn't have stood out against the pony in the same way as someone wearing a coloured cloak, or even a leather jacket.'

'That makes sense,' admitted Nuala.

'The trouble is that Conor then said that he couldn't remember what colour the cloak was, and by the end of it all, it was hard to know whether he had seen anything at all. He doesn't seem like a king's son, does he?'

Mara nodded. She had felt sorry for Turlough. His eldest son, and *tánaiste* – heir – did not look like kingship material. The clan were not happy with him. He had grown out of his earlier delicacy and now looked much stronger, but he was still a shy and diffident young man. She decided to turn the conversation back to the scene on the mountain.

'Who was talking about a row in the flax gardens?' asked Mara. She was still annoyed with herself that she had not heard that story. She had been too lost in her concerns about Conor.

'Just Ulick.' Nuala's tone was dismissive.

'Oh, Ulick!' Mara was disappointed. Ulick might or might not have heard something going on, but the chances were strong that he had only said that to make mischief.

'Just Cathal shouting at his son and calling him stupid; that seemed to be about all there was to it. I'll make a note of everything when I go back to my bedroom,' said Fiona in a businesslike way. 'Did you hear anything else, Nuala?' she asked sweetly.

Nuala shrugged her shoulders. She took down from a high shelf a soft ball made from segments of cloth and stuffed with sheep's wool and rolled it along the floor. The two babies scrambled after it. Art reached it first, but Cormac took it from him. Art made no protest, but seized the ball between his white new teeth, tugged it out of Cormac's hand, and set off crawling rapidly with the ball dangling from his mouth. Cormac followed him with a cry of rage.

'I thought that Donán said something about a tall man coming to the edge of the flax garden and looking up? Did either of you notice that?' asked Mara.

'Yes, I did,' said Nuala turning back from her game with the children. 'I remember thinking that he probably meant Owney. That's Cathal's son,' she explained to Fiona.

'Do you know him then, Nuala?' asked Mara and Nuala smiled broadly.

'I don't think there was a Saturday or Sunday for the whole of my childhood when he didn't turn up at my father's place wanting doctoring. He was either bleeding, or stunned or with a broken finger or something like that.'

'My lads admire him immensely. He is supposed to be the best hurler that the Burren has ever fielded,' said Mara. Nuala's words had made her think of something.

'Did your father ever give him any advice about avoiding injury?' she asked.

'He kept telling him to stop or he would kill himself,' said Nuala wryly. 'I remember telling Owney that I would make something out of leather to protect his head if he would wear it, but he said that he couldn't because it would slip and get in his way. He begged me not to do it. Didn't trust my sewing, I suppose.'

'So you told him that he could be killed by a blow to the head,' said Mara thoughtfully. 'How old were you then, Nuala?'

'I suppose that it was about four or five years ago,' said Nuala, thinking back. 'It was just about the time that the housekeeper kept trying to make me stitch a sampler. I wasn't very successful at that so I don't suppose I would have been too good at making a protection for Owney's head. I must have been about eleven.'

'I remember you then,' said Mara with a smile. 'You told everyone in great detail about what you were studying. I bet that Owney got a lecture on the dangerous places to be hit on the head or even the body.'

'I suppose so – all long words, too – the longer the better

I used to think in those days.' Nuala stopped, her smile vanished and she didn't look surprised when Fiona said, 'If that's true, then I suppose Owney would know all about the windows to the soul and where was the place to hit if you wanted to kill a man.'

'He might have remembered.' Nuala spoke guardedly, her dark eyes wary.

'Do you remember mentioning things like temporal fossa and occipital fossa and thyroid cartilage to him?' asked Fiona sharply.

Nuala shrugged. 'I may have done,' she said in a casual tone. 'Mara, now that the king is going to Aran, do you know whether I am going back to Thomond tomorrow? I just came for the christening. I want to get on with my studies.'

'I'm not sure. I'll talk to him tonight about you.'

'It's just that Seamus MacCraith said that he was riding back tomorrow.' Nuala shot a quick, questioning and slightly triumphant glance at Fiona as the door opened and Cliona came in.

'It's time for them to be fed now or we'll be having tears soon,' she said, sitting down on a low chair and allowing the babies to scramble up on to her lap.

'We'll go then and leave you in peace,' said Mara rising to her feet. 'Nuala, I'll find out if there is a suitable escort to take you back to Thomond tomorrow. If there isn't, then it would be lovely to keep you for a week until the king and his entourage get back from Aran.'

What about poor Fachtnan, she thought, as she followed the two girls upstairs. Is either of them wondering where he is and what he is thinking at this moment?

Ten

Brecha Nemeɒ Coísech
(The Laws for Professional People)

There are two kinds of poets, the fili and − inferior in status and accomplishment − the bard. A bard receives only half the honour price of a fili of the same rank.

The poet is a lay professional who has full nemed *status. His honour price is ten* séts, *five ounces of silver or five milch cows. A woman poet is known as banfili and her honour price is the same as that of a man poet. The poet's main function is to praise or to satirize. A poet derives his status from three skills:*

1. imbas forosna: *encompassing knowledge which illuminates*
2. teinm laeda: *breaking of marrow − going to the heart of the matter*
3. dichetal di chennaub: *coming from the head − he is able to extemporize on any occasion.*

For every poem commissioned by a patron the poet should receive a duas *(fee) depending on his rank and the nature of the composition. He must produce quality; if he doesn't, he loses his* nemed *status. If the poet is not paid he has the right to satirize his patron.*

'Ulick has it all planned out. We're going to go in two *pucáns*. We'll put most of the men − all of them except the two bodyguards − into one *pucán* and then Ulick, myself, Conor, the O'Brien of Arra, Donán, and Fergal and Conall, of course, into the other one. We'll have great *craic* altogether.' Turlough was like a schoolboy planning his boat trip, thought Mara indulgently. He was such a sweet-natured man. He was not fond of either O'Brien or of Donán but he was set to enjoy his holiday and, good-humouredly, would make the time to be a pleasure for all around him.

'Isn't a *pucán* a bit small,' observed Mara idly, her mind on the affair of Eamon. 'I'd have thought that you would go in a cog or carrack or a hooker. Wouldn't that be more suitable for a king?'

Turlough's only answer to that was a hearty laugh so she decided to leave his affairs to him and to go back to her own.

'Nuala is anxious to go back to Thomond. Is it all young men riding back there tomorrow, or is there anyone suitable to put in charge of her?' she asked. I sound like an old hen with one chick, she thought wryly, but after Fiona's escapade she would prefer to be careful. Nuala was very dear to her and, despite her formidable intellect, was, in some ways, just a child.

'Keep her until next Saturday,' advised Turlough. 'Tell her that I will enjoy her company on the ride. Seamus MacCraith is a talented young fellow, but he has a bit of a reputation. The women and most of the others are only going as far as Inchiquin – they'll spend a few days there and join us on the way back.'

'I think that Seamus MacCraith is more interested in Fiona than in Nuala,' said Mara, 'but you're right. I'll be firm with her. Tell her I need her help with my investigation. Turlough, what am I going to do about our little Cormac?'

'Cormac? You're not worrying about him, are you? He's looking great. He grows every time I look at him. Bright little fellow with a will of his own! Loved coming up on my horse, didn't he?'

'And threw a tantrum when you took him down!'

Turlough laughed with pleasure. 'That's what I mean. Got a great will of his own. You compare him to that pasty-faced son of mine Conor! Our little Cormac is the image of the great Brian Boru himself.'

'Or Teige the Bone-Splitter,' said Mara wryly. 'He's not going to become a warrior; I plan for him to become a Brehon,' she said firmly, 'but he is not a year old and now we have to think what happens next. Cliona wants to go back to her own farm and that is understandable, but now I have to face the decision whether to wean Cormac, find a nursemaid for him. Brigid has too much to do to care for him and . . .'

'Would Cliona foster him? Take him with her? That would be the best thing for him,' interrupted Turlough eagerly. 'He's getting on so well with her. We could always look for another fosterage when he is a little older, if you think that is not grand enough for him.'

'She proposed that,' said Mara. She felt her heart sink. She was not surprised when Turlough said enthusiastically, 'That's wonderful. He has his little friend, his little brother. What's his name? Little Art. They are great friends together. It makes sense, doesn't it?'

'It does,' said Mara.

Turlough was on his way out, but stopped, his attention alerted by something bleak in her tone, she supposed.

'But you're not happy with it, is that it? What would you like to do?'

Mara gave a deep sigh. 'I'm just being stupid,' she said. 'It's just that I don't seem to see too much of him even as it is. At least, at the moment, I can go in and look at him when he is asleep, or snatch the odd moment . . .'

'So you'd prefer to have someone in the house, would you?' queried Turlough anxiously.

Mara thought about it. It might be difficult to get another wet nurse, so Cormac would have to be weaned before he was ready; would, at the same time, have to face a parting between himself, Cliona and his little friend Art.

'I'm just being stupid. Of course it would be better to leave him with Cliona for another couple of years,' she said, endeavouring to produce a light laugh. It worked, of course. She knew that it would. Turlough was not the sort of man who looked beneath things. His face cleared instantly.

'I'm sure you're right,' he said heartily. 'It isn't as if he will be on the other side of the country – Cliona's place must be only about five minutes from Cahermacnaghten. Where did you say? Baur North, wasn't it?'

'That's right,' said Mara. 'Baur North.' Her son would grow strong in that fertile limestone valley, would play in the flower-studded meadows with his friend and foster-brother,

would embrace the curly coated, newborn lambs, help to
herd the sheep from field to field, as she had seen other small
boys do, lug heavy bales of straw, shut the barn against wolves.
He was an active, wilful child. He would not be content
to sit in the corner of the schoolhouse with a lump of clay to
mould or a piece of cloth to sew as her daughter Sorcha
had been. This was the best decision for him. Resolutely,
she got to her feet. The customs of Ancient Ireland sancti-
fied it. Good sense applauded it as the best possible of all
decisions.

'I'll have a word with Cliona now,' she said.

The sun had moved over into the west by the time that
Mara went down the steeply spiralling staircase. As she glanced
through the narrow arrow-slit window she could see that the
sky over Aran was crimson with streaks of blue and the sea
had that evening stillness, which comes before a frosty night.
A couple of large, white-sailed boats glided across it, making
for the islands, and a solitary seagull, ignoring the boats,
scanned the seas near to the coastline.

There was a buzz of conversation from the great hall – peals
of laughter, voices raised merrily, an atmosphere of jollity
and good-humour that had been a feature of the short holiday
at Ballinalacken castle. Mara was glad that it still prevailed,
despite the fact that the hostess had been preoccupied with
the unexpected and puzzling death of the young lawyer. She
was about to join them when she heard a soft sound from
behind her.

A large three-mullioned window had been placed on
the landing outside the door to the great hall. It was set into
the six-foot-thick wall on the western side of the castle. It
gave a wonderful view over the Atlantic Ocean to anyone
descending the stairs but now the thick velvet curtains were
closed in front of it, cutting off the cushioned window seat
from view. Two pairs of feet showed below the curtains and
there was a soft murmur from behind them. A murmur that
flowed mellifluously – the alliterating words and the rhyming
syllables chiming melodically like bells struck in a rhythmic
sequence.

Mara paused. The poem was very beautiful, a hymn of

praise to loveliness: to hair more gold than the treasures of kings; to lips more red than rubies; to eyes that held the blue of oceans. It was easy to guess which couple sat concealed in the window seat.

Turlough will have to wait for his poem about the joys of hunting, she thought with a smile. Seamus MacCraith had found in Fiona a more worthy subject. She was about to continue downwards when the words suddenly ceased, midline, and then came a strange sound. Strangled sobs from the man and Fiona's voice murmuring consolation. Mara frowned. This seemed more serious than she had realized. The poet had only met the girl a few days ago. Still, love could flare up quickly in the young. She hesitated for a minute before going on down the stairs towards the nursery. She had no desire to play the part of an eavesdropper, but as Brehon she had a responsibility to investigate that secret and unlawful killing. If Seamus MacCraith had been completely bowled over by Fiona's beauty, had fallen madly in love with the girl, with all the intensity of feeling which a poet possessed, what had he felt when Fiona disappeared for that midnight ride with Eamon? Was it possible that he was the secret follower of the pair, that when Fiona parted from Eamon, he had watched her safely cross O'Briensbridge, then turned back, followed the young lawyer and killed him? Whether the killing was murder or an unhappy accident was a matter that Mara had still not decided.

This made her think of the party that night. Fiona had been dancing with Shane, then she seemed to disappear. But Seamus MacCraith had not disappeared; quite clearly Mara remembered seeing him dance with Nuala. This decided her. Cliona, and Cormac's future had to wait for the moment. She went soundlessly back up the stairs to Nuala's room. As she had guessed, Nuala was there, lying on her bed studying an old, tattered book.

'Was that belonging to your grandfather?' asked Mara with a nod towards the book.

'No,' said Nuala. She gave a slight smile. 'I think that I have every word that grandfather wrote engraved on my brain. My professor, Donough the healer, as they call him in

Thomond, gave me that. It belonged to his father. He told me to take great care of it as it is meant for his son who is studying in Italy at the moment.' She shut the book and turned, swinging her legs to the ground. 'Mara,' she said abruptly, 'is there any news of Fachtnan?'

'I wanted to ask you about Fachtnan.' Mara postponed the discussion of the poet for the moment. Fachtnan was very dear to her and Nuala was a clever girl whose opinion was always worth having. 'What do you think happened to him?'

'I've been thinking about that,' said Nuala seriously. 'I even made a little list here of possible reasons for his disappearance.' She flicked though the pages of her book and then produced a leaf of vellum filled with her strong, slanting handwriting. 'I copied this from your scholars when they were debating a murder,' she added, and then read aloud:

'Motives: *Fear, anger, revenge, greed.* That's right isn't it?'

'I should have made a lawyer of you – life might have been easier for you, if I did,' said Mara studying the dark-skinned, dark-eyed face of the girl opposite and thinking of her struggle for knowledge. Nuala's father had been a physician, but he had no sympathy with his daughter's desire to follow in her father's footsteps. She didn't have the over-whelming beauty of Fiona, but to Mara's eyes she was an extremely attractive girl; tall, slim and her very black hair had the high gloss of expensive silk. Why had Fachtnan chosen to fall in love with Fiona when this girl offered herself and her fortune to him?

'I think to be a physician was bred in the bone,' said Nuala with a dry smile. 'Anyway, to go back to Fachtnan's disappearance, when I went through that list, I thought that there was something left out. Quite a few extra possibilities occurred to me.'

'And to me, also,' said Mara. 'Because this, I pray God,' she went on quietly, 'was not a murder. Or if it was, there is no strong reason why it should have been committed by a fellow scholar. Perhaps Fachtnan just felt bad and decided to go home a few days early. We know that he was in the schoolhouse early on Saturday morning, so no harm came to him on that moonlit night when Eamon and Fiona went on that disastrous expedition. There could be lots of ordinary, everyday explanations as to why a boy of nineteen suddenly goes missing.'

If only Fachtnan were not Fachtnan, she thought. If he were any of the other boys; Moylan, Aidan, or even Enda who, after a turbulent adolescence, was now soberly working as a lawyer in Thomond. Her mind ranged through all of her scholars through her almost twenty years of teaching. Fachtnan stood out amongst the cheerful, noisy throng as well behaved, sober, considerate and polite. It was just so unlike him to disappear like this that wild notions of abduction had begun to race through her mind.

'You haven't asked me what I would add to the list of possible motives.' Nuala was watching Mara's face with her intelligent dark eyes.

'Tell me.' Mara tried to smile, but she had a feeling that all this was getting too much for her.

'I wonder whether he has decided to test whether he could be a Brehon,' said Nuala tentatively. 'You know he feels that he has failed twice. Only once, in fact, I know, the year before he was due to take his examination, but you advised him to leave it and then he did fail last summer. He told me once that he has no interest in being just a lawyer. What he wanted was to be a Brehon like you and keep the peace in a community.'

'And I've always thought that was what he was suited to,' said Mara. 'How well you understand him.' Perhaps, she thought, Fachtnan will come back to Nuala and forget this obsession about Fiona. He seemed to have confided his dreams and hopes to her. However, that was probably before the delicate, blonde beauty of Fiona had enraptured him.

'So,' continued Nuala, 'I just wondered whether he had decided to go off and to solve the murder himself. You know. Hunt down the murderer and bring him back in triumph to lie at the feet of the wronged maiden.'

'Don't be sarcastic,' said Mara with an amused smile. 'Still there is something in what you say and I'll think about it. You've cheered me. Now I must go. There's just one more thing I want to ask you about that night. Do you remember that you danced with Seamus MacCraith? I think it was just after Fiona danced with Shane and everyone was looking at her. And then the music started up again and I saw you dance with the poet.'

'That's right,' said Nuala indifferently. 'The king told him to dance with me and so he obeyed.'

'Just the one dance?' queried Mara.

'Just the one. I didn't see him for the rest of the night. In fact, he didn't even finish the dance with me. Do you remember? It was the *Rince Fada* – long dance – and when I came back up to the top again, he had disappeared. I had to call Hugh over to stand opposite to me.'

'I see,' said Mara. She frowned thoughtfully. It looked as though once Seamus MacCraith noticed that Fiona had disappeared, he also left the hall. But where did he go? Did he follow the two? Or did he merely retire to the guards' room, along with other non-dancers, and have something to drink there? That might be something that Moylan would have noticed as he had been popping out and in with great regularity and once came back wiping his mouth with his sleeve.

'Don't start making matches for me, Mara. I'll do my own work there.' Nuala was watching, her lips twisted in a wry grin. 'After all, I am a woman of fortune. I should be able to find a husband somewhere.'

'I wasn't making a match, I promise.' Mara laughed. 'You find yourself a husband when you are ready. I'm not in favour of early marriages. It's a big decision. Get qualified first before you rush into marriage. That brings its own strains. You no longer just have to think about yourself but there is also a husband, and then, perhaps, a baby to think about. Now I must go. I have to talk to Cliona about Cormac. I have a problem I must solve.'

'I take your point.' Nuala nodded condescendingly. 'A professional woman has many problems when they take on a husband and a child. I'll probably remain single. I'd like to travel around the world and meet other physicians, like the son of my teacher, Donough Og O'Hickey, does. That would be interesting.'

Nevertheless, there was a bleak note in the young voice, thought Mara, as she made her way down the stairs, passing the window seat where the young poet and Fiona still sat, concealed except for their feet.

Eleven

Oíre
(Text on Honour Prices)

Fosterage is the way that children are reared. It is known as the 'shared cradle'. The foster mother is known by her foster child as Muimme and the foster father as Datan.

Fosterage can be undertaken for affection, perhaps by a relative, in which case no fee is paid. Otherwise fosterage is for a fee. The fee is calculated according to the honour price of the child's father.

The fee for the son of an ocaire *(small farmer) is three séts or one and a half ounces of silver and four séts for a daughter. The fee for the son of a king is thirty séts or fifteen ounces of silver and forty séts for a daughter.*

Cáin Iarraich
(The Law of Fosterage)

The son of a king must be supplied with a horse for riding and with clothing worth seven séts, or three and a half ounces of silver. He must be educated according to his rank, taught to play chess, horsemanship, swimming and marksmanship. A daughter of a king must be taught how to make silken garments and how to embroider.

The son of an ocaire *must be taught how to care for lambs, calves and pigs. He must know how to dry corn, chop firewood and comb wool. A daughter of an* ocaire *must be taught how to use the quern, the kneading-trough and the sieve.*

Mara went on down the passageway and stood outside the nursery for a moment listening to the shrieks of excitement from within. This was a room where she had envisaged her son would spend up to six months every year. She had prepared with such care for this child. How much time would he spend there in the future?

But plans don't always work out and Mara now faced that possibility. Cormac was a strong-willed, active child, not a mirror image of his mother or of his half-sister. His needs were perhaps different to those that she had envisaged. Companionship of his little foster-brother was essential to him and this would continue as he grew and became even more active. Unlike her daughter, Sorcha, he would not be content to sit in the corner of the schoolhouse with a piece of sewing, or to model little cups and figures of animals from a lump of clay. Cormac, unless he changed, would be bored to fury by such a regime. He would be better leading an active life on a farm, standing in gateways brandishing a stick as the animals were herded to different fields, carrying bales of hay for winter feeding, leading a life of fun and companionship with his foster-brother, skating on icy ponds in the winter and swimming in the sea in summer.

The matter had now been decided. She had to bear herself with dignity and grace and do the best for this late-born son of hers, the young Prince Cormac O'Brien, born of the union between Mara, Brehon of Burren, and Turlough, king of Thomond, Corcomroe and Burren.

Inside the room there was a happy scene. Cliona was on her knees racing around the room, barking like a dog and the two little boys were shrieking and crawling rapidly across the room after her. Cormac saw his mother, stopped, then approached Cliona fiercely shouting 'no' and then smacked her hard on the head.

'You are getting too bold for your own good,' exclaimed Mara, picking him up and holding him in her arms. For a moment she strained him to her and then put him down again.

'No!' shouted Art and they wrestled together sprawling on the floor, cheeks flushed with excitement.

Cliona beamed at both boys. 'They're so clever,' she crooned. 'They'll be picking up new words every day now.'

Mara watched the two babies. They were making such a noise that any conversation would be impossible. Perhaps she could postpone her talk with Cliona. She sat on the window seat, looking out towards Aran. The day was very clear and she could see the gold sand on the island beach and above it the castle belonging to Brian the Spaniard, rearing up towards the blue skyline. It was a day of no wind and a few large white-sailed boats seemed to stand quite still in the middle of the sea. Two or three black coracles, rowed by the islanders, made rapid progress by contrast and they seemed to be on their way across to the becalmed ships.

A silence made her turn her head. Art had quite suddenly fallen asleep on a large floor cushion; Cormac stared at him for a minute, but then his blonde eyelashes drooped over his eyes. He put his head down on the cushion beside his foster-brother, put one arm around the other baby's chest, snuggled into him and in a moment was sleeping peacefully, also. Mara found her eyes wet with tears.

'They're like that,' said Cliona softly. 'They're great children. When one sleeps, the other drops off straight away.' She took from a carved chest a cover woven by Brigid from soft lambs-wool, and tucked it around the two children. Then she put some more turf on the fire and tidied away all of the playthings, avoiding Mara's eye. Both women were tense; Mara recognized that and knew that she had to speak now.

'I've been thinking about what you said, Cliona, and I've discussed it with the king.' She paused for a moment and then hurried on, 'We both feel that it would be very wrong to take Cormac away from you now; he is doing so well and is so happy with you and with little Art.'

Cliona was rigid, but her eyes filled with tears. 'Do you mean you want me to go on living with you or that you agree to allow me to foster him?' she asked and Mara could tell from the note of fear that although she might hope for the second, she feared the first was the most likely.

'I want you to foster him until the age of five, but I want to see as much of him as I can, perhaps borrow him for short holidays as he gets a little older. Is that too much to ask?'

Cliona smiled radiantly, drawing a hand across, first her right cheek and then her left. Her eyes were bright with tears, but also delight. 'Not too much to ask at all!' she exclaimed. 'We live so close. We can visit you after school is finished for the day, or you can visit us; whatever is easiest for you. I'm so happy. I feared that you would not agree.'

She hesitated and then said in a rush of words, 'I must tell you the whole truth. I want to get back to my own place because I am thinking of getting married again.'

'What! Well, the king will be pleased to hear that. Who is the lucky man?'

'He's another O'Connor, but from a different clan, from Corcomroe, not far from here. He's a fisherman from Doolin. He has his own boat. His name is Setanta. Cumhal knows him. He'll tell you all about him. Brigid buys fish from him. That's how I got to know him; met him often in the kitchen in Cahermacnaghten.' The sentences came out jerkily from Cliona and she watched Mara carefully.

'I know who you mean!' Mara felt very relieved. Setanta O'Connor had been bringing fish to the law school at Cahermacnaghten on Fridays since he was a boy of ten years old, or even less. He had been a sensible, grown-up young man even then, competently driving a donkey and cart and conscientiously refusing invitations from her boys to join in a game of hurling, explaining that he had to deliver his fish quickly so that it was nice and fresh.

'Setanta O'Connor is lovely. I'm so happy for you both,' she continued. For a moment, after the first exclamation of pleasure, but before the name was mentioned, she had begun to worry a little. She had been completely happy with Cliona's care of her son, but she wasn't sure about a new man in the household. Would he take to the two babies, neither of whom was his? But Setanta – well, that was different. She knew him well. He would make a wonderful foster father.

'And about the fee—' started Cliona, but Mara interrupted her, laughing gaily.

'I'll draw up the deed, Cliona, don't worry about that, but I'll just tell you now that the usual fee for the son of a king is fifteen ounces of silver, or fifteen cows. It can be either – whatever suits you.'

'I don't want a fee. I will foster him for love,' said Cliona, 'but I want to ask a favour of you. I want Art to have an education just like Cormac. Do you think it is possible? It would be like a dream coming true for me to have my son a lawyer. I'm teaching myself to read so that I can teach them once they learn to talk. Look!' She crossed over to the chest and took out some scraps of vellum and Mara could see lots of three-letter words neatly written on the old scraps. 'Brigid gave me these – you don't mind, do you? She's been teaching me. She said you taught her when you were a little girl – you were only three years old, that's what Brigid told me. She said that you were the cleverest child in the world.'

Mara laughed. 'Don't believe everything that Brigid tells you,' she warned. 'She brought me up, you know. She's more like a mother to me than anything else.' She looked carefully at Cliona. She was an intelligent woman and this had best be said now, rather than allow false hopes to build to great heights.

'Cliona,' she said carefully, 'I will start both Art and Cormac off in the law school when they are five years old, but nothing is sure so far as children are concerned. It's possible that neither boy will be of the right material. The training is long and arduous and they need to have perseverance, brains and a very, very good memory. My own daughter Sorcha did not have any interest in the law and I didn't force her. The same thing will apply to Cormac and Art; if they enjoy the work and prove to have an aptitude for it, then well and good, but if not, we will be just beating our heads against a stone wall. In fact,' she ended lightly, 'from what I see of Cormac I imagine that he will want to be a hurling player.'

Cliona laughed also. 'And Art will be a wrestler,' she said, trying to match Mara's light tone, but her eyes were shining with excitement. She was unable to keep still, but busied herself around the room, straightening cushions, getting nightshirts out from a chest and putting them to warm in front of the glowing fire.

'I'd better go now and let you put them to bed,' said Mara rising to her feet, but wishing that she could be the one to undress her son, give him his bath and put him to bed. It was not practical, though. She was Brehon of the Burren, wife of the king, hostess at Ballinalacken castle. She had a husband to organize for this sudden and unexpected trip to Aran, guests to speed on their way, and, foremost in her mind, a murder to solve.

'There's Setanta now. I know his footstep.' Cliona rushed to the door, but closed it behind her. No doubt she wanted to tell the good news in privacy. Mara waited, listening to the soft breathing of the two sleeping children.

They were before her in less than three minutes, both glowing with happiness. Mara smiled on them, gave her best wishes for their future happiness, but quickly went to the matter that was worrying her.

'I would like you to reconsider about the fosterage fee,' she said carefully, addressing her remarks to Setanta as well as to Cliona. 'It will be a sum of fifteen ounces of silver as Cormac is the son of a king – or else it could be fifteen cows.'

'Cows would be no good to me. I prefer the fish – they feed themselves, physic themselves, and find their own pastures,' said Setanta firmly.

'But what about the silver? What about a new boat?' asked Mara.

Setanta laughed. 'I have a boat that's a match to any boat in the sea,' he boasted. 'My grandfather made it, cut the hazel rods, covered it with the best leather. My father greased it three times every year and I do the same. That boat can fly across the water with only one man rowing – not like those English boats.' He nodded contemptuously towards the window. 'No, let Cliona try to make a lawyer out of little Art and that will be fee enough for us.'

Twelve

Brecha Nemeð Oéiðenach
(Last Laws for Noble People)

Every Brehon needs to have great knowledge. He must understand all ways of life in the kingdom that he presides over – knowledge of all occupations, trades and of all professions must be his.

Mesbretha *(estimation judgements):*

Every judge should be able to estimate at a glance the value of produce or artefacts. He should know:

1. *Value of the cloth on the loom*
2. *Value of the lambs on the mountain*
3. *Value of a breeding cow*
4. *Value of the crop in the field*
5. *Value of the leather on a shoemaker's last*
6. *Value of a woman's embroidery needle*
7. *Value of a heap of scutched flax*

When Mara and Fiona arrived at the law school on Monday morning, the boys were already there at their desks, shining with soap and enthusiasm. They rose to their feet politely to welcome Mara, but the excitement was so evident that instead of the customary morning greetings she just smiled and said, 'Well?'

'Well . . .' said Moylan teasingly as he slid along the second bench to make room for Fiona. 'Well . . . we had an interesting time yesterday afternoon.'

'Oh, indeed!' Mara gave him an appreciative smile. She was glad that Fiona had not been left to sit on her own on the front bench, where she normally sat between Fachtnan and Eamon. 'Come on, Moylan, tell me,' she said with feigned impatience.

'There was a fight,' said Moylan. 'He, Eamon, had been in a fight. He was hit over the head.'

'We found a stick,' supplemented Aidan.

'What do you mean "we"? I found it,' said Hugh.

'That's right.' Moylan took the matter back into his own hands. 'Hugh found it. And very well done to him,' he added in a patronizing manner.

Mara concealed a smile. Moylan seemed to be taking over the role of senior scholar at the law school. Fachtnan would have said something like that, though without the condescending overtones. Fachtnan's own learning difficulties always made him very sensitive to Hugh's problems.

'We've marked the spot, Brehon,' said Shane. 'When you see it you'll understand why. You tell her, Moylan.'

'There must have been a fight,' said Moylan wisely. 'We could see lots of skids . . .'

'On the patch of grass there.'

'And horseshoe prints.'

'The horse must have got worried . . .'

'And then bolted . . .'

'Found his way back to the stable . . .'

'There was a bit of blood on the stick . . .'

'And it was cracked . . .'

'Here it is, Brehon.' Moylan rushed over to the large wooden press containing the law books and documents and took from on top of it a stout, wooden stick.

'Heavy,' he said, balancing it between his hands and then placing it carefully on the empty front desk.

Mara bent over it. It was a typical stick – every farmer of the kingdom had a cudgel like that made from well-seasoned ash and tipped with iron. Few people in the community left home without something like this. It could be used to guide the footsteps over the uneven stone of the fields, to help in the scaling of high ground or mountain pastures, to herd the cattle or the sheep, or to guard against attack from a bull.

'Here's the blood,' said Moylan, pointing to the iron tip.

'There was not much blood on the tip even when I found it,' said Hugh taking ownership of his find. 'But look, Brehon, you can see that there had been some. Look how it has seeped into the ash.'

'We should have brought Nuala,' said Fiona. 'She could

examine the stick and say whether she thought that the wound
was made by it.'

'You're right,' said Mara. 'Aidan, would you go and fetch
her. You and Fiona,' she amended. A ride in Aidan's cheerful
company would be good for the rather silent and still pale
Fiona. 'Also, give this note to my lord, the king.' She took a
scrap of vellum from her own desk and scribbled a quick note
to Turlough asking him to send a man to guide O'Brien of
Arra to the flax garden after his midday meal at Ballinalacken.
'We'll take some food. It's fine and dry and we can have an
outdoor meal and stay there. We'll have the auction at two
o'clock. Shane, would you go and ask Brigid about the food,
Moylan would you go and tell Muiris O'Hynes about the
auction.' She pondered for a moment about whether she had
an obligation to let the rest of the kingdom know about this
auction, but decided that it was unnecessary. She had done her
legal duty before the first auction – had advertised it in the
kingdom's judgement place at the ancient dolmen of
Poulnabrone, had requested that time and place would be given
at every Mass in every church on the Burren. Only two people
had bid and the matter was now between these two.

'There is one more thing, Brehon, before we all fly off, like
angels, on different errands,' said Shane with a humorous quirk
to his mouth.

'You got that bit about angels being messengers from the
sermon two weeks ago,' accused Moylan.

'I'm glad you all listen so well in church,' said Mara, slightly
guilty as she realized that she had not heard that particular
sermon. She usually spent that time in church planning for
the week ahead. On that particular Sunday, she remembered,
she had been going through the arrangements for the flax
garden auction, mentally checking through the deed that she
needed to draw up with reference to the O'Brien of Arra
marriage settlement deed, dating from her father's early days
as a Brehon. 'What was it that you wanted to tell me, Shane?'
she said aloud.

'I just wanted to show you something,' said Shane, drawing
his pen case out from the satchel beside him. It was a beautiful
case, made from engraved leather. Shane's father had given it

to him as a present last summer when Shane had received a very high mark at his end of year examination. Shane was very proud of it and kept it beautifully polished and his carefully trimmed quill pens neatly arranged according to size within it. Now, as he took the lid off, Mara could see that there were no pens there, just a small heap of ash.

'I took it as I was afraid that it might blow away before you had a chance to see it, Brehon. There's more there, but I wanted to show you this.' He pointed and Mara lifted the case carefully and took it to the light of the window.

Then she could see what Shane's sharp eyes had spotted. As almost always happened when something is burned, a scrap of vellum had escaped the flames. And this scrap, by a miracle, contained a whole word: *aithech* – rent-payer. Mara looked up and around at the smiling faces of her boys.

'The deed was burned!' she said with certainty. 'This certainly changes matters. It begins to look . . .'

'Let me make the case, Brehon!' exclaimed Moylan. 'Unless you'd rather do it, Fiona, would you?'

Fiona shook her head humorously. 'No, go on, Moylan. You're bursting with it, I can see.'

Moylan cast a quick, defiant look at his juniors and took centre stage, standing by the fireplace and arranging an imaginary gown on his shoulders.

'Let me make the case for the murder of Eamon the Aigne from Cahermacnaghten law school. Eamon was murdered by . . . let us call him *the unknown man*—'

'Or woman,' interrupted Fiona. The colour had come back to her face and somehow she seemed to be more of her old self. Mara wondered whether Fiona had felt under suspicion and now had begun to think that the affair had been concerned with the deed for the flax garden.

'Let me refer to him or her as *the unknown*,' Moylan rushed on before any more interruptions occurred, 'who met Eamon, whether by appointment or by chance, and wrestled with him, trying to take away the deed before it could be delivered to the safe-keeping of the successful bidder, a man called Muiris O'Hynes.

'According to my junior friend, here, young Shane –' Moylan

bowed, almost overbalanced, straightened himself abruptly and glared at Aidan who had given a snort – 'according to my friend, there were two or three droppings on one spot which we think showed that the horse stood for some time while the murdered man and *the unknown* stood and talked.'

'Only one horse, we thought, Brehon,' interrupted Aidan. 'And that points to someone from the flax garden.'

'Am I making this case or is it you?' Moylan glared at his friend and added with heavy sarcasm, 'Of course, if you think that you can . . .'

'And then they struggled,' said Shane rapidly. 'You will see for yourself, Brehon.'

'So it seems to me,' said Moylan, hooking his thumbs under his armpits and inflating his chest, 'that a struggle took place, resulting in a fatal blow by *the unknown* and then the deed was burned and the body tumbled down the hill. Gentlemen – and ladies, of course – I make the case that this unlawful killing of Eamon the lawyer was committed by one or both of the two people who benefited from the deed being seized and then destroyed. And here in the privacy of the schoolhouse with the door well guarded by our faithful dog, Bran, I put forward the names of either Cathal O'Halloran, the flax manager, or of his son, Owney.'

'I see,' said Mara. It was an obvious solution, but somehow she felt vaguely dissatisfied with it. There was one obvious flaw, but, as she could see by Shane's eager face that he had spotted it, she said nothing but just smiled encouragement at him.

'I hear what my learned friend has to say, but would put forward the objection that he has not accounted for Eamon the lawyer's presence at the flax garden in the morning following his moonlit trip to O'Brien of Arra.' The words burst from Shane's lips.

Fiona flushed uncomfortably, but said coolly, 'I've already told you that he went north when we left Arra.'

'Instead of turning south and then crossing at O'Briensbridge; but that still doesn't explain why he did that. You said yourself that you quarrelled over his decision so that makes it even more surprising that he didn't give you a reason since he and you were such great friends.' Shane's voice was bland, and without the underlying note of innuendo which Moylan and Aidan would probably have inserted. He was young for his age in some ways, thought Mara, but his brain was sharp and he had put his finger on the most puzzling aspect of the matter.

'You are absolutely sure, Fiona, that he gave no reason to go north, did he?' asked Moylan, a note of disappointment in his voice.

Fiona shook her head. Her face had gone pale again and Mara intervened quickly.

'I think that you made your case well, Moylan, and that the next step for us is to talk to Nuala and then we will make our way up to the flax gardens. So, Aidan and Fiona, will you fetch her now and don't forget my note to the king, Aidan.' The others were on their feet by now and she allowed them to go without further instructions. Regardless of the investigation into the murder, the first consideration now had to be the auction. No doubt the result would be the same. Muiris O'Hynes was considered to be a wealthy man and Cathal, no matter how hard he tried, was unlikely to be able to raise more than the two ounces of silver originally offered. Mara sighed, took a clean sheet of vellum from the wooden press, trimmed her pen with her knife, dipped it into the ink pot and began to write out a new deed of contract.

What would Cathal, his family, and his clan who depended upon him, do if Muiris won the contract? Go back to scratching a living from the salt marshes of his homeland? A place where the grass itself could be poisonous to the cattle that munched it. All those years of gaining knowledge and expertise in the growing of flax, the spinning of the fibres, the weaving, the dyeing – all wasted effort. Would a man kill to avoid all of this being taken from him?

Mara was forced to say yes to her own question.

Thirteen

Berrad Qirechta
(Summary of Court Procedure)

An adult son whose father is still alive usually has no legal capacity of his own. However, he can annul any contracts of his father that would damage or diminish his future inheritance, as long as he fulfils his duties as a son (i.e. doesn't leave the land of his father without being given leave, obeys his orders, etc.)

'That stick has blood on it – blood soaked into it,' said Nuala sharply, eyeing it as Hugh held it under her nose.

'That's right.' Hugh nodded happily. 'So it's the murder weapon, isn't it?'

Nuala heaved an impatient sigh. 'Don't you boys ever listen,' she said. 'I told you. Eamon was killed by someone pressing on the thyroid cartilage. There was no blood – the fragile bones were cracked and the man died.'

'But he had a scalp wound,' said Moylan indignantly.

'That was inflicted after death – probably tumbling down the mountain. There's far too much blood on this stick – look at it carefully.'

'Perhaps there was another murder!' suggested Aidan with a hopeful note in his voice.

'It's strange though, Nuala, because I found this just at the place where there were marks of a struggle and also Shane found burned pieces of the deed of contract there in the same place.'

'And droppings from a horse that had stood for a while,' supplemented Shane.

'I think we will have to leave the matter of the stick for the moment and get on our way – just leave it in the press in the schoolhouse, Moylan.' Mara surveyed the well-filled twin satchels attached to the sides of each pony. The auction would be when the bell sounds for vespers. The boys would have to eat their lunch before then and she herself wanted to have plenty of time to survey the possible murder scene and to be able to turn matters over in her mind. Muiris, apparently, must already be at the flax garden. He had not been at home when Moylan went to carry the message and his household did not know where he was.

'By the way, Mara, Seamus MacCraith will be joining us,' said Nuala in a bored tone of voice. 'The king and the others have gone for another day's hunting and he doesn't want to go. He's afraid that if he does he will be forced to write a poem and *"the subject does not offer any scope"*, or so he says. I tried to put him off but he wouldn't be dissuaded. He said that he would hover at a distance.'

What a nuisance, thought Mara, but she said nothing. Fiona was blushing self-consciously and the boys were grinning. It was fairly obvious that they knew why Seamus MacCraith had not chosen to join the hunting party and was going to honour them with his presence. That was all very well and she was sure that Fiona could handle him, but today was a working day and Seamus would just be a nuisance. As soon as the poet arrived Mara drew her horse up beside his and suggested that he would work on his poem better if he kept at a distance from them.

'In any case,' she added, 'all of my scholars are working on a case and Nuala, with her medical knowledge, is assisting us. I'm sure that you understand how work like this cannot go forward in the presence of a stranger – anything said at times like this has to be highly confidential. Perhaps you would like to go ahead of us now. Would that be best? Like that you can absorb the beauty of the mountain without our presence inter-rupting your thoughts.'

He stared haughtily at her and without a word spurred his horse and thundered across the stone-paved fields of the High Burren towards the lower slopes of the Aillwee Mountains. Nuala caught Mara's eye with such a comical expression that Mara found herself biting her lips in order to suppress a laugh. No, she thought, that young man would not be right for Nuala, nor for Fiona, either. He might be intelligent, but he lacks a sense of humour. He, himself, and his sense of his own genius, would always be more important to him than any girl. Let him go ahead and admire the scenery.

And certainly the scenery was worth admiring. The day was warm but with a hint of crispness that seemed to forecast a frosty night. Between the clints, those massive slabs of stone that paved the fields of the High Burren, the early spring grass sprouted, looking fresh and appetizing for the cows that wandered over the firm surface. Here and there between the field boundaries a blackthorn bush had grown and the snow-white blossom gleamed in the noontime sunshine, rivalling in its intensity the almost silver gleam of the limestone slopes. The flowering season of the Burren was beginning and gradu-ally, amidst the splendour of the glistening limestone, patches of colour showed themselves to the eye. The purple orchids dotted among pure white ones, azure clusters of bugle, mats of purple-flowered thyme and here and there a few early gentians, specks of intense blue, showed up between the creamy daisy-faced mountain avens flowers.

'Do you miss this place when you are in Thomond?' Mara almost regretted her question once it had been uttered, but Nuala showed no emotion, just glancing around at the moun-tains and distant view of the sea with a fairly indifferent face.

'I never really think that much about it,' she said. 'I've so much to do. I suppose I am just focussed on my work.'

'You always were,' said Mara. 'Even as a ten-year-old your dedication was there. That's why I trust you implicitly when you tell me that the blood-soaked stick was not used in the murder of Eamon. But where did it come from?'

She expected no answer and got none. Nuala would only speak if she knew the answer and if the answer could be a scientifically proved fact. Mara clicked her heels against her horse and increased her speed until she drew level with her scholars.

'Why should a bloodstained stick, that was not used on Eamon, be found at the place where we think the murder took place?' She threw the question out and immediately five pairs of eyes were fastened to hers. 'One answer from everyone.'

Moylan looked around. 'I say that Nuala might be wrong

and Eamon might have been hit on the head first and then punched in the bottom of the neck.'

'Eamon wrestled it from the murderer and hit him with it, so the blood belongs to the murderer,' came back Shane's quick response.

''The stick has nothing to do with the case.' Hugh sounded doubtful, but Mara gave him an approving nod.

'What about the stick being left there as a false clue?' asked Fiona.

'Why?' queried Moylan.

'Use your brains,' said Fiona crisply. 'If we discover that Owney or Cathal, or any other obvious suspect does not have a stick, then our attention is immediately focussed on them. The blood could have come from anywhere – it could be from a butchered animal.'

'Let's think who would have a stick,' said Aidan. 'Would flax workers have sticks?'

'Good point.' Moylan nodded at his friend.

'Could do, I suppose, to climb the mountain.' Shane sounded doubtful.

'Or to defend themselves against a wolf,' suggested Hugh with a glance across the mountain where the shouts of the wolf hunters bounced against the echoing rocks.

'Or against a bull, or even a ram,' said Fiona. 'The trouble is that most people will have a few or even a lot of these sticks – just like you have, Brehon, at Ballinalacken, just standing in a barrel in the guardsmen's room.'

'Still, we'll bear it in mind, though, Brehon,' said Moylan. 'We might just notice someone asking about a missing stick.'

So will I, thought Mara, as they began to cross the fields at Baur North. Perhaps Fiona's surmise about the stick being left as a false clue was the most interesting and most likely idea.

If, however, Shane was right then it should be easy to spot a man with a wound. Neither Cathal O'Halloran nor his son, Owney, would be able to hide a wound that had bled so much.

'Look, the spring lambs are being taken up from Lissylisheen to the slopes of the Aillwee Mountain,' shouted Shane, interrupting Mara's thoughts.

'The O'Lochlainn himself is with them, Brehon,' said Moylan.

Mara smiled to herself. Moylan was taking his role as eldest scholar in the law school seriously. He was making sure that she knew of the presence of an important person and was ready to exchange greetings. Ardal O'Lochlainn, the O'Lochlainn, as the head of the clan was known, was probably the most important man in the kingdom of the Burren after Mara herself as representative of King Turlough Donn. In the centuries past the O'Lochlainns had been kings of the Burren, but now there was no more loyal subject of the king than Ardal, the present *taoiseach* or chieftain of the clan. He was a handsome man, tall, lean and athletic with those intensely blue eyes and his red-gold crown of hair and Mara gazed with pleasure at the picture he made on his beautiful thoroughbred strawberry mare.

'You're moving the lambs, Ardal,' she called out. 'Does that mean that you think the weather will be warming up?'

'That's right, Brehon. The wind is going around to the west. Might even be raining before dawn, I think. The grass is beginning to grow. I was up the mountain earlier and there are all sorts of herbs for the flock to eat. That reminds me, Brehon, I was looking very closely at the ground up there beyond the flax garden and I found this. I'm sure it must belong to you.'

Reining in his well-trained mare, Ardal bent down and picked something out of his satchel. It took him a moment to find the object and when he produced it Mara could see why. The object was no bigger than his little finger – just a scrap of pink linen tape, tied in a loop.

Moylan gave an exclamation, but Mara silenced him with a sharp look. She held out a hand and smiled graciously. 'Thank you, Ardal,' she said. 'How clever of you to have spotted such a small object!'

'I knew it must be yours.' Ardal's very white teeth flashed in a mischievous grin. 'I remember when you were a little girl you told me how you had persuaded your father to get his linen document tape dyed pink, instead of black or white like other lawyers.'

'That's right.' Mara returned his smile while, behind the polite mask of neighbourly friendliness, her mind was racing. How could a second piece of pink tape have been found at the very same place? She glanced at it. Yes, it definitely had come from Cahermacnaghten, but once again, the bow had not been tied in her characteristic knot. 'Stand back, everyone,' she said aloud, hoping to forestall any queries from her scholars. 'Stand back and allow the O'Lochlainn to take his flock through the gap.'

She waited until he had moved on before holding up the loop to her scholars and to Nuala.

'Definitely from our law school,' said Moylan with conviction.

'And it is just the right size to be used to tie a scroll,' observed Fiona, assessing it with her eye.

'Did you tie it, Brehon?' asked Shane shrewdly.

Mara shook her head. 'No,' she said. 'I always make a loop with one side of the tape, then wind the other around it. You can see that this has been made by having two loops knotted together.'

'Do you think that Eamon had two deeds with him, Fiona?' asked Moylan.

'Not that I know. Why should he?' said Fiona.

'Perhaps it belongs to a deed of contract from last year and Cathal, the flax manager, dropped it,' suggested Hugh.

'Birdbrain,' scoffed Aidan. 'That piece of tape hasn't been out in the open for a whole year.'

'I didn't say that,' retorted Hugh. 'It might be that Cathal destroyed the old one when he thought he would be getting a new one in a couple of days. In fact, he might have burned it and what Shane found might not be the fifteen eleven deed, but the fifteen ten one.'

'What, took it out of his house, carried it up the hill and burned it there?' exclaimed Moylan.

'Why not?' Hugh was standing up for himself. 'These pieces of vellum really stink when you burn them – smell of dead calf.'

'How do you account for the two pieces of tape, then?' Aidan thrust his face aggressively towards Hugh.

'Use your own brains, don't borrow mine,' retorted Hugh.

'That's enough. Let's ride on now and see what else we can discover. Let's take the Glenisheen route and then we'll keep out of the way of the O'Lochlainn and his sheep.' Mara understood their ill temper, which stemmed from frustration. This seemed to be a case where every step forward seemed to be followed by a step backwards.

There was no sign of Seamus MacCraith, the poet, she was glad to find, as they made their way up the winding road, passing the flax workers' cottages and the flax garden itself until they reached the small plateau above.

The boys had been keen and observant. There was no doubt that there had been a scuffle of some sort here, and there was no doubt that a horse had stood there for some time. Mara stared thoughtfully at the droppings.

'But only one horse,' said Nuala from behind her.

'Looks like it,' said Mara quietly. A feeling of great relief came over her.

'So not Fachtnan following him then?' said Nuala shrewdly.

'Thank goodness, no,' said Mara. She turned and gazed down at the flax garden, lost in thought. It began to look as though the murderer came from there. Perhaps it wasn't a murder; perhaps it was just a fight that went wrong. A taunt from Eamon, a quick and unfortunate blow from Owney or Cathal. Most likely Owney, given the fact that he had been informed by Nuala about the vulnerable 'doors to the soul' parts of the body. But if it had been an accident why didn't he come and confess the deed to the Brehon? These fights between young men happened from time to time and provided that the correct fine was paid to the family then no further retribution was demanded.

Mara's thoughts were interrupted by a hastily suppressed moan. With amazement she turned towards Nuala. This girl never cried. Even the death of her father, even his rejection of his daughter months earlier on, had not drawn a single sound from her, but now she stared across the mountainside with tears running down her face, her whole body heaving with sobs. She had her back turned to the law school scholars and seemed to be desperately striving for self-control, her knuckles jammed against her mouth.

'Moylan,' called Mara, 'could you all go a bit further up the mountainside – go towards the north. See if you can see any tracks of Eamon's horse up there.'

She waited until they had moved off, Moylan with an air of great self-importance, assigning different routes to each one. When they were out of earshot she turned to the girl beside her. Nuala had ceased to sob, but her olive-skinned face was sallow and there were dark circles around her brown eyes. Her cheeks were wet and her hands still clenched tightly as she desperately fought for self-control.

Mara put an arm around the girl, felt her stiffen, but then slightly relax. She did not move nearer or appear to seek any comfort, but she did not reject the arm, just continued to stare bleakly into the distance with the air of one who sees nothing.

'What is it?' asked Mara softly.

Nuala struggled for a moment and then her iron will came to her aid and she said in a flat voice, 'I think Fachtnan is dead.'

'What!' Mara stared incredulously at the girl and then common sense reasserted itself. She was used to the young. Everything was dramatic to them.

'How can you tell?' she asked gently. Nuala avoided her eyes, staring bleakly at her feet.

'Do you know anything that you are not telling me?' Mara realized that her tone was sharper than she intended – only she knew how much Fachtnan meant to Nuala. Instantly she softened her voice, saying, 'Nuala, you are only guessing Neither of us knows what happened to Fachtnan. The chances are that he was so fed up and disgusted with Fiona's behaviour that he decided to go home a few days early.'

Nuala raised her dark eyes and looked very directly at Mara. 'You don't believe that, do you? Not Fachtnan. He wouldn't do a thing like that. He knew that Eamon had been killed. He knew that you would be starting an investigation. He wouldn't run out on you like that – give you all the worry about him to add to your other burdens. He wasn't like that.'

Mara was silenced. It was only what she had thought herself.

'There was only one other possibility,' continued Nuala. 'He might have been the guilty one. He might have followed Eamon on that strange route from Arra to here. They might eventually have come to blows. Fachtnan in his anger punched Eamon in the neck, killed him, returned to the law school, found that he could not face telling you what he had done, and then went . . .'

Home, or to his death. Were those the words that Nuala suppressed, biting her lips and clenching her hands? Mara waited. Nuala was an intensely private person. Her love for Fachtnan was probably greater than Mara had realized, used as she was to thinking of the fifteen-year-old girl as just a clever child. The face opposite her own was not a child's though, but a woman's and a woman who was coming face to face with a nightmare.

'You see, if Fachtnan had come here with Eamon, we would see signs of his horse; I checked in the stables. His horse had definitely disappeared,' said Nuala after a few minutes during which she seemed to be breathing deeply, sucking in some courage or resolution from the sharp bite of the mountain air.

'I don't think the lack of signs is any indication one way or other,' said Mara, purposely making her voice matter-of-fact and judicial. 'Let's just stick to what we know. Fachtnan was alive and well and sitting in the schoolhouse on Saturday morning. He then disappeared. The chances are that he set out to investigate the murder. That, I think, is probably more likely than the idea that he would just go home without leaving word. If there is no sign or message by tomorrow morning then I will get Cumhal to organize a search for him. Now, here come the others. Try to put this out of your head. Fachtnan will turn up safe and well. He's a sensible young man and I don't think that he has an enemy in the world. Dry your eyes, let's not talk of this in front of the others.'

Nuala would be best left to herself for a few minutes, thought Mara, as she went forward to meet her scholars. They looked keen and cheerful, she noticed, and waited for them to give her the news.

'He came from the Galway side, definitely,' said Moylan with an air of satisfaction. 'Show the Brehon what you found, Fiona.'

'These are definitely from his horse,' said Fiona. She delved within the pouch she wore strapped around her waist and came out with a small handful of white horsehair.

'See how long the hairs are and there are a few black hairs mixed with the white ones,' she said. 'I'd say these are tail hairs and Eamon's horse had some black hairs mixed in with the white in his tail. I found them on one of those stunted blackthorn bushes and that makes me think that they came from the tail, also.'

'I know what you mean.' Mara considered the handful of hair. This part of the mountain would be open to gales of wind from the west and the blackthorn would seldom grow beyond a foot high, even over a time span of fifty or a hundred years. She had often marvelled at the thick gnarled branches of something that was no larger than a garden flower. Eamon's horse had been a showy one with a tail that swept the ground. There now seemed little doubt that he had circled the mountains of Thomond and come around to enter the kingdom of the Burren from the north.

But why?

'Would you like to see the place where I found the ash, Brehon, before it disappears?' Shane broke into her thoughts and followed with a reminder of what Ardal O'Lochlainn had said about the wind from the west. She followed him and called to Nuala to join them. It would be better for the girl to avert her mind. Nothing could be done about Fachtnan until they were back at Cahermacnaghten and she could consult with her farm manager about the possibility of a search party. Fachtnan was unlikely to be anywhere on the Aillwee. It was a low mountain with quite a few shepherds' and cattlemen's huts. Already, many cows had been moved up there and the few pathways suitable for a horse would have been well trodden.

Shane had built a low wall around the ashes of the burned deed of contract. He had even roofed it in with some branches of thick, springy heather. Now that she was there he uncovered it carefully. Mara bunched up her gown to protect her knees from the sharp edges of the limestone and knelt down. Yes, there were some more unburned pieces of vellum.

'Nuala,' she called over her shoulder. 'Come and help. Your eyes are amazingly sharp. If we could find a date we would know that this year's deed was burned here.'

Nuala joined her rapidly and they crowded around the little pile of burned ash and scraps of vellum.

'Got it,' said Fiona after a minute's silence. 'Look.' She pointed a slender finger adorned with a silver ring. 'Look, Brehon, there.'

Mara narrowed her eyes, but already Shane had shouted. 'Got it. "XI". That's it, Brehon, that's certain. It's this year's deed.'

'The rest has been burned off,' said Hugh.

'Doesn't matter, we've got what we need; you can see the space after the two numerals. It has to be eleven, that's right, isn't it, Brehon?'

'No other possibility.'

'Good old vellum.'

'This proves that the murder is connected with the flax garden.'

The voices chattered on while Mara remained on her knees staring at the remains of the roman numerals which had been written on the top of the deed. Memory had swept over her and for a minute her feelings of desolation almost overwhelmed her. Suddenly, and she had not thought of this for years, she remembered teaching the child Fachtnan how to record numbers in Latin. 'Look,' she had said, 'the number five is written like a "V".' Carefully, she had arranged the chubby five fingers, moving the small thumb so that it and the fore-finger made the letter. 'And then you make a ten with all of your fingers, cross your wrists and you will see it looks just like an "X".' He had been such a sweet child, such a hard worker, always trying to remember things, grateful for her help, so intelligent and yet so handicapped by his bad memory. Could he really be dead?

And if so, was his murderer the same person who had crushed the throat of Eamon and cut short that young life?

Fourteen

Crích Gablach
(Ranks in Society)

Each kingdom has a Brehon to act as a representative of the king's law and the king's judgement.

Heptad 25
There are seven fees that are due to a Brehon:
1. The payment for attendance at a judgement place.
2. The payment for listening to witnesses.
3. The payment for accumulated wisdom.
4. The payment for knowledge of artefacts.
5. The payment for clear judgement.
6. The payment for responsibility.
7. The payment for legal language.

The bell had not yet sounded for vespers when Mara and her scholars descended into the flax garden. Nuala had wanted to go home and Mara suggested that she look for the young poet and accompany him back to Ballinalacken, whereupon Nuala instantly changed her mind and decided to accompany them to be a spectator at the auction. Mara had smiled at her decision. Obviously Nuala had no interest in the poet. Stop trying to play the matchmaker, she told herself. In any case, from what she had seen of Seamus MacCraith she doubted whether he was worthy of Nuala, or of Fiona, either.

The mountain today was no place for a dreaming poet. The flax garden was full of noise and, from the sounds to the south of the Aillwee Mountain, Mara guessed that the hunt was still in full progress. Perhaps Seamus MacCraith had decided to give composing a rest and had joined them. She hoped so, as she felt guilty about the poet's isolation. If he joined the hunt it might take his mind off the lovely Fiona! Turlough, his son,

his son-in-law and Ulick Burke – as well as the guards and
men-at-arms, of course – were making enough noise for a
hundred men.

When the sun began to set lower over the sea they would
gather up their sticks and their dogs. Tired but happy, they
would make their way back to Ballinalacken for their supper.
It was an easy way of disposing of her guests, a day spent out
in the mountains, though she suspected that the Aillwee
Mountain would, by now, be denuded of wolves. Ardal
O'Lochlainn was a careful and knowledgeable farmer and he
would not be sending his lambs and their mothers up there
unless he was fairly sure that there would be no threats to the
flock.

The flax garden seemed to be full of tension when they
arrived down. It was probably about half an hour before the
time for the vespers bell to ring, Mara calculated, and the work
was going on at a frantic rate. Thuds of wooden battens beating
or scutching the flax came from the shed nearest to them and
shuttles pinged violently from the weaving shed. Near to the
dyeing vats Cathal and his son Owney were having a violent
argument. '. . . *always imagine you know best . . .*' were the only
words that Mara could distinguish. She moved hastily in the
other direction towards the spinning-wheel sheds. Gobnait,
Cathal's wife, was standing at the door shouting back in. She
sounded incoherent with rage as she yelled, 'I leave you for
an hour and look at how little you have done. Nothing but
gossip and slacking. Well, it's your livelihood as well as mine.
If you can't do the work I can easily get those who can. There's
not a woman in Burren who couldn't spin as well as you lot.'

Mara wondered briefly whether any of the women would
have the courage to point out that Gobnait might not be still
in the flax gardens by the next day, but they might. Muiris
O'Hynes, if he was wise, would be likely to employ some of
the experienced workers while he built up an expertise among
his own people, but Cathal, his wife, Gobnait, and his son,
Owney, would certainly not be one of those who would be
retained. Muiris would want to stamp his own authority on
the business, and he had spent long enough observing, at a
safe distance, how that business was carried out. In any case,

he would not want to employ Gobnait, who had a reputation of being a quarrelsome woman. Mara smiled to herself remembering Brigid's words about Gobnait being just the sort to send a swarm of bees after anyone who displeased her.

And then her smile vanished and was replaced by a puzzled frown. Where was Muiris? By all accounts, he had spent the last few days here in the flax garden, so it was surprising that as the hour for the auction approached he would not be in evidence. Unobtrusively, she beckoned to Moylan and, when he came over, said quietly, 'When you went to Muiris's house today, who did you see?'

'I saw his wife,' said Moylan promptly. 'And she told me that Muiris had already gone up to the flax garden. She said that he was carrying a satchel and she said it with a bit of a smile. I think that she was hinting that he brought a bag of silver with him. He's supposed to have lots, you know,' added Moylan. 'He gets good prices for his leather at all the fairs. I've heard that he goes to Galway and sells it to English merchants there.'

'I see.' Mara nodded. She was not surprised at what Moylan said. She herself had guessed that Muiris was wealthy. A man like him, who had made his own wealth, always wanted to make more. Muiris was hugely ambitious for his children. His eldest son and daughter had both made good matches and both had been well endowed by him, but there were other sons and daughters coming to marriageable age and the flax garden was a good business opportunity for Muiris and his wife.

But where was Muiris now? Áine would be in his plans. Husband and wife worked side by side in all the enterprises. She would know what he intended. Was he planning a dramatic late entrance, just as had happened the last time? There would be sense in it, if he could time it exactly. No doubt the price would be lower if Cathal and Muiris were not capping each other's bets during the ten minutes that preceded the fall of the pin. Perhaps that was the meaning of the smile, which Moylan had interpreted as referring to the contents of the satchel.

There's someone coming now, Brehon. I can hear the horse,' said Moylan.

'Good,' said Mara walking over to the entrance into the flax garden where the rest of her scholars stood grouped and waiting for instructions.

'O'Brien of Arra is coming, Brehon,' said Hugh as she joined them.

'Interesting what a view you can have from here, Brehon,' said Shane. 'Anyone from the flax garden could stand here and see all over the mountain, up as well as down.'

'Which makes it all the more peculiar that none of them saw what happened to poor Eamon,' put in Fiona and Mara nodded agreement. There was something very strange about the lack of knowledge shown by the flax workers.

'I think I'll wait here,' she said. 'The rest of you can go and find Cathal and tell him that the O'Brien of Arra will be here in a minute or two. We might as well get ready, and then the candle can be lit as soon as the bell from the abbey tolls.'

The sooner it's all over, the better for all concerned, she thought, as she watched the horse with Brian Ruadh on its back make its slow way up the zigzag pathway. There was little doubt in her mind that Muiris could match and outmatch any silver that Cathal and Gobnait had been able to piece together. Even if they had frantically scoured every possible corner for resources they were unlikely to be able to win this auction. Perhaps that was why Gobnait had been missing from the spinning shed this morning. Perhaps she had gone to see relatives of hers near to Galway on a hunt for a loan.

'Good day to you, Brehon,' called Brian Ruadh. 'That was a better path than I expected. I declare I don't think that I've been here since I was a child.'

'Yes, Cathal O'Halloran has looked after your property well. All is in good order. Perhaps after the auction we could have a look over it in the company of whoever wins the lease.'

'Oh, are you expecting many bidders?' Brian Ruadh's face lit up with a touch of greedy anticipation.

'No, only two bidders as far as I know. Would you like to tie up your horse here, next to ours?' As she spoke, Mara scanned the horizon and looked back down the hill. Shane was right. From this position in the flax garden there was a great view of the Aillwee Mountain – even of the valley below, but there was no sign of Muiris O'Hynes anywhere. What had happened to the man?

The table, the chair, the stools, the benches were all in place when Mara accompanied the O'Brien of Arra into the shed. The candle was on the table, the pin and the tinder box lay beside it, but no mead, this time, Mara was pleased to see. She disliked the overly sweet honeyed taste of the stuff and, as it was highly alcoholic, thought her scholars were just as well without it. She took from her satchel the deed awaiting the insertion of the name of the successful bidder and the official measure. Carefully, she carried the candle to the light from the door, making sure that all saw her use the measure before inserting the pin an exact inch below the top. She stayed there for a moment inspecting the wax vigilantly, but this time, as far as she could see, there was no hard knot of tallow that would delay the length of time before the pin fell.

'Ah, I remember this happening when I was a boy,' said the O'Brien with a sigh of nostalgia. 'The old ways are always the best ways.' He gave another sigh, but no one agreed with him. Cathal and his wife stood like stone statues, gazing stolidly ahead, Owney prowled the shed, bending his head so that it did not crash against any of the low beams, exchanging an uneasy smile with Nuala who was pretending to examine the bales of linens. The law school scholars stood with solemn faces, each of them probably remembering that Eamon and Fachtnan had been there the last time that this ceremony was held.

There can only be a few minutes left for Muiris to arrive, thought Mara, as she waited with outward indifference. Her feeling for time was good, but even so she was taken aback by the summons to prayer. The wind must have turned to the west because the clang of the abbey bell for vespers was unexpectedly loud. Everyone jumped at the sound.

'Close the door, will you, Shane. And Moylan, will you light the candle for us.' Mara handed her eldest scholar her own tinder box. Let everything go according to the exact procedure laid down in the law document. Mara was determined that this auction would be conducted with dignity and authority.

This time the candle was of fine beeswax. The honeyed smell soon filled the shed and the candle burned steadily. It would burn to its allotted time; the pin would fall and the last bid would gain possession of this fertile flax garden and all its possessions for the year to come.

Cathal O'Halloran did not make his bid immediately as was his wont. This time he sat and waited, sat with furrowed brow, staring eyes and compressed lips, sat until he could bear the tension no longer and then, eventually, he snapped out the words,

'Two ounces of silver.'

O'Brien of Arra looked disappointed, the scholars' faces brightened; eventually something was happening. Owney, the heir to his father's heritage of the salt marshes and to this prosperous flax garden, stopped his prowling and came to rest behind his father's stool. Mara sat very still, very upright in her chair, her eyes fixed on the sharp bright flame of the candle and the translucent wax beneath it. O'Brien cleared his throat and looked hopefully at Cathal and then at the door, but nothing happened. Gobnait sat solidly, her face calm, her hands folded peacefully on her lap. She had the look of the one who had come to rest after the day's work was done.

Only a narrow strip of unburned wax now remained above the shining pin. Everyone stared at it. It was a pity that the poet had not come, thought Mara. This scene in the half-dark of the storage shed might have given material to his quill. The immense shadows, the half-seen forms, the triangular flame . . .

And then, quite suddenly, there was a thud of running footsteps outside, a question shouted, and an answer given, the door wrenched open, sunlight pouring in, the slim young figure of Seamus MacCraith himself standing in the doorway.

'Come quickly,' he said. 'There's been a terrible accident.'

And at that very moment, as had happened before, the candle flared wildly sideways, the wax around the pin dissolved and as fast as he could utter the words, Cathal O'Halloran shouted the words: 'Two ounces of silver.'

And then the pin dropped. The auction was over. Stiffly and awkwardly, Cathal held out his hand to the O'Brien for the traditional handshake and Brian Ruadh took it and held the hand for a moment, then dropping it as if he did not quite know what to do with it.

'Who is it?' Mara asked. Her heart thudded and then slowed down. Now I must be very calm and take charge, she told herself, though her first thought was that Fachtnan's body had eventually been found.

'I don't know,' wailed the poet. 'I've never seen him in my life before.'

'Not Fachtnan, my eldest scholar?' It was an effort for Mara to force the words out, but they had to be said. Nuala's face had gone as white as bleached linen so Mara knew that the girl's thoughts had followed hers.

'No, no,' said Seamus MacCraith peevishly. 'This is a middle-aged man.'

'Alive?' Automatically, Mara reached over and picked up the pin from the table feeling its point with one finger and then slotting it into the sleeve of her cloak.

'I . . . I think so. He . . . he . . .' His voice was hesitant and it trembled to a halt. Nuala grabbed him quickly by the arm as his colour ebbed away.

'Here, Aidan,' she shouted, 'sit him down on the stool. Push his head down. Fiona, bring him around as fast as you can by any means. There's probably someone bleeding badly out there. He's the type to faint at the sight of blood. Bring him out as fast as you can once he's back to his senses. I don't want to waste any time with him. I'm going to check my medical bag. Get me some scraps of linen, Owney, long ones.'

'Here you are, lad, tear that up.' Cathal grabbed an unbaled length of linen and lobbed it at Owney.

'I'll get some water.' Gobnait bustled off. 'We'll follow you with some men and a board to carry him back, Brehon.' Suddenly the flax manager and his wife were back to their usual cordial selves – all tension had disappeared.

'Give me a jug and I'll slosh some water over the poet.' Aidan was off to the well in a second and returned almost instantly holding the jug full of water over Seamus MacCraith's pallid face. Fiona grabbed it from him and dipped her own linen handkerchief in it, patting the poet's brow.

'Come on,' said Aidan impatiently. 'He can walk. Nuala will be furious if we delay any longer. Grab his other arm, Hugh. Come on, Seamus, be a man and get marching.'

Out in the sunlight, one of the workers was standing holding Seamus MacCraith's horse. Others were being organized into groups to carry a board, to carry water. Gobnait even had a ewer filled with her precious mead in one hand and a pewter goblet in the other. She thrust it at Moylan with whispered instructions and then retreated to the door of the spinning shed. Her face, under a conventional wide-eyed shocked expression, looked expansive and relieved. Whether this unknown man was merely injured or was dead, it probably would not matter much to Gobnait. Her family, relations and workers were probably all here and their livelihood for the year to come had just been assured.

But who was the man? Not one of the hunters, thought Mara, reassuring herself. Turlough could stir nowhere without his two bodyguards at his back and the other men-at-arms were never far behind. The threat from the O'Kelly on the other side of the hill towards Galway was too real for any let-up in the blanket of safety which surrounded her husband at all times; and where Turlough went, his son, son-in-law and friend would not be far away. Turlough had been lecturing them on that the other night at suppertime, pointing out forcibly the dangers of one man going off on his own and meeting with an accident.

Nuala was already mounted on her horse, her face calm, her brown eyes focussed. 'Which way, Seamus?' she called. There was no hint of impatience in her voice, now, unlike the boys who were shouting queries into the poet's dazed ears.

Seamus MacCraith raised his head, but that was a mistake. The setting sun shone into his dazed eyes. He blinked, staggered and would have fallen except for Aidan's grip.

'Let's get you up on your horse, then you'll feel better.' Owney, with the strength of a young giant, heaved him up on to the horse. For a moment it looked as though he were a little better, but then he leaned over and spewed up all of the water that Moylan had been pouring down his throat.

Hugh and Aidan jumped aside neatly, uttering sounds of

disgust, and a few expletives, but Owney, more compassionate, kept a tight grip on the poet's cloak until he ceased to vomit.

'Better now,' he said, slapping him heartily on the back. 'Come on, now, tell us where this man is lying.'

'Give him a chance,' said Gobnait tranquilly. 'He'll feel better in a few minutes.'

'And a man can die in a few minutes,' exploded Nuala. 'Come on, Seamus, which way?'

'Which way, Seamus?' Mara put an authoritative note into her voice. Nuala was right – the injured person could die while they waited. What a self-indulgent young man this poet was.

He responded to the whiplash of authority. 'In the quarry, down there,' he muttered, pointing to the south of the flax garden.

In a second Nuala was off her horse, hitching up her long gown and *léine*, allowing them to overflow her leather belt until they were just knee-length. The boys were beside her, Moylan grabbing the heavy medical bag. All of them ran until they reached the steep slope beside the winding path. Without hesitation Nuala scrambled down the steep, rocky incline and the four boys followed her. Owney abandoned the poet and went thundering down behind them.

Mara wavered wondering whether she was too old for scrambles like that.

'Come this way, Brehon,' shrieked one of the spinning women. 'There's a path to the quarry over here.'

Behind the scutching shed there was a narrow path of well-trodden limestone. It was steep but the surface was good and had been used regularly. A few bushes of juniper and of blackthorn grew beside it, well sheltered by the towering walls of stone on either side. From behind her Mara could hear O'Brien telling Cathal how this path had been cut through solid rock in order to drag building stone to the flat land above.

'Used wooden sledges and ropes to drag them up, my father used to tell me. I remember him saying that they watered the surface until the limestone on the path was as smooth as a frozen lake. Tons of stone were carried up, built all of the sheds, and the workers' houses, too. It was a great job, a great piece of property.'

'It was, indeed, my lord.' Cathal's voice was soothing, the voice of one who had got what he wanted and was willing now to make any concessions.

It was strange, though, thought Mara, that neither man seemed to be speculating on the identity of the person who was lying injured in the quarry. She would have thought that at the news, both Cathal and Gobnait would have checked their own workers, but they had shown no sign of doing that – where a few simple queries could have elicited the information.

The path was deeply shaded by the overhanging bushes, so when Mara stepped out into the quarry the setting sun, shining on the limestone, almost blinded her for a moment. She stepped forward and scanned the scene. The stones from this quarry had been hacked out carefully leaving large, solid sections of rock protruding at twenty-foot intervals in order to support the towering cliffs behind. The effect was to create a series of alcoves on the eastern wall of the quarry.

The four boys and Nuala were in one of those alcoves, kneeling down and bending over something. As Mara arrived, Hugh looked over his shoulder and then got to his feet, moving aside to allow her to see.

There, lying on the ground, his head broken, with flies buzzing around the thick clots of blood, was Muiris O'Hynes, the man who wanted to bid for the flax garden.

Fifteen

Cis Lire Foðra Cire
(How Many Kinds of Land Are There?)

Land is valued according to type, not area. The value of a 'cumal' of land, that is about 34 acres, varies. The very best land, land fit for arable crops, is valued at twenty-four milch cows, or twenty-four ounces of silver for a cumal. The worst land, bogland, is only worth eight dry heifers or two milch cows or two ounces of silver for this amount of land.

'Is he dead?' Mara knelt on the hard ground beside Nuala whose hand was on the man's wrist.

Nuala took a long moment before answering but then shook her head. Mara asked no more questions. Nuala must be allowed to do her work unhindered. The four boys, used to Nuala and her physician's work from their earliest years, stood ready to help. The life of Muiris would now be in her hands and could be safely left to her.

Mara got to her feet and waited until O'Brien of Arra and Cathal O'Halloran arrived. Nuala had her task, but so had Mara. This had to stop. Murder stalked the land like a ball among a set of ninepins. First Eamon, then Fachtnan's disappearance, and now Muiris. The suspects were ranged in her mind. The most obvious had to be either Cathal or Gobnait, or even Owney. Muiris had not been able to take possession of the flax garden even though he had successfully topped Cathal's bid because the first deed, the signed deed of lease, had been wrestled from Eamon, his throat punched so that he died instantly.

And now it looked as if once again Muiris had been foiled – perhaps this time at the expense of his life.

'What a terrible thing!' The O'Brien stared at the bloody mass which had once been a head with a look of sick horror on his face.

'Terrible!' echoed Cathal.

'Dreadful, indeed,' said Mara quietly. She beckoned to Shane. 'Go and fetch Fiona. I want the two of you to go down to Poulnabrucky and fetch Áine. Break the news to her. Say that he is alive, but don't hold out any false hopes. Tell her that Nuala is with him.'

The wife of Muiris had the right to be with him if he died here on the mountainside, she thought, and then turned her mind back to other matters, scrutinizing Cathal's face carefully. This valuable land of sixteen acres had been a means of livelihood for him and for his clan for many years. This year, his possession of it had been threatened and now the man who had made that threat was lying, almost dead, in the quarry literally within a stone's throw of the precious land.

'Let's see if we can help in any way.' Mara beckoned to the two men and urged them forward watching carefully. Now they were so close that they could smell the black clotted blood and hear the buzz of the greedy flies. Aidan was on his knees ineffectually swotting at them but every time that the insects were dislodged they came back again.

'I'll see whether I can make contact with the king. We might need those men-at-arms to help move him.' O'Brien of Arra was restless. The warrior breed found it hard to remain still. Mara gave him a nod. There was nothing that he could do and she had no suspicions of him. Why should he try to kill Muiris? He might have been able to double the yearly rent for the flax garden if Muiris had been at the bidding. In any case, she had watched him come up the mountain towards the valley.

'Will he live?' asked Cathal in an undertone when O'Brien had strode towards the entrance to the quarry.

'Nuala is very skilful,' Mara assured him, looking closely into the man's face. What could she read there? Concern, horror, fear – yes there was fear, but was that surprising? Everyone feared death; saw in it their own vulnerable mortality.

Nuala said nothing, just worked steadily, feeling around the broken skull with sure, sensitive fingers and from time to time laying her hand on the neck of the dreadfully injured man. Feeling for a pulse, thought Mara, and she hoped that Muiris's struggle for life would last at least until his wife of over twenty years could be by his side. She held out a hand and immediately Moylan came forward with the medical bag and held it open while Nuala rummaged within and then took out a phial and a tiny spoon. Carefully and steadily she dripped three large drops on to the spoon. Moylan seemed to guess what she wanted as he quickly inserted a finger into the man's mouth, pulled down the slack jaw. Deftly Nuala poured the dose deep into the throat.

White lips, white gums, white tongue, thought Mara. Could this man live? She looked again at Cathal. He was looking back over his shoulder. Gobnait had just appeared. Mara looked back at Nuala, but she was on the alert, every nerve strained to hear what husband and wife said to each other.

And they said nothing. Nothing. That was strange, thought Mara. It was odd that no question was asked by that vociferous woman, odd that no information was offered by the man. Perhaps a long look had been exchanged between them. Mara remained on the alert, but turned her thoughts back to the terribly injured man.

'Nuala, will he be fit to be moved?' she asked so quietly that Nuala could ignore the question if other matters needed her attention. A cluster of flax workers were coming into the quarry by the main entrance, Owney and another man carrying a large board between them. As they came nearer, Mara could see what had delayed them. They had used some strips of wood to nail two boards together and now the improvised litter was as wide as a single bed.

Nuala nodded approval of the litter to Owney as he placed it carefully beside the injured man. He kept his eyes on Nuala, Mara noticed, and did not glance even once at the injured man. Of course, hurling could be a violent game with that rock-hard leather ball and those heavy ash hurleys continually swinging at head height as the teams strove against each other. Perhaps Owney had often seen a man with his head broken like this.

'I'll get some sheepskins to pad it and some strips of linen to tie him securely. We don't want to risk a fall on the mountain ground.' Gobnait went bustling off at a surprisingly rapid pace for such a big heavy woman. These were the first words that she had spoken and they were practical and more to the point than lamentations and exclamations of horror. However, Mara still felt that there was something odd in the reaction of the whole O'Halloran family. She had been Brehon of the kingdom of the Burren for almost eighteen years now and had found that most crimes stemmed from greed and insecurity.

Moylan had moved away from the body and was prowling around restlessly. Then he stopped and stood staring fixedly at something, reminding Mara of her dog Bran searching for a buried bone and then suddenly discovering it. Moylan was looking across at her so she rose from her knees and went quietly across to him.

'Look at that stone,' he whispered when she came near. Mara looked around. Owney was looking at Nuala, waiting for a command, Cathal's eyes were on the fast-disappearing form of his wife and the flax workers were looking across to the north of the mountain where shouts and excited barking showed that the hunters were descending towards the valley.

The stone was a large one. It had been roughly squared and still bore the marks of a chisel. It was undoubtedly the murder weapon; there was blood on one side of it and, as Mara could see when she bent down over it, there were a few splinters of bone and a couple of iron-grey hairs.

Nuala turned her head and Mara moved back beside her. 'I think that we'll have to move him,' she said in a whisper. 'I can't really be sure whether it's the right thing to do but we can't leave him out on the hillside on an April night and it would be best to get him home where Áine can nurse him.'

'I should have told Shane to have her come with a cart,' said Mara, vexed with herself. 'Hugh, go after him, go as quickly as you can.'

By the time that Áine, Fiona and the two young boys arrived back the four men-at-arms from the hunting party had come on the scene, accompanied by O'Brien of Arra.

'The king sent you a message, Brehon, to say that he would take the guests straight back to Ballinalacken. He did ask whether any had seen the injured man, but none had. They had mostly hunted to the south side of Aillwee and above Glenisheen.'

Mara nodded her thanks. She could interview the hunting party herself back at Ballinalacken. Now she would concentrate on the flax garden workers. She looked across at Nuala, thinking that the girl was looking a little happier. Muiris was breathing better and now only time would tell whether he would make a recovery or would die. The third possibility, that this hard-working, ambitious farmer would be nothing but a living vegetable for the rest of his life was one that she preferred not to consider.

'How long ago was the blow struck, Nuala?' she asked in an undertone. 'Would you have any idea?'

'A couple of hours, perhaps,' said Nuala doubtfully. 'Not less, I would think. Look how the blood has clotted and turned black in colour.'

Mara nodded. A few hours would make sense. Even longer perhaps. Muiris had been missing from his house from morning. The quarry would have been an obvious place for him to visit if he had plans to expand the business, build more sheds, take on more workers. Perhaps he had even planned to purchase the land outright from O'Brien of Arra. Muiris was a man whose ambition was limitless. He and Áine would have discussed their plans thoroughly, and they would have costed everything.

Áine was wonderfully brave. She uttered no exclamations, no cries, shed not a tear, but helped with moving her husband on to the wide litter. Although Owney's face was running with sweat by the time that the move had been accomplished – more from anxiety and tension than from the weight, as Muiris was a small man – Áine remained calm and practical throughout. Four men-at-arms who had returned with O'Brien of Arra straightened their backs and sighed with relief as the move was accomplished.

'We'll go down the mountain with them and hold on to the four corners of the cart, Brehon,' the leader of the four told Mara. 'We'll take the strain if there are any jolts. It's not a bad road, though.'

'I'll come with you, if you like, I'm quite strong,' said Owney eagerly.

'I think we'll leave it to these four trained men, Owney,' said Mara mildly. 'I would like to talk to you, so I would prefer you to remain.'

'I'll walk down with you, Áine; try not to worry too much. He is alive and we'll keep him alive between us,' said Nuala, with that calm, compassionate demeanour which had made her so beloved in the kingdom of the Burren from the time that she was a child. She had always been trusted by the sick and the injured and great tales had been told by the old people of the kingdom of how her grandfather's spirit had come back to inhabit the young girl and imbue her with his skill and knowledge.

Now to solve the puzzle. There must be no more murders or attempted murders, said Mara to herself and aloud she said sternly to Cathal, 'I will need to see every one of your workers immediately, Cathal. Could you please gather everyone into one of your sheds so that I can talk to them?'

He bowed his head, touched Gobnait on the arm and started to go back up the narrow path leading to the flax garden. O'Brien of Arra gave her an uncertain look and then followed the flax master. As they went, Mara said in her clear, carrying voice, 'Moylan, pick up that stone, be very careful with it. Avoid touching the blood and other evidence. Can you manage it?'

Moylan, she noticed, had no problems at all with the stone. He swung it up lightly and carried it without the slightest strain. Even a woman without particular strength would have been able to handle it, would have been able to lift it and throw it over the cliff of the quarry, down on to a man standing or sitting below.

Moylan walked respectfully a few feet behind her and Fiona and Aidan flanked him on either side. Hugh and Shane brought up the rear. None spoke. There was a feeling of tension in the air. Seamus MacCraith was sitting on a stone just inside the gateway when they arrived at the flax garden. Mara sent Shane over to ask him to wait for the moment and she would speak to him soon when he was feeling a little better.

It did not take Cathal long to assemble his workers in the baling shed. They stood around the walls with the children in front, clustered around the table with its candle and its blackened wick still standing in the centre of it and beside it the pen case and ink pot.

And that was all that was on the table. The deed had disappeared. Mara looked around in bewilderment. For a moment she fumbled in her satchel, thinking that she may have put it away there without thinking, but it was not there.

'Here's the deed, Brehon, I have signed it.' To her surprise O'Brien of Arra handed her the scroll, before taking himself off. With relief she tucked it into her satchel and then turned to the waiting men and women and nodded as he explained that he would now ride back to Ballinalacken.

'Last week a man was murdered just outside of this flax garden,' she began. 'I questioned you all on that occasion and none knew anything. Now, once again, just outside this place, another man has been brought to near death, or to death itself. Only God himself knows what the outcome will be. I ask you all now that you will let me have any piece of information, however small, which will lead to the uncovering of this murderer. If you hold anything back, there may be another death, and this time –' she allowed her eyes to dwell for a moment on the small faces near to her before resuming in a grave voice – 'this time, it may be someone very near and very dear to you, someone perhaps whom the murderer fears may have seen the killing last week or the attempted killing today. I want to know whether any person was missing from their place of work during the last three hours. Most of the reasons will be innocent, of course, but we must know who had the opportunity to kill or try to kill Muiris O'Hynes.'

She waited for a moment for her words to sink in and then asked Cathal how many workers he had. There were twenty-one of them and Mara divided them into three groups, seven for each of her three older scholars, to be interviewed, one by one, in the privacy of a shed. Every mother was to be responsible that her children were also interviewed, one by one as well. Shane and Hugh would marshal the queues.

Her scholars were used to this procedure and they rapidly

agreed upon sheds and then shepherded their little flocks away leaving Mara alone with the flax manager his wife and his son.

'If I could talk to you, Gobnait, first,' she said briskly and then concealed a smile as Cathal and his son almost fell over each other in their efforts to bolt from the shed.

'I think that we'll have this door shut, don't you?' remarked Mara taking her tinder box from her pouch, relighting the candle and shutting the door carefully so that the small flame did not waver too much.

Gobnait lowered her bulk on to a bench and did not reply. Her face in the candlelight looked old and heavily lined, the skin rough and dry.

Probably not much more than ten years older than me, but a hard life, thought Mara. The O'Hallorans had toiled at the business, had acquired the skills and established the markets. It must have been very difficult to see it all about to disappear. Gobnait, of course, had been working at weaving since a young girl. That, no doubt, was how she acquired the massive shoulders and large hands. A dangerous woman to cross, thought Mara, as she smiled amiably and then plunged into the interrogation.

'So where did you meet Muiris this morning?' she began, allowing the words to come out with an air of assurance.

Gobnait was taken aback. 'How do you know that?' She thought for a moment and then blurted out. 'I thought he was unconscious.'

'That's the thing with head injuries; people float in and out of consciousness,' said Mara, vaguely watching the colour flame in the woman's weather-beaten cheeks.

'Well, I did see him,' said Gobnait defiantly after a moment's thought. 'I felt that I would never forgive myself if I didn't make one last effort. He's been skulking around and Cathal kept saying to ignore him, but in the end I thought I would talk to him, that I would tell him that it was not as easy, that Cathal and I had to learn the business as we went along, that it was our only hope of making a living and of providing a living for others. He didn't need this. Not him. Not with his good farm down there in the rich valley with the limestone underneath and his grazing land on the mountain. I've seen the cattle they have here in the Burren; fat, and with their udders full of milk. You should see what cows are like in our place. Scabby and bone-thin with their ribs showing.'

'And what did Muiris say to you?'

Gobnait faced her defiantly. 'He said that I was probably right. He said that he had been thinking all of these things himself. He said that he would probably back off and not bid. Perhaps next year, that was what he said. Or perhaps he would be content with his farm and with his leather business.'

'So you weren't surprised when he didn't arrive for the auction?'

'No, I wasn't surprised,' agreed Gobnait. Her eyes in the candlelight were uneasy, but she sat very upright and stared boldly at Mara.

'And that was the end of the conversation, was it?' queried Mara.

Gobnait nodded. 'That was that.'

'And you came back up to the spinning wheel shed. You must have felt in a very good humour. After all, you had got what you wanted. You and Cathal would be the sole bidders for the lease of the flax garden.'

Gobnait hesitated. She was beginning to suspect that things were not going according to plan. She glared suspiciously at Mara, but said nothing.

'It's just that I overheard you talking to the women and you appeared to be in a bad humour. I wonder why that was,' said Mara gently.

'They had been idling,' returned Gobnait. 'Now, if that is all, Brehon, I'm sure you wish to see my husband and son and to start on your return journey before twilight. These mountain paths can be treacherous in bad light.'

'Indeed,' said Mara smiling. 'How thoughtful of you. One last question. Did you see anyone on the mountainside after you had spoken with Muiris – someone who was not with my scholars and me, or with the king and his hunting party?'

Gobnait thought for a moment and then nodded her head. 'Yes, Brehon,' she said. 'I saw a man. A man in a *bánín* cloak. He had his back turned. I didn't recognize him. But he was standing very still for a few minutes, standing facing the cliff side.'

Sixteen

Berruð Oirechta

(Summary of Court Procedures)

A witness is known as fiadu *(one who sees) and is only a true witness if he or she has seen for themselves. What does not take place in front of the witness's eyes must be considered invalid and an oath must be taken that all has been personally seen or noticed.*

One man is not proper for giving evidence. Preference must be given to two or three who all tell the same story.

'Standing facing the cliff side – standing for a few minutes, doing nothing, that seems very odd,' said Moylan. 'Do you think that Gobnait was telling a lie, Brehon?'

'No, I don't,' said Mara reluctantly. 'She seemed to be puzzled about it. After all, if she was going to make up a story, surely she could make a better one. Say that she saw a man hiding, lurking behind a rock or something. That story was an odd one and in my experience, odd stories are often true.'

'But why would someone stand facing the cliff?' Fiona furrowed her brow impatiently. She was a girl who always liked to understand puzzles instantly.

'I know why,' said Aidan nonchalantly. Mara glanced back at him in surprise. Aidan was not usually the sharpest of her scholars.

'Well, go on say it,' said Moylan impatiently.

'I don't like to in front of Fiona.' Aidan had a superior note in his voice and he stared straight ahead between his pony's ears, but the corners of his mouth twitched.

'He means that the man was urinating, Brehon,' said Fiona with a sigh. 'Boys are so stupid.'

'I think that was rather clever of Aidan,' said Mara admiringly. 'That's the perfect explanation.' The two younger boys ahead were sniggering and then all, even Fiona, laughed openly, the tension of the last hour releasing itself into snorts and giggles. Every law school should have an Aidan, thought Mara. He wasn't notable for his brains or his working ability but his sense of fun often defused the pressure and strains that were an inevitable part of their life as hard-working law scholars and assistants at crime scenes.

'But Gobnait refused to admit any responsibility for the attack on Muiris; did you believe her, Brehon?' asked Fiona thoughtfully when they had all finished laughing.

Mara thought for a moment. 'I'm not sure,' she said reluctantly. 'What do you all think?' She reined in her horse and they all gathered around her. She wished that she could go back to the law school, stand in front of the board and debate the matter with her quick-witted scholars. However, this could not be. A glance to the west showed her that the sun was setting over Aran, the sky streaked with bars of blue, crimson and the palest of yellows. It was important for the hostess to be present at the evening meal at Ballinalacken and, also, she wanted to see her little son before bedtime. This deserted space at the foot of the mountain would have to do for now.

The scholars took a minute to think matters through.

'She's a big woman,' said Fiona eventually. 'She would be capable.'

'Hands like a pair of hams,' offered Aidan.

'Bad tempered,' said Hugh.

'Capable of what?' Moylan turned his pony's head towards Fiona.

'Of lobbing a stone down the mountain at a man's head.'

'Or picking it up and smashing it against his skull.'

'Not the last, I'd say,' said Shane. 'That would be hard for anyone to do. Muiris mightn't have been big, but he was immensely strong. I've seen him heave around huge flagstones as though they were feather-beds.'

'I said "capable of what" because I was thinking that we are forgetting about Eamon's murder. The chances are that whoever committed today's crime is also responsible for the first crime.'

'I don't agree,' said Fiona. 'I think that we should keep an open mind about that. The two crimes may not be connected in any way. What do you think, Brehon?'

'An open mind is always good,' said Mara cautiously, 'but I don't think that you have answered Moylan's question.'

'Could Gobnait have the strength to take Eamon by the throat and punch him in the thyroid cartilage?' Fiona mused for a moment and then said decisively, 'I don't see Eamon allowing a woman to do that.'

'Oh, but you see a woman is just the person to do that,' said Shane eagerly. 'A woman could say to Eamon, "you've got a wasp on your neck; let me brush it off," and then punch him before he knew what was happening.'

'You've forgotten one thing, my young friend,' said Moylan in the judicial manner which, as eldest at the law school, he now seemed to have acquired.

'What?' Shane glared at him aggressively. Mara did not interfere. The scholars needed to sharpen their skills and hone their belligerence if they were to argue their cases in a court of law. There was time enough for Shane to learn to hide that aggression under a smooth exterior before he went out into the world, but she was a realist enough to know that without a certain toughness none of her scholars would survive the work. Moylan, she thought, had begun to acquire that polish and she was glad to see it. He replied to Shane now with lofty condescension.

'My dear young comrade, in order to know that a punch in the thyroid cartilage would kill a man, a certain knowledge, either medical or legal, has to be assumed. Does anyone think that this large, tough lady with hands like hams, possesses this knowledge?'

'Good point, Moylan,' said Mara. 'What are the thoughts on this?' She looked around but all heads were shaking.

'What about Cathal and his son, Owney, Brehon? Did you get anything out of them?' asked Fiona.

'With thumbscrews,' muttered Aidan.

'Cathal was bewildered,' said Mara slowly. 'That was the impression I got. Bewildered . . .' She hesitated for a moment and then added, 'I may be wrong in this, but I slightly got the idea that he was afraid.'

'Afraid!' exclaimed Fiona alertly. 'That's interesting. Afraid of what?'

'Well he kept talking about terrible luck and about signs in the sky and about a black cat . . .'

'Perhaps he was trying to fool you,' said Hugh innocently and then blushed with embarrassment when Moylan glared at him.

'He may have been,' admitted Mara hastily before his elders could round on Hugh for disrespect to the Brehon. 'The funny thing is that I sensed that he didn't believe all of this "black cat" nonsense, but I did feel very strongly that he was frightened, although you would expect him to be happy.'

'And Owney, he had the knowledge—' began Shane but was interrupted by Moylan.

'That's if he remembered what Nuala said to him years ago. But Owney is not too bright. A few too many knocks on the head, that's Owney. You know what those games of hurling between the kingdoms are like – savage!'

'So at the moment you are thinking about Gobnait, Brehon,' said Fiona quietly, with a quick look around to make sure that no one was passing.

'That's right,' said Mara. She hesitated and then said firmly, 'Now I must go and Fiona, I'd like you to come with me. We'll stop at Poulnabrucky and ask about Muiris and then go back to Ballinalacken. I can trust you to go across to Cahermacnaghten on your own, boys, can't I? I'll see you in the morning.'

'Don't worry too much, Brehon,' said Aidan with easy assurance. 'We'll have it all worked out for you before tomorrow morning.'

'What would I do without you all? I would be lost entirely!' Mara spoke jokingly, but there was a feeling in her mind that she had spoken the truth. She had never really regretted her decision not to give up the law school and her work as a Brehon when she became the king's wife. There were days when it all felt too much for her, but she would not change her position with anyone in the country.

There were no new developments in Muiris's case, but Nuala was calm and hopeful, explaining that it would take a while for the man to recover his senses. The family were hanging on her every word so Mara did not push for further explanations. There was nothing that she could do for Muiris now except find out who did that to him and demand retribution. She and Fiona went over and over the facts again on their way back to Ballinalacken but still the puzzle remained.

'If only we could find out what happened to Fachtnan,' she said eventually. 'Nuala is afraid that he is dead, but somehow I don't think so. Fachtnan was always wise, always careful. He had learning problems, but he was always full of common sense and wisdom. I can't see him trying to tackle a murderer on his own and he wasn't the sort of boy who would try blackmail. It's such a puzzle. I always felt that I could rely on Fachtnan to do the right thing.'

'He did a stupid thing that night if he followed us and that was my fault, I suppose,' said Fiona.

'Yes, but he didn't try to cause a fight as one of the other boys might have done,' argued Mara. 'He just went along quietly and made sure that you were safe. I'd say that he followed you the whole way home and that once you were safely back at Ballinalacken he went over to Cahermacnaghten. Then, of course, came the shock of the news about Eamon's body being found just above the flax garden . . .'

What would Fachtnan do then? she silently asked herself, unwilling to distress the girl further. Being Fachtnan, he would feel a certain responsibility, he would feel that he should perhaps have intercepted Eamon, have persuaded him to return.

But where did he go? And who did he meet? He had disappeared last Saturday and there had been no sign of him since.

'You go up and get ready for supper,' she said to Fiona when they arrived. 'I'll just look in at the babies first.'

The noise from the children's nursery floated down the stairs towards her as she mounted up from the guardroom. She smiled as she heard Turlough's booming voice, and then another man's voice, a laugh from Cliona and two high-pitched shrieks of excitement from the little boys.

When she pushed open the door, both children were on their feet staggering around the room, Art stumping along in a serious, determined way, the lighter and smaller Cormac making sudden runs, taking a tumble and getting back on his feet almost instantly.

'Look at the two of them,' yelled Turlough in a voice that
was trained to reach across battlefields. 'Look at them! What
do you think of that for walking?'

'Walking! That's running!' returned Mara, just managing to
catch Cormac before he collapsed at her feet. She snatched
him up and covered him with kisses, lifting up Art with her
other arm and holding the two children closely to her, and
then smiled a welcome at Setanta O'Connor who was sitting
on the window seat, looking very much at home.

'My lord took the ball from them, because they were fighting
over it, and put it on the table across the room. Art started to
crawl over, but Cormac got on his feet so that he could see
it better and then he started to run to keep his balance and
Art was after him in a second and there they were the pair of
them, walking like two-year-old children.' Cliona was bursting
with pride.

'I'll have to make them a hurley each,' said Setanta, smiling
at the excited face of his wife-to-be. 'I can see it won't be
long until they are out running around the fields.' He got to
his feet, stretching his long legs. 'I'd better be going,' he said.
'I was just delivering some fish to the kitchen for your supper,
Brehon. You'll be having lobster and salmon tonight, my lord.'

'Good man,' said Turlough, as much at ease with a humble
fisherman as he was with his noble friends or kinsmen, thought
Mara, feeling fond and proud of her kingly husband and wishing
that they had more time to spend together. Next week, she
promised herself, next week when the boys have gone on their
holidays. And then she thought of the murder, of the two
crimes, and set her lips. These things were only solved with
a lot of hard work and plentiful allowance of luck, she knew.
With a suppressed sigh she handed over the two babies to
Cliona and tucked her arm into her husband's.

'Let's talk for a few minutes before we have to go down to
supper,' she said quietly as they went out of the door together.

'Bad day?' he asked as they walked up the spiral stairs together.

'Bad day,' she echoed with a sigh. There wasn't much room,
but she found his bulk strangely comforting and clung to his
arm as, side by side, they squeezed their way up.

'I just don't understand,' she said and then paused. These

stairways acted like a funnel for sound. She would say no more until they were in their bedchamber with the solid, wooden door closed between them and the rest of the world.

'And that comes hard,' he said with an understanding grin, but he also knew the hazard of listening ears, so he contented himself with dropping a quick kiss on the shining black loops of braided hair.

'What has Muiris to do with all of this tangle?' he asked as he shut the door. He didn't wait for her answer but walked across the fireplace and lifted a flagon of hot wine from it and poured some into a goblet holding it out near to her mouth. It smelled delicious and she gulped it down eagerly.

'What is it? What's in it?' she asked curiously.

'Lemons and cloves and a bit of cinnamon powder,' answered Turlough. 'Brian the Spaniard, the man from the Aran Islands, sent it over today. He is looking forward to our visit, he told me. In the meantime he sent the fruits, molasses — that's a sort of dark honey, I suppose, sort of powdery crystals — and spices to keep me warm until he can welcome me.'

'Very cordial of your cousin from Aran,' said Mara, sipping the hot wine. It was delicious, she thought, though perhaps slightly too sweet. She could have done with half the amount of these molasses.

'Very cordial,' agreed Turlough with a grin. 'I wonder what he wants. I never trust Brian the Spaniard. No doubt, I'll hear as soon as we land on Aran tomorrow. I wish you were coming.'

I don't, thought Mara, but there was a wistful note in Turlough's voice so she just smiled at him and reminded him that she had the murder of Eamon the lawyer and an almost fatal attack on Muiris to solve.

'I wish that I could help you with that,' said Turlough eagerly. 'I've been asking Ulick and two boys whether they saw any stranger on the mountain. None of us saw anyone except Ardal O'Lochlainn — we kept a distance from him in case the dogs would frighten his flock — oh, and Donán thinks he saw a stranger over near to the flax garden, but that's probably just Donán, he likes to make himself interesting. I wouldn't take much notice of that if I were you. He thought it looked like your scholar Fachtnan, poor lad, but you and I know that is impossible. If Fachtnan were . . .' He hesitated and then continued hurriedly, '. . . if Fachtnan were anywhere near, then he would immediately join you, not skulk at a distance on the hills.'

If Fachtnan were alive, that's what he was going to say, thought Mara, but there was no sense thinking along those lines so she said idly, 'And what about Seamus MacCraith, the poet. Didn't anyone see him?'

'Oh, yes, of course, we all saw Seamus – striking attitudes against the skyline, thinking deep thoughts, no doubt.' Turlough laughed with nervous relief at the turning of the conversation from the missing Fachtnan. 'Calls himself a poet, but can't even produce a few verses about hunting. Not the man that his father was, that's for sure.'

'They say the same about your son, Conor,' said Mara quietly. 'You'll have to look after yourself. The clan cannot do without you. Don't take any chances on those mountains. You don't want to break a leg, or your neck for that matter.' Something occurred to her and she slipped a question in quickly while he was blustering about how strong he was and how he had many long years of life still ahead of him to enjoy the company of his wife and his new son and how much more energetic he was compared to Ulick Burke who spent half the day stretched out asleep on a patch of heather. 'And I am as sure-footed as any of the young men,' he finished.

'I hope you all had sticks with you on the mountainside, did you?' she asked her question as nonchalantly as she could manage.

'Yes, I think so,' he said after a moment's thought. 'Anyway, there's always a barrel of those iron-tipped sticks in the guard-room so anyone who broke a stick the last time could help themselves. I seem to remember telling someone to help himself – no, I can't remember who,' he added as he saw the question in her eyes.

So, no clues there, thought Mara. It would have been one of the guests – the guards would have armed themselves – but which one? It could have been any of them. Donán thought he saw a man; Ulick was wandering around by himself; the poet, Seamus MacCraith, was loose on the mountainside for most of the day, and during that time a strong, energetic, quick-thinking, courageous man like Muiris was assaulted and left for dead.

'We'd better be going downstairs,' she said with a sigh. 'The others will be waiting for us.'

The Great Hall was looking magnificent for the last ceremonial meal of the king's visit. Twenty-foot boards, covered with snowy-white bleached linen cloths, were set on trestles in the middle of the room. The amount of food was astonishing. Silver bowls and platters were edge to edge in the centre of the table, filled with every delicacy that the king's cooks could devise. This was going to be a seafood evening. Already, large pink crabs had been positioned by every place and scarlet lobsters lined the centre of the table. Great bowls of green samphire, of carrageen moss and of sea-lettuce were there for those who liked their seaweeds; carrots, turnips and dried mushrooms for those who did not. As soon as the king took his place at the top of the table, Mara sat down beside him. She felt too tired and too discouraged to do her normal arranging of the guests. The few guests left would just have to sort themselves according to their inclinations.

Which they did. Ulick claimed a place beside Fiona, cold-shouldering Seamus MacCraith so adroitly that the poet almost overbalanced. Turlough called to Conor to sit beside him, assuring himself that his delicate son was not tired after the day in the open air. Donán, after a moment's thought, took the place on the other side of Fiona leaving Mara to entertain Seamus MacCraith.

'The salmon! The king of fish!' exclaimed Turlough.

'Remember the old legend about the salmon of wisdom that we were all told when we were young? Burn your thumb on the side of it and acquire the wisdom, my lord,' said Ulick languidly. 'Or perhaps we will allow our young poet to be the one to do that. He is more in need of wisdom than you and I, my lord. We have acquired wisdom on the battlefield of life.'

Seamus MacCraith gave him a contemptuous look and turned his attention to Mara who asked him whether he had a fruitful day.

'Alas, no,' he shook his head. 'There is a certain monotony about the Aillwee Mountain. Just white everywhere. It lacks the sculptural sweep of Mullaghmore Mountain. I don't find it inspiring.'

Mara gazed at him. Was it possible that any man could be so completely self-centred? 'I don't think that it was a monotonous week on the Aillwee Mountain,' she said drily. 'You do realize that one man has been killed there and another man almost killed – he may well die tonight.'

'Oh, that.' He waved his hand dismissively in the air. 'I spoke only of the scenery.'

'I'm glad to have an opportunity to speak to you,' said Mara and then paused while a portion of salmon was ladled on to her plate and next on to Seamus's. It was not ideal to be cross-questioning a witness at a dinner table, but Ulick and Turlough were shouting witticisms at each other across the table and little could be heard above the two battle-trained voices.

'I wanted to ask you if you saw anyone that you didn't know on the mountainside.'

He had seen several but by the time Mara had elicited, word by painful word, some vague descriptions of what these, uninteresting to a poet, strangers looked like, she decided that they were probably Ardal O'Lochlainn and his shepherds.

'And you saw no one else, outside of the flax garden, I mean.' She hesitated, unwilling to put words into his mouth but judging by his abstracted air he had already lost all interest in the subject so eventually she was forced to ask him straight out whether he had seen a woman anywhere near to the flax garden or to the quarry.

'I saw Fiona, of course. I could see the sun shining on her hair.' He gazed fervently across the table at Fiona's lovely face.

'And me,' suggested Mara.

He looked at her with astonishment as if he had only just noticed her. 'Oh, and you, of course,' he said hastily and his eyes went back to Fiona, who had thrown her head back and was laughing heartily at one of Ulick's jokes.

'Red lips . . .' he murmured.

'Have some more wine,' said Mara signalling to an attendant

to fill the glass. 'Now, tell me exactly how you came to discover the body of Muiris.'

He had little to tell. He had been wandering around aimlessly, getting tired of the monotony of sun on white stone, had wandered into the quarry in search of something that might look different or might inspire him. He hadn't really noticed anything else, but the buzzing of flies had attracted him towards the corpse, as he put it, and Mara did not contradict him – for all she knew Muiris might by now be dead. She would not trouble the family tonight, but would send a messenger tomorrow morning to find out how he did and whether Nuala needed any supplies.

Seamus MacCraith had turned a delicate shade of pale yellow at the thought of the corpse and the flies buzzing in the blackened blood, so she decided to get rid of him. He had pushed away his platter of uneaten salmon and the servants were busy clearing off the first course and replacing it with clean plates and new dishes. She lifted a finger and beckoned to Turlough's son-in-law, Donán O'Kennedy.

'You go and entertain Fiona with some young company,' she said kindly to the poet. 'I want to have a word with Donán.'

Ulick gave her a grin and she knew that he had overheard, but she didn't care. If it were not for Turlough's sake Ulick would not receive any invitations from her, though she supposed that from now on, as godfather, he would have to be included in Cormac's birthday celebrations. In any case, he was three times Fiona's age and should have more sense than to be flirting so outrageously with her.

'Did you have a good day?' she asked Donán once he had taken his place beside her. He considered the matter in his pompous way and she ate some bread to conceal her impatience. Why on earth had Turlough picked out this dull young man to be a husband to his daughter?

'There was no sport to be had,' he said eventually. 'We didn't kill a single wolf.'

'I suppose it was rather dull,' she conceded. 'You would have plenty of time to be looking around, scanning the mountainside for any sign of wolves. Turlough was telling me that you thought you saw a man. It wasn't Seamus MacCraith, was it?'

'No, everyone would recognize Seamus in that madder-red cloak of his. No chance of missing him.' His voice was scornful.

'Who do you think it was?'

'I have no idea, Brehon. He was wearing a *bánín* cloak.'

Mara sighed. The fact was that most people of the kingdom wore the undyed wool cloaks unless it was a grand occasion when yellows, greens, reds and even purple cloaks made an appearance.

'It couldn't have been my scholar, Fachtnan, could it?' She asked the question with little hope. 'Would you know his appearance? He was here at the feast last Friday night.'

'Was he the one with the pimples?' asked Donán sounding bored.

'No, that's Aidan.' Mara felt irritated with him. Donán was typical of a man with a grudge against life. He lived in a castle provided by Turlough, his servants and men-at-arms were Turlough's, his children's foster fees were paid by Turlough; not an enviable position for any man, but he did nothing to try to regain his own lost inheritance.

'So there is nothing that you can help me with, nothing you saw or heard today?'

Donán crammed his mouth with honey cake and nodded languidly, his eyes on Ulick Burke. He had nothing to say and did nothing to entertain his hostess.

Mara turned to Turlough and he immediately bent his head towards her. 'What is it?' he asked and the concern in his voice almost brought tears to her eyes.

'Nothing. I'm tired. I think we should all have an early night. You, Ulick, Donán, Conor and Brian Ruadh will be off early in the morning.'

'That's right,' he said looking anxiously at her. 'I've given orders that I am to be woken quietly. I won't disturb you. We'll go off very quietly and you have a good sleep in and a good rest. You're looking tired.'

'I'm all right,' said Mara. She concealed a smile at the thought of Turlough doing anything quietly. On the other hand she might accept his offer. There was no point, really, in accompanying him and his companions to Doolin harbour and hanging around there waiting for the tide to turn and the boat to be ready. It would be a slow and tedious proceeding with plenty of drinking at the alehouse and silly jokes from Ulick. She would make her farewells to Turlough in private and stay in bed until they had moved away from Ballinalacken. Then she would get someone to saddle her horse and go straight over to the law school, and try to get this matter solved. In the meantime, there were a few other matters to uncover first from the house guests before she turned her attention to the inhabitants of Aillwee.

She looked around the table. O'Brien of Arra had finished his food and she smiled an invitation to him.

'Come and sit by the fire with me,' she said, standing up and moving close to him. 'This has been a terrible day.'

'Terrible,' he echoed, following her. 'Dreadful shame about that man, the farmer.' He hesitated a moment, taking his seat and leaning forward to poke the fire before saying, 'I wonder what he might have offered for the lease.'

'I have no idea.' Mara tried to make her voice sound soft and regretful, having suppressed her first instinct, which was to give him a tart reply.

'Nothing we can do now.' O'Brien of Arra heaved a sigh.

'No, indeed.' Mara decided to come quickly to the purpose of her interview before they were interrupted. 'I saw that you had signed the document, and that Cathal had made his cross – no doubt in your presence.'

'That's right.' O'Brien of Arra looked slightly embarrassed. 'We should, of course, have waited for you, but you had gone off with young Seamus MacCraith and Cathal O'Halloran was very insistent. You can understand, after all that had happened before.'

'Oh, don't worry, it's all perfectly legal. Your signature acts as witness that Cathal made his mark. I've countersigned it and will deliver it to the O'Hallorans to keep until next year. There is no problem with it at all.' Mara hastened to assure him. It was interesting that Cathal, even with the alarming report of a dead man lying nearby, had taken the time to ensure that the deed was signed and witnessed.

'I wanted to ask you whether you saw anyone that you didn't know when you were on your journey up the mountain

– that is apart from the men with the flock of sheep,' she asked.

He started to shake his head and then paused. 'I think I may have seen someone. A tall young man, dark, curly hair, wearing a *bánín* cloak. Do you know,' he went on, 'I have a feeling I might have seen this young fellow before – about this time last year. You sent your two eldest scholars to me with the flax garden deed for signature. I think it might have been one of these.'

'Fachtnan and Enda,' said Mara. 'But Enda had blonde hair.'

'That's right. He's the young man who works for the king, isn't he? I've seen him recently. No, it's the other one that I meant.' He looked around the room. 'I don't see him here today. Is he back at the law school?'

'No,' said Mara. 'Fachtnan has been missing since last Saturday. Do you think it was he that you saw?'

He shook his head. 'Probably not,' he said. 'And yet . . .' He looked up and narrowed his eyes. The door had opened and a tall, middle-aged man, well dressed in a blue woven cloak, had come in and stood hesitating at the door.

'But that is my steward,' he said. 'There must be some business for me to attend to. Will you excuse me, Brehon?'

'Ask him to have a meal and to stay the night,' said Mara hospitably. 'In fact, there is no reason why he should not stay here at the castle until you arrive back from Aran and then you can ride back together across the Shannon. I'll send an order to our steward and he will arrange matters.'

When he left her she heaved a sigh. From time to time it appeared as if she were about to solve the mystery of the missing Fachtnan but hopes always ebbed away. Was it possible that he was still alive?

Seventeen

Bretha Déin Checht
(The Judgements of Dian Checht)

Every injury brings with it its own fine. There are six different fines for an injury to teeth with the largest sum given for an injury to a front tooth as that exposes the victim to ridicule for ever afterwards.

A Brehon must not be too hasty in giving judgement in the case of any injury as the physician's report must be awaited and the long-term effects of the injury calculated.

The amount of compensation will be a set fee for the injury and an additional fine which will take into account the honour price of the victim.

Mara slept little that night and once dawn arrived she abandoned the effort and slipped out of bed, being careful not to disturb Turlough. She dressed quietly and then stole down the stairs, startling the night guards.

'You're never tempted to sleep?' she asked them with a smile as they jumped alertly to attention, greeted her and then at her request undid the massive bolts of the huge oak front door of the castle.

They both looked shocked at the idea. 'What, with O'Kelly just ten miles away?' one exclaimed.

Mara tried to look shocked, too. She had been hearing about the threat from O'Kelly since the time that she had first invited Turlough to her house and the man had never materialized. No doubt he would marshal his men if the Great Earl, the Earl of Kildare, gave the order, but in the meantime he stayed peacefully in his good, fruitful limestone land east of Galway. She had begun to wonder whether she would ever see the man or whether he would remain as a distant bogeyman, used by mothers and foster mothers to frighten badly-behaved children.

The morning was still grey when she came out and the
ocean was a sombre purple-blue. Turlough and his companions
would have a calm day for their crossing to Aran, she thought
as she went down the steep bank towards the kennels and
stables. There were no lights in the cabins where the attendants
slept and no sound from the stables. A dog barked as she
approached the kennel door, but she spoke quietly to Bran,
her own dog, and his whine of welcome reassured the other
wolfhounds.

Bran was a beautiful dog. He was very large, a good three
feet high at the shoulder with a noble head, small pricked ears,
and a slim muscular body. Most wolfhounds were grey, or
brindle, but Bran was pure white, his rough coat matching the
limestone on the hills. He was the son of a dog that Mara had
grown up with, her father's dog, and he was a magnificent
creature. He was utterly devoted to his mistress and so intelligent that he hardly needed a command to do her bidding.

Together they went down the steep hill from where the
castle stood. Normally Mara walked on the seaward side, but
the morning air was chilly and she turned almost instinctively
towards the rising sun. The hill on this eastern side of the
castle was almost perpendicular and the pathway little used, so
until she and Bran got to the bottom of it, she did very little
thinking.

At the end of the overgrown path there was a large flat
stone, with a small, lower stone beside it, almost like a table
and chair, or even a desk and a stool. The Burren was littered
with these giant stones, seemingly flung down on the landscape
in a random fashion. Giants' stones, she had named them as a
small girl reading old legends from her father's precious collection of books. She seated herself on the lower of the two and
turned her face to the warmth of the sun. There was a temp-
tation to daydream, to think about her little Cormac, to make
plans for his future, but she resisted this and turned her disci-
plined and well-trained mind towards her problem. Usually
she found it easier to hammer out her ideas with the eager
cooperation of her young scholars, but not this time. This
murder of Eamon and especially the disappearance of Fachtnan
touched them all too deeply. No, this was a matter that she

had to solve herself and strangely she almost imagined another presence beside her — that of her father.

Mara had been the only child of Seamus O'Davoren, the Brehon of the Burren. Her mother had died when she was still very young and her father had not wanted to place her in fosterage so she had formed a habit of straying into the law school and listening to the scholars chant their lessons. She had learned to read with immense rapidity, took to Latin like a duck to water and was very soon outstripping scholars twice her age. Her father had always warned her that it would be hard for a woman to make her way in the law; she would only manage, he warned, if she were better than any of the male scholars, and he always insisted on logical thought as well as on the huge bank of knowledge that every lawyer had to possess.

Now, one by one, with her arm around the warm coat of her beloved dog, she took out her thoughts and laid them on the slab before her. She imagined them there, all the puzzles written down on vellum, rolled into neat scrolls, carefully labelled and tied with pink tape.

And the one that stood out was not labelled Eamon, or even Muiris, but had the word 'Fachtnan' written on it. Continually she had pushed the question of Fachtnan aside, feeling that the verified murder had to be solved before the disappearance, but now she allowed the matter to take her full attention and brain-power.

Intuition can come first if you wish, she could hear her father say, *but it must be followed up by logic.* Her intuition was nudging her to consider the matter of Fachtnan but she must be careful to pin her thoughts to the facts available. Fachtnan had disappeared without a word or a line of writing. He had gone out last Saturday and since then there had been no message. That was so unlike him — and she had known him for over fourteen years — that she had to find a reason why he had neither returned nor sent word. Suppose that Nuala, who, after all, loved him very dearly, was correct. Suppose that Fachtnan went off to try to solve the murder of Eamon; and that seemed, knowing his character, to be the only reason for his sudden disappearance. But why had he not returned? The obvious answer was, as Nuala had speculated, that he was dead. But there was another answer and this had to be explored now. He might be imprisoned.

But why would a murderer imprison the young man? What would be the point? Mara stared fixedly into the distance. She had to stop asking herself questions, she thought severely. Let the answer float into her mind and then test her theory with rigorous logic.

There were some shouts from the top of the hill where the castle perched on the highest spot in the surrounding landscape. Doors were slammed, horses neighed, orders yelled. The sounds floated down to her from what almost seemed to be sky level.

It was a magnificent place for a castle, she thought. It was perched on top of a stony outcrop on the summit of a high, steep hill. The castle itself, with its new extension, took up almost the whole of the stone platform and beyond it the land fell away quite sharply making any form of moat or wall unnecessary. No enemy could capture that castle without terrible slaughter as they toiled up the almost perpendicular height from the base.

And, of course, the guards on the roof could see into the next kingdom. A battalion of soldiers from the Great Earl, or from the infamous O'Kelly, could be spotted while still miles away. Turlough was as safe in Ballinalacken as he was in Thomond, she thought. She wondered whether she should go back up to wish them goodbye and to send polite messages to his cousin the ruler of Aran, Brian the Spaniard, as he was known to distinguish him from the many other Brian O'Briens that were scattered over the three kingdoms and in Limerick as well. She decided against an undignified scramble up the steep hillside, though. The chances were that by the time she reached the top Turlough, his son Conor, son-in-law Donán, cousin Brian Ruadh O'Brien of Arra and friend Ulick Burke would all have moved off to ride the mile or so to the port. In any case, she rather disliked Brian the Spaniard and did not feel that she could be sincere in her wishes. Turlough would say what was necessary and the appearance of O'Brien of Arra, the man from Aran's foster-brother, would be a great and welcome surprise to him.

The sun was strengthening in the sky now and its heat was comforting to her. She loved the sun, her olive skin soaking up the rays and turning brown in the very earliest days of summer. It gave her a feeling of well-being to sit there in the warmth and she decided to indulge herself a while longer. It was still early and she could afford to sit and doze for another a few minutes. She placed her folded arms on the flat surface of the rock in front of her, laid her head on to them. Just a few minutes, she promised herself.

When she woke the sun had moved. For a moment she hardly knew whether she had been asleep or whether she had actually experienced a journey – watching as an eagle does, from a great height, floating along but observing the creatures on the ground. A young man with dark curly hair and an earnest expression, a man with a mission, a man who was determined to prove himself.

Hastily she got to her feet. No time now for the leisurely, scholarly weighing of the evidence, balancing of the probabilities. Somehow she knew that she was right; the truth had lain with the disappearance of Fachtnan. Everything else now fell into place. She had to see Turlough. Hopefully he would still be at the harbour.

It took Mara quite some time to struggle up the steep and overgrown path. She wished that she had brought a rope or a leather lead to thread through Bran's collar. His strength and agility would have helped to pull her up. The path was so narrow and so grown-in with bushes that there was no room for them to go side by side. He went ahead, turning his head from time to time to check that she was still following, and she struggled and panted behind him. She made a mental note to order that the path be cleared. The castle had staff who were probably quite idle during the long periods when the castle was not occupied. She made the note and firmly repressed the thought that it should have been noticed and dealt with long since. Now she had to turn all her energies to her task in hand.

No one was on the terrace in front of the castle when she arrived, but the gravel was churned up as if a dozen lively horses had pranced and wheeled there before turning and trotting down the gentle slope towards the sea. She went instantly to the stables, but no one was there. The stable staff had probably gone indoors to eat their breakfast. She would not bother to waste the time that it would take to summon them. Her beautiful mare, Brig, a present from the king before their marriage, stood there in her stall, ears pricked as she eyed her mistress. Rapidly, Mara got down the saddle and within a few minutes, with a quick command to Bran to go to his bed, she was galloping, as fast as the mare could go, down the road to the sea.

How long had she slept? Her common sense and her knowledge of the sun's position in the sky told her that she had slept for at least an hour but she kept hoping that it was less. There was no one on the road in this early morning and she hoped that she was making much faster progress than the king and his companions had made. They would have gone slowly, exchanging jokes and comments over shoulders, those ahead waiting for those behind to catch up. Turlough would have been in no hurry. Though he enjoyed his visits to the islands, he hated the actual journey itself and invariably felt sick. With some luck, he would still be at Doolin bolstering his courage with a few glasses of wine or of the potent *uisce bheatha* – water of life brews – sold in those wayside inns.

But luck was not with her. And somehow she knew it as she thundered across the small stone bridge that spanned the River Aille before it made its way into the sea ahead. Somehow there was an absence of sound, a strange stillness and emptiness ahead of her.

But the sea was not empty. Its broad, heaving, dark-blue and white masses were dotted here and there with a couple of large-sailed ships, various familiar boats, such as cogs, hookers and caravals, as well as the fishermen's curraghs. Quite near to shore was a *pucán*, but only one. Where was the other? As well as the fisherman a *pucán* could scarcely hold more than four or five men. It was a small boat, entirely open with no cabin or deck.

Mara touched her heels to the mare and in an instant the highly bred animal launched herself forward flying over the road to the sea as if she were about to rival the seabirds that flew overhead. In a few minutes they were at the harbour. The second *pucán* was still there tied up to a mooring post and gathered around it were Fergal and Conall, Turlough's body-guards, three men-at-arms and Ulick Burke.

Mara flung herself from her horse, hastily tossing her reins to a waiting hand. 'I'm coming with you,' she said firmly to what looked like the boat owner. 'Set off instantly. I want you to catch up with the other *pucán*.'

He looked at her hesitantly and muttered something. He had a strange voice, husky and with an odd note in it. Something unfamiliar about it. She didn't know whether he had under-stood her or not and in a raised and clear voice she repeated her command.

'The boat has been holed, Brehon,' said Ulick stepping forward and inserting his small neat frame between her and the boat owner.

'What?' she exclaimed.

'That's right,' he said, and added soothingly, 'Don't worry about it. They will send back the other *pucán* for us once my lord and his family have landed. You look so upset. Now you mustn't worry about us, Brehon,' he went on with his usual mocking tone of faint amusement. 'We'll be in time for the feast this evening and that's the reason why everyone visits, is it not?'

Mara stared in disbelief and then she rounded instantly on the guards. 'And you allowed my lord to go without you, without any protection! Not a single one of you went with him.'

'Sure, what protection could the man need, there he is with his loving family, his cousins and his sons, what more could a man want?' Now Ulick was openly laughing at her and she fought a desire to slap his face.

'A king, my lord,' she said icily, 'does not go without a guard. I cannot believe this of you,' she added addressing herself to Fergal and Conall.

'With respect, Brehon, the king himself ordered us to stay,' said Fergal, flushing a deep red, though he spoke in a dignified manner. 'His family wished to be with him on the first boat; none of them wanted to wait, and we could not go against our orders. We suggested that we should go with the king but he would have none of it.'

'How long will it take you to mend that boat?' Mara decided that this matter had to be left for the moment. The first priority had to be for her to talk to Turlough.

The man muttered something and Ulick obligingly translated. 'He says that it could take a week, Brehon. No, there is nothing for it, but to wait with patience. Your presence will make the time so much more pleasant.'

Mara looked out to sea. The first *pucán*, despite its sail, was making very poor progress. It hardly seemed to be moving. There was a strong wind blowing from the west and there was a moment when the boat seemed to go backwards. She endured a moment's panic when she wondered whether that boat, also, had been holed, but then realized that the problems were wind and waves. Even from where she stood, she could see that a strong springtime tide was flowing, bringing the water in so fast that the beach was visibly being lost, yard by yard, under its onslaught. She gazed around, wondering what to do. She had the fastest horse in the kingdom, but no horse could go through these enormous waves that seemed to be tossing the *pucán* around as if it were a toy boat. She narrowed her eyes trying to see whether anyone was looking towards the shore. The *pucán* must have made better progress earlier as it was now quite a distance out to sea, probably about halfway between Doolin and Aran, she reckoned. The figures on it, of Turlough, Conor, Donán and O'Brien of Arra were tiny. There was no possibility that any shriek or any signal could reach them.

There were no other boats around. All the fishermen of the port were out trailing nets through the incoming tide. These boats were nearer and Mara could see that every head was turned towards the shore. No doubt they had seen her dramatic ride down the road that led to the sea and were speculating about what had brought her.

And then one fisherman stood up in his boat, balancing carefully, legs wide apart, at one with the motion of the waves. He held one hand at his brow to shield his eyes against the glare of the morning sun. Something about the sturdy figure caught her attention and she knew who it was. It was Cliona's husband-to-be, the fisherman Setanta O'Connor. He seemed to look at her for a while, as if wondering what brought her to the port but then his net caught his attention and he sat down again, turning his face away from the shore and towards the islands.

'Setanta,' she shrieked but then knew that there was no chance that her voice could reach him in the teeth of the roar of wind and water. There was only one thing to be done. Her experience as the only girl brought up in a schoolful of boys would stand her in good stead. She put two fingers into her mouth and blew hard. The whistle was loud enough to start all of the seagulls cawing wildly. Whether Setanta heard it, or whether he heard the birds, however it was, he turned around once more and this time she was ready for him, snatching the scarf from her neck and waving it frantically in the air and then beckoning to him with her spare hand. For a moment she wondered whether he had understood and then she saw him take a second oar from the bottom of the boat. In a minute he had turned the boat around, rowing with long strokes, his light boat riding the waves and allowing the tide to sweep him back to the shore.

'Setanta, can you catch the *pucán*? I must speak to the king about a matter of urgency.'

His answer was to throw a rope ashore and in a moment Fergal caught it and tied it firmly to one of the mooring posts.

Mara stepped down into the boat and then she hesitated. Her own words came back to her. A king should not go unescorted. She looked at the tiny curragh made from a framework of hazel branches and covered with leather.

'Setanta, can you take the king's bodyguards as well?' she asked. She could not quite see how as there were only two seats and the spaces between the seats were filled with squirming blue and silverfish, but she knew that they should go. Perhaps another fishing boat would come back to the harbour . . .

But in a moment Setanta had lifted the net of fish, tied its opening with a fine rope and without hesitation thrown it into the shallow water. One of the men-at-arms, with a rather shamefaced glance at Mara, came forward at his shouted request and tied the end of the rope to one of the mooring posts.

'Sit on the floor and for God's sake balance your weight.' Setanta was a man of few words.

Mara wondered whether he should give one of the body-guards an oar, but then decided not to interfere. It would horrify Setanta if she sat on the floor and she had no idea if either Conall or Fergal could row. Thomond was an inland kingdom; men from Corcomroe, like Setanta O'Connor, were out on the sea as soon as they could walk.

Mara shut her eyes to stop herself from obsessively measuring the distance between the *pucán*, which had set out over an hour ago, and the small, fragile shell in which she sat. After a while she cautiously opened them. Already they had left the harbour and were on the open sea. She turned her face towards Aran. The *pucán* had not appeared to have moved any nearer to the island, but she knew that on the sea distances were deceptive.

Setanta O'Connor was an expert with his curragh. He seemed to put very little effort into every stroke, but the boat leaped forward at each sweep of the oars. He used the wind and the tide cleverly, rowing hard when the wave came towards them and then allowing the boat to drift back as the wave retreated. What was it that Setanta had said about his boat? '*I have a boat that's a match to any boat in the sea,*' he had boasted. '*That boat can fly across the water with only one man rowing – not like those English boats.*'

'The men in the *pucán* are taking down the sails, Brehon,' said Conall after a few minutes. He spoke tentatively and she forced herself to smile at him. After all, it wasn't their fault that Turlough had so little idea of what was due to him as king, so little suspicion that anyone would undermine him in any way.

'That's where we're going then, is it?' Setanta O'Connor glanced quickly over his shoulder. 'Heavy, these things, unless the wind is with you. Still, better than one of those Galway hookers, though.'

'More sails on a hooker, though,' said Mara trying to make conversation. She had no need to think about anything now; she just needed to rejoin Turlough and to be by his side like any good wife. She thought of Gobnait and of Gobnait's famous predecessor, the Abbess, who released a swarm of bees into the faces of the incoming army. She thought of Andraste, the female god of war, and of Maeve, Queen of Connaught, victor of battles, and then she straightened her back and gazed steadily out to sea as the small boat scrambled through the waves.

'It will be a bit hair-raising for a while, Brehon, best hold on tight,' shouted Setanta. 'Don't you worry, though. They say that an O'Connor of Doolin can never drown. Fishermen like us always bob up again.'

Not true, thought Mara. Many, many fishermen drowned every year. The Aran islands were full of widows and orphans. Still, she appreciated his spirit and hoped that her impulsive act had not taken him into a danger that he would normally have avoided. She gripped the wood of the board beneath her tightly and gazed steadily ahead.

An enormous wave, taller than any tower house, was approaching. It was a giant wall of translucent water, glinting in the morning sunshine. And yet not a wall, more like a giant slab of glistening blue glass. The bottom of this monstrous body of water seemed to be about twenty foot thick, but it tapered upwards to a thin curl of creamy white.

'Now!' shouted Setanta. Incredibly, he was laughing.

The wave slid under the tiny, frail boat, lifting it high in the air. For a moment they seemed to be suspended between sea and sky, like standing on a mountain top.

And then they were sliding down, sliding into a pit of churned up colours of greens, blues and broken creams. The boat's prow was pointing downwards and Setanta himself was almost submerged.

'Oh, Jesus be merciful!' shrieked one of the bodyguards.

And then, by some miracle, the boat straightened out. Setanta was now frantically bailing out the water with a leather bucket, working like a madman for a second and then tossing it to Conall.

'That got interesting for a moment!' he shouted as he began to row again. His eyes met Mara's and he gave her a cheerful grin.

'Very interesting!' called back Mara. Her courage was high and she was amazed to find how she had enjoyed the moment, once the danger was past. Cumhal, her farm manager, often took the boys sailing on summer Saturdays or Sundays and she could understand now why they enjoyed it so much. There was something about pitting one's strength against the elemental winds and waves and surviving it. She doubted whether Setanta would ever settle down to be a sheep farmer on Cliona's land.

'Tide's turning,' shouted Setanta joyfully. 'Look at the birds, Brehon. They always know.'

Mara looked towards the shore. The noisy seagulls had now alighted on the harbour wall and were greedily watching the water below. After a few minutes she saw them swoop down and alight on the stony beach below. A few succulent crabs or even a few sprats would probably be entangled in the seaweed and the seagulls would get a tasty meal. She remembered her observation of the white-sailed boats from the window of Ballinalacken.

'How's the wind, Setanta?' she shrieked and she saw him lick the corner of his mouth and turn his face.

'Might be shifting,' he shouted back. 'Bit slacker, anyway.'

Mara licked a finger, tasting the intense saltiness of it, and then held it out moving it hopefully towards the north. The *pucán* lay south of them on its route to the smallest and nearest of the three islands. If the wind moved to the north or even to the north-west it would aid them very much but give no help to the other boat, which could need an easterly or north-easterly wind.

The master of the *pucán* and his men had sensed the change in the wind also. They had scented some hope for themselves. A second, rather tattered white sail was being run up the mast. For a moment it hung there, limp and motionless, and the wind caught it. The boat spun helplessly for a moment. Setanta's boat chopped a few hundred yards off the gap between them; the men on the *pucán* made some adjustments to the sail. It spread out and took the wind flat against it and then the boat began to move slowly, with several helpless spins, but it was moving to the south-west, moving towards the island.

Well, thought Mara, it worked once and it will work again. For the second time this day she stuck two fingers in her mouth and sent forth the penetrating whistle. Every head in the *pucán* turned and then came the familiar, battlefield-trained roar. The sail was immediately hauled down.

Setanta redoubled his efforts, sending the light boat skimming across the sudden calm that had smoothed the waves. In a short space of time they had reached the *pucán* and Turlough was there, bending over the bars, his face lit up with an expression of pleasure. At his quick command a ladder was dropped over the side and Setanta grabbed hold of it quickly, resting one oar in its rowlock.

'You go up first,' said Mara to the two bodyguards. 'Your place is beside the king.'

They were on their feet instantly, the useful-looking throwing knives conspicuous on their belts, their faces set and determined. Once they were on deck Mara climbed the ladder. Her cloak, woollen gown and the *léine* beneath it were all soaked with salt water, but she climbed with as much dignity as she could manage.

Turlough held out a hand to her, a warm hand that squeezed hers as she mounted the last few rungs of the ladder and stepped on to the deck. She returned the pressure of his hand, but did not look at him.

All of her attention was focussed on the tall figure standing beside the mast.

'Donán O'Kennedy,' she said, 'I, as Brehon of the Burren, accuse you of the murder of Eamon the lawyer on Saturday the eighth day of April and I call upon you to answer for your crime in front of the people of the Burren on judgement day on the eve of the feast of Bealtaine in three weeks' time.'

Eighteen

Brecha Écgid
(Judgements of Inadvertence)

The law does not punish a man whose actions led to a death if his intentions are pure and if the risk was thoroughly understood by the victim.

For instance, a death of a passenger on a boat by drowning is not deemed to be a crime:

1. If the weather was inclement.

2. If the owner of the boat had done his best to ensure that the boat was in good repair.

3. If his seamanship was as good as could be expected.

4. If the victim had realized how bad the conditions were.

Donán's hand went immediately to his dagger and Mara smiled grimly. She had not needed that for proof, but it was good that Turlough saw it. He stared in horror at his son-in-law, now in the grip of one of the bodyguards, and then back at his wife's face.

'The murder of Eamon the lawyer,' he said, his strong voice almost faint. 'But why? Why on God's earth would you do a thing like that, boy?'

The king's son, Conor, who had been lying on the deck beside the railing, raised his head in astonishment, turned a delicate shade of green and then vomited over the side of the boat. By the look of him, that was not the first time. He tried to gasp out something but Mara ignored him. She had work to be done. Conor was a delicate young man without much spirit. Normally he was quietly affectionate towards his father, but no one felt that he would make a good king. He had been elected *tánaiste* – heir – when he came to age of eighteen, but had proved to be a disappointment. Unlike the position in England, where the king's eldest son automatically became king, in Ireland the king was elected from the most promising and warlike of an extended royal family group. The hope of the clan was that Turlough would live to a ripe old age and that when he came to the end of his days there might be a better choice than Conor for successor.

'Turn the *pucán* around,' said Mara authoritatively to the ship's captain. 'We are not going to Aran today. Turn around and go back to Doolin. Sit down over there, Donán, and you, my Lord of Arra, sit beside him.'

They did her bidding, almost helplessly. Both bodyguards, with a quick glance at the king, stood threateningly over them. Conall held out a hand and in a dazed manner both took knives from their pouches and handed them to him. Mara gave them one glance and then went back to the side of the *pucán* and leaned down, looking into the young fisherman's smiling face.

'Setanta O'Connor, you have a wonderful boat and you managed it marvellously. Someday I hope to go in it again. I hope you have a good trip back to Doolin and find your fish safe. I'm very grateful to you.'

She would not insult him by offering silver, she thought. At some later date she and Turlough would make a present, perhaps a wedding present when he and Cliona married. 'Bring the fish up to the castle when you get back,' she ordered. 'We'll take your whole catch. The cook won't be expecting so many for the evening meal.'

'Tell him to tie that cockleshell of his to the stern; with a wind like that behind us we'll be back at Doolin long before he could row the half the distance.' The owner of the *pucán* had a thick, strong Connaught form of Irish, hard for anyone to understand him on the boat. Mara had been puzzled by the choice of two *pucán*s to convey the king, his relations and his men-at-arms on his annual visit to Aran. These boats were normally used to carry turf to the Aran as they had neither peat bogs nor trees on the islands. Now she understood the whole business, but nodded affably at the man, before passing on the message to Setanta.

In a moment, Setanta was on board, holding a rope in his hand which he made fast to an iron spar at the back of the *pucán*. He did not come forward to join the others, but perched there, keeping an eye on his precious boat.

Mara gazed after it for a moment as it bobbed behind them on the ocean. A cockleshell, the owner of the *pucán* had called it and it was an understandable description. Certainly it looked very small and very fragile there on the waves. I'll never eat fish again, she thought, without remembering the peril that these dauntless men may have undergone in order to put food on the table for those who could afford to buy. She reflected on the young Setanta, bred to a life of toil and danger, working hard, sometimes frightened, surely, often wet and cold, while others of his age played.

Her eyes went back to Donán O'Kennedy, who would never have had to lift a finger, as Brigid would say, and who now sat sullen and silent, leaving as much room as possible on the bench between himself and O'Brien of Arra. He had been fostered by the Earl of Ormond, a strange choice by his father. Why send the son of a Gaelic chieftain into the household of an English earl? Even though the family of the Earl of Ormond, like the Earl of Kildare's family, had lived in Ireland for over two hundred years they had never broken their connection with England and had always paid homage to the English king, dressed like the English, brought up their children to be English and to despise the laws and the customs into which they had been born.

'Take off that wet cloak.' Turlough was at her side removing the cloak as he spoke. Quickly he took off his own cloak, lined with wolf fur, and placed it on her shoulders.

'You will be cold now,' she said, but smiled her thanks. He did not question her, she thought with amusement. He had complete faith in her judgement. His only question had been to his son-in-law. *What made you do it?* he had asked and it had been a good question.

So what did make Donán do it? Not shortage of money. He and Ragnelt lived in as much luxury as Turlough himself and worked far less – not at all, in fact. Donán's life was a self-indulgent one of eating, drinking and occasional hunting. Already he was beginning to show the signs of that over-indulgence. His skin was sallow and his waist had thickened.

So what had made him do it? It depended, thought Mara, on which crime you thought of.

Because there had been three crimes.

And then she thought of Eamon. What had made him do it? Could his upbringing have had anything to do with his eventual fate? She knew what his upbringing would have been like. Not for him the indulgence of English castle life, of being served on bended knee, of days filled with idleness. Eamon was brought up in a law school and in their own way, the young law scholars worked as hard as the sons of fishermen and perhaps even harder than the sons of farmers. The learning went on from first thing in the morning almost to last thing at night. Thousands and thousands of law texts, whether couched in triads or heptads, or else presented in large, indigestible chunks, had to be memorized, learned and relearned, until they were safely and permanently stored in the young brains. Latin, with all its difficulties, all the horrors of the pluperfect subjunctive and the ablative absolute, was started at the age of five and by graduation they spoke it as if it were their native tongue. The self-discipline acquired by these young scholars was immense; Mara had experienced some who would conceal illness to the moment of almost collapse in case they fell behind with their studies by taking to their beds.

So what had happened to Eamon? Why had he done that? Did he, sometime in his youth, acquire false values that told him a bag of silver was worth more than integrity?

'They're signalling from Aran, from the castle, my lord.' The shout from the owner of the *pucán* interrupted Mara's thoughts.

'Waving a flag,' said Conall, taking his eyes from the two on the bench and turning back towards the island.

Mara narrowed her eyes but could barely see the flag waving frantically. The turn around of the *pucán* had been noticed, she thought.

'Keep heading for Doolin,' she said firmly and avoided Turlough's enquiring eyes. What a very good-tempered and trusting man he was not to deluge her with enquiries!

The next moment, they were almost deafened by an

ear-splitting explosion. Mara had never heard anything like
it in her life before. It was louder than any storm sound and
seemed to rent the sky. The seagulls flew straight up into the
air, a panic-stricken flock, in a cluster of white feathers and
wide-open squawking yellow bills.

'My God! He's got a cannon!' yelled Turlough, more in
admiration than in fear or shock.

'Where would he have got that from?' inquired Mara. There
was only one answer to that, she thought, as she realized the
significance of the cannon shot. The picture that had formed
in her mind during that hour of solitude at the foot of the
castle mound had been correct in its broad outline, but only
now were all the small details coming to light.

The sea was full of boats, white-sailed boats that were more
like small ships than the familiar red-sailed hookers and cogs
of these Atlantic straits. What was it Setanta had said that day
when she had met him in Ballinalacken? He had been boasting
of the excellence of his boat and had compared it, contemptuously, to 'those English ships'. Why had she not noticed
that word?

And now they were in danger. Some sort of signal had
been given by that cannon shot. A large ship with many sails
darted out from the harbour at the eastern end of the island.
Another followed it.

Even more alarming, a third ship that had been tossing on
the waves not too far from them now turned its prow in
their direction.

'Sail as fast as you can,' said Mara to the boat owner in
fluent Connaught Irish. 'Quick, get every ounce of sail up. I
want us back in Doolin before that English ship can reach us.'

'English!' echoed Turlough, catching that word. In a moment,
he had understood everything and there was a harsh, angry
look on his face. He cast a look of disgust at his son-in-law,
unbuttoned the short leather jacket that he wore and revealed
a formidable collection of throwing knives, each in separate
pockets.

'Let any man try to board this ship and he'll get a knife
in the guts,' he said grimly.

'Go and join my lord,' Mara said to the bodyguards. 'Give

me one of those knives and I'll guard your prisoners. For pity's sake, Conor,' she said over her shoulder. 'Get up off that deck; seasickness is purely imaginary. Forget it.' And then she swung around rapidly as O'Brien of Arra made a half attempt to stand up. 'Stay where you are, my lord, and you, too, Donán. Any attempt to move and I'll feed you to the fishes.'

The two English ships from Aran were travelling fast, but the *pucán*, she judged, was going faster still. They were out in the open sea and felt the full force of the west wind; the ships were still in the lee of the island.

'Faster,' she muttered. All of the English ships had more sail and presumably that meant a faster speed; they had to get well ahead in the next five minutes or so. She gave a hasty glance at the prisoners and then back out to sea again. The lone English ship was the danger now. Would it try to accost them or would it wait for the other three ships? That might be more deadly, she thought, and tried to remember the accounts of naval battles described by the Roman author Tacitus. Grappling irons, she thought, and quickly picked up a pair of oars from beside the mast and handed them to Conor who had staggered to his feet and stood swaying uncertainly.

'Use these for pushing away the ship if it gets too near,' she said encouragingly, but spoke loudly enough to be heard by the king's bodyguards. Turlough also heard and he gave her a grin, but then once more the air was split by the thunderous explosion from the cannon. This time it was fired towards them and something hit the sea and a sparkling jet of water shot upwards.

'Missed by a mile!' yelled Turlough shaking his fist at the island. 'By God, if I ever get a chance to catch hold of Brian the Spaniard I'll strangle him with my own pair of hands, cousin or no cousin.'

Turlough's other cousin, O'Brien of Arra, looked startled at that, Mara was glad to see. He thrust his hands into the comfort of his warm cloak, hunched his shoulders and stared apprehensively over his shoulder at the bulk of the island with its castle perched halfway up the slope.

Strangling or knives, neither was a weapon that would avail against cannon and handguns. Turlough was living in the past, thought Mara. If only they could get back to Doolin, reunite him with his men-at-arms, and then get everyone in behind the wooden door of Ballinalacken Castle. An iron cannon would be too difficult to move by road, too slow, too cumbersome with its escort in continuous danger from the lightly clad Irish, armed with their throwing knives. But by sea was different; a cannon could have been shipped across from England and landed at the safe, sandy harbour of Aran and then dragged by islanders up the short, steep slope to the castle.

'Brehon, that ship, the one that's been out there all the morning, that's holding off deliberately.' Setanta had decided that his boat was safe and had joined Mara, casting a curious eye on the knife in her hand and on the two men huddled on the bench before her.

'Holding off deliberately,' repeated Mara and her heart sank. Her eyes went to the two ships, now out of the lee shore of the island, now moving faster, blown by the west wind. The third boat had to tack in order to make the best of the wind, but each long diagonal movement was bringing them nearer and nearer to the *pucán*.

'They're going to try to surround us,' she said, half to herself but half to Setanta. 'Now let me think of the battle of Actium; what did Tacitus say? What did Octavius do?'

'Never heard of either of them,' said Setanta firmly. 'My lord,' he called. 'These three ships will have you surrounded before the sun moves away from the cliffs of Moher.'

'Let them try anything,' growled Turlough. 'I'm ready for them. I have my son by my side . . .' He cast a quick look at the pallid Conor, his *tánaiste*, and added hastily, 'And two good bodyguards at my back.'

'With respect, my lord, that is not enough,' said Setanta firmly. 'The sea is no place to be fighting three against one battles and these ships are probably packed with armed men, wearing metal jackets, too. I've seen the sun glint on them. No, what you must do is to get the sea to work for you.'

'What do you mean?' Turlough sounded annoyed. 'Don't

you go dictating battle strategies to me, young man; I was fighting battles when you were in your cradle.'

'My cradle was the sea,' said Setanta with a grin. He jerked his thumb at the helmsman. 'Does that fellow there speak any decent Irish?'

'Tell me what you want and I'll translate for you,' said Mara quickly. She herself could see how the ships advanced like a pack of dogs about to bring down a wolf.

'This is a chance — just a chance, my lord,' said Setanta. 'See over there where the gulls are rising and the water is a different colour.'

Mara's eyes followed his outstretched hand. She could see what he meant. One patch of the water was not a deep greeny-blue but was translucent with white spray rising from it. As she watched a wave approached, shuddered and broke.

'There are rocks there,' she said with alarm.

'That's right, Brehon, a whole line of them, stretching from that spot almost on to the shore. Many's the time that I sailed over them. You can find great lobsters, lurking there.'

'Sailed over them?' queried the king.

'That's right, my lord, they're further down than you think. Ask that man what sort of keel he has, is it smaller than a hooker's keel?' he said urgently to Mara and she quickly translated his question.

'He says not as deep as a hooker's but he doesn't want to risk the rocks.'

'He'll risk it or I'll put a knife into him.' In an instant Setanta produced a wicked-looking knife, all stained with blood, from his pouch and held it menacingly at the man from Connaught. 'It's our only chance, my lord,' he said to the king. 'We go that way, they follow us. These ships have deep keels; I saw one a couple of days ago when I and two other boats went out far after a shark.'

'You mean that they will go on the rocks? Good man.' Turlough hugged his son's thin shoulders with glee and then punched Setanta on the arm.

'I'll stand beside you and translate,' said Mara. 'Conor, you watch these men. Take this knife; don't hesitate to use it if necessary.'

The knife wavered in Conor's hand, but it would probably serve to keep his mind off the seasickness. Both Donán and O'Brien of Arra looked quite cowed and the king was flanked by his two bodyguards. Mara moved across to where the boat owner was standing, tiller in his hand and his eyes fixed stubbornly ahead.

'To the right,' said Setanta. 'Just a little. Don't want the ships to take too much notice.'

Mara translated and the *pucán* altered course very slightly.

'Just a bit more,' said Setanta indicating with his hand and nodded with satisfaction when his order was obeyed. Now the boat was pointing slightly away from the harbour at Doolin. The three white-sailed ships followed discreetly.

'Bit more,' said Setanta. Now he put his own hand on the tiller for a minute and nodded with satisfaction. 'Nice boat,' he said admiringly. 'Answers to a touch.'

Mara translated, but there was no change in the boat owner's surly expression. He had been in the plot, she thought, he and his comrade who had no doubt been heavily compensated for the hole in his boat. She glanced over her shoulder and then stiffened with alarm. The English ships were no longer sailing three abreast. One had shot rapidly towards the south, the centre boat remained behind them but the third boat was sailing directly towards the harbour.

'The pincer movement,' said Mara aloud. 'You remember your Livy, my lord, and you, Conor, from your studies. Livy wrote about Hannibal using the pincer movement in his battles – one detachment to the back and two on the flanks of the enemy.'

Both men gave her a look of total incomprehension and Mara half smiled to herself. She would have to tell her scholars about this. Their knowledge of the classical writers was fresh and profound, but she had always found that a practical analogy was what made the knowledge stick firmly. She would have them make small models of the *pucán* and of the three English ships and they could reconstruct the sea and the rocks in the pond beyond the orchard. It would be a fun activity for the last day of term next Monday.

Mara felt quite confident now in Setanta. He knew what

he was doing. By now she no longer needed to translate. The young fisherman had his hand on the tiller and, inch by inch, was nudging the *pucán* towards the ominous pale patch in the sea. And where the *pucán* went, the three English ships followed – one to the back and now one on either side.

The man from Connaught was looking more and more worried. It was understandable that he did not want to risk his boat and the lives of all upon her, but Mara was cheerfully secure in her belief in Setanta. She could see now that this was their only hope. Those three English ships had so much more sail and the west wind still blew hard. They would, by now, have caught up with and surrounded the *pucán* if Setanta had not changed its course.

'Take it easy, take it easy!' suddenly shouted Setanta with alarm as the boat owner rudely pushed him aside and took over the tiller himself. 'Don't jerk it like that! Slow and easy – that's the way to do it.'

Mara translated rapidly, struck by the note in Setanta's voice.

'Should you take over the boat?' she asked him in a low voice. 'I can easily get one of the king's bodyguards to put the man under arrest. I'm sure that he was part of the plot.'

Setanta shook his head. 'No, a man knows his own boat. I wouldn't like anyone to take my boat. He'll know the feel of it.'

The boat owner gazed straight ahead, but Mara had an uneasy feeling that he might have understood what she said. Perhaps in his dealings with Aran he had picked up more Munster Gaelic than he pretended.

'That's it,' Setanta was saying, breaking up his phrases in order to give her time to translate. 'Straight ahead, now . . . Let's keep them guessing . . . We don't want one to be stuck on the rocks and the other two free to make mischief . . . Turn a little to the right . . . Take it easy . . . Don't wheel too suddenly . . . Just a few inches at the time.' He seemed quite at ease, quite confident, this fisherman's son with the lives of the king, the king's wife, and his *tánaiste* in his hands. A man who lived by the sea, for the sea and on the sea. He was the only one on the *pucán* who did not hold on to something when the boat wallowed in the shallows or climbed the waves. His balance was perfect and the slight movements he made to retain it were almost imperceptible.

'We're right over the rocks now, my lord, and the *pucán* is sailing beautifully,' he called.

'Good man,' returned Turlough while Conor paled and Donán half stood up and then sat down again, shivering violently.

The three English ships held off for a moment, but then the ship on the right began to close in on them.

'This run of rocks is about half a mile wide,' said Setanta to Mara. 'We'll be able to go most of the way to the shore on it, but hopefully the ships will get stuck on it before then.'

'Tell him that I'd like to send a lump of lead down just to test the water,' said the boat owner abruptly to Mara.

'Don't let him do that!' exclaimed Setanta with alarm. 'These fellows are not stupid. They'll know that he is sounding the depths if they see him doing that. It's only if they see us sailing confidently along that they'll follow us. They probably don't know what a shallow draught the *pucán* has.'

The man shrugged fatalistically when Mara had translated. 'A woman at a fair in Connemara told me that I would die in my bed,' he observed. 'Let's hope that she was right.'

'Could we go a bit faster here? Put up some more sail. I'll hold the tiller steady.' Setanta gestured and the man understood, leaving his position and altering the sail slightly to the right.

'That's it,' said Setanta with satisfaction as the boat leaped forward. 'I thought there was a bit of a change in the wind a minute ago. A touch of north into it. Now we're catching every breath of it.'

Setanta was enjoying this immensely, thought Mara, despite all his pretended disdain for bigger boats. She began to plan a splendid sailing boat as a wedding present for Setanta and Cliona. She looked over her shoulder. His manoeuvre had worked. The *pucán* had drawn well ahead of the three English ships. The one at the back accelerated and then slowed down and stopped.

'Stuck!' shouted Setanta.

There were shouts from the rear ship, shouts of warning, probably, but the wind was very loud and the waves were crashing. The men in the other ships would probably take them as encouragement. Mara found herself crossing her fingers and endeavouring to pray at the same moment.

'It's working, my lord,' called Setanta. 'It's working! Watch!'

Mara's head turned first in one direction and then in the other. Both events happened almost simultaneously. The ship on the left struck the rocks first. There was a slight lull in the roar of the wind at that moment and they heard the dull boom and then the ship on the right lurched violently and then stayed very still. One of its masts cracked and the sails tumbled to the deck.

'We've done it, by God!' yelled Turlough and at the very same instant, the boat owner, the man from Connaught, handed over the tiller to Setanta. He went forward towards the central mast. He seemed to be fiddling with something and then opened a box there.

He's trying to put up more sail, thought Mara vaguely, and concentrated on looking ahead towards the harbour at Doolin. She could see the figures on the shore; they had looked tiny the last time that she had looked, but now they could almost be recognized. She was sure that she could see the small, slight figure of Ulick Burke standing amongst the tall figures of the burly men-at-arms.

Setanta was still at the tiller, whistling a dance tune as he looked ahead with a lively anticipation on his face. He had slightly altered the course of the *pucán* and now they were heading directly for the harbour. No doubt they would soon be off the rocks, but this course was taking them more in the direction of the English ship on the left, still securely stuck on the rocks. Its men were leaning over the deck's bar and as Mara looked suddenly a hail of arrows flew from the ship, aimed directly at the *pucán*.

'Missed!' shouted Turlough. But the two bodyguards seized him immediately by the arms, both expostulating vehemently, and dragged him away from the side of the ship. Mara noticed with amusement that neither bothered about Conor who had thrown himself flat upon the deck.

And then while everyone was looking at the English ship and at the arrows which still fluttered out from it, there was a deafening crack. The single mast in the centre of the *pucán* had swayed then fallen to one side, bringing down the red sail with it.

Nineteen

Di Checharsllicht Athgab
(Dealing with distraint)
Sellach (the *onlooker*)

The witness to an offence who does not prevent the crime is also guilty, in this instance his offence is called cin súlo *(the crime of the eye).*

These onlookers are divided into three categories:
1. *The man who, though he did not commit the crime, has been the instigator. He must pay the full penalty.*
2. *The man who accompanies and takes pleasure in the crime. He must pay half of the penalty.*
3. *Also guilty is the man who looks on and makes no attempt to stop the crime. He must pay one quarter of the penalty.*

In a moment the bodyguards had twisted the axe from the boatman's grasp and knocked him to the ground. One sat on his chest and held a knife to his throat while the other cut a length of rope and bound his hands and feet together until he was trussed like a parcel. He swore and struggled but eventually lay still, looking up at his ruined mast. His face was not ill-satisfied. No doubt he felt that somehow or other his rescue would be achieved; that the *pucán* would be boarded and that the plan could go forward.

The *pucán* glided to a halt and rocked gently on the waves. There was a shout of exultation from the nearest ship. Mara looked around desperately and saw a fourth ship, large and with many sails, rounding the end of Aran and pointing directly towards them. There were some bulky objects on the deck and she narrowed her eyes, trying to make out what they were.

'It's carrying boats; they've guessed what has happened to the ship. They'll launch the boats when they get near the ridge of rocks. They'll probably have guns, too. I've heard that they

have two hand guns at the castle on Aran.' Setanta's eyes had
followed hers. 'Hold this,' he said. Quickly he had passed the
tiller to her. 'Keep it straight,' he instructed and a minute later
was at the back of the boat, his fisherman's knife catching a
glint of the sun which had just emerged from the clouds.

In a moment he was running along the side of the boat,
holding the rope in one hand. 'Keep down, my lord,' he yelled
as a flock of arrows came across. Mara winced and felt herself
duck automatically. One hit the side of the *pucán*, but the rest
sank uselessly into the turbulent sea.

'Keep them busy,' shouted Setanta and quick-witted Fergal,
the younger of the two bodyguards, stripped the red cloak
from Donán, draping it over the broken section of the mast.
The cloak fluttered in the wind and looked most realistic and
the men on the ship shouted and raised their bows.

Another score of arrows came across and once again one
reached the deck while the others fell short.

'Only one man among them can shoot properly,' shouted
Turlough. 'What the blazes is that young fellow doing?'

Setanta had reached the prow of the ship. He had tied his
rope to a bar there and had quickly slipped overboard. Turlough
pushed his protesting son aside and followed him quickly.

'Merciful God in heaven,' he yelled. 'The lad is going to
tow us!'

Mara longed to look, but she clung to the tiller. 'Keep it
straight,' Setanta had said and she would obey his orders. Was
it possible for a tiny boat made from hazel sticks and covered
with cow hides, like the curragh, to pull the much heavier
pucán, she wondered and then remembered the delight of her
youngest scholar Shane, when, as a homesick eight-year-old,
exiled from the inland sea of the Great Lake in northern
Ireland, he had been allowed by a friendly fisherman to pull
a large hooker along the length of the harbour wall. If a rather-
undersized child of that age could pull a boat of that weight,
perhaps Setanta, rowing hard, might be able to tow the *pucán*.

And so it seemed to be happening. After a couple of jerks
the *pucán* began to move – definitely moving. But, of course, the
pace was so slow. Without the sail the wind was of little use
to them and the tide was receding.

Mara cast several anxious glances over her shoulder. The fourth ship, profiting from the strong west-northwest wind, was making great progress. It seemed to be bounding through the water, its sails fully expanded. At this rate it might catch them before they reached the safety of the harbour. She longed to join Turlough, to go and look over the prow and watch how Setanta was doing, but he had asked her to hold the tiller straight and she held on grimly.

Turlough was shouting encouragement and jokes down to Setanta, although there did not seem to be any response – he would probably be sensibly saving his breath for rowing. Mara smiled with pleasure. She could imagine what it must be like for Setanta to be on such familiar footing with the king of three kingdoms, Turlough Donn, the most popular king of Thomond, Burren and Corcomroe in living memory. Turlough was a great king, a great leader of men, an honest and sincere person, gentle and affectionate. She felt tears blur her eyes as she thought of all his virtues and then she looked across at the two men who had plotted against him and her mind filled with anger. They would pay the full penalty of the law, she promised herself. Once they had arrived back safely she would make sure that the news of their ignominy would be known across the length and breadth of the three kingdoms.

If we get out of here safely . . . she said to herself, but then caught a glimpse over her shoulder of the fourth ship. For a moment, she thought it was impossible that it had moved so far in so few minutes, but no, it was definitely the same ship. She looked back at the harbour. It was a little nearer, but nothing dramatic. However, the *pucán* continued to move and Turlough continued to shout robust words of encouragement to Setanta.

And then something strange happened. Dotted all over the broad blue-green surface of the sea were curraghs. Fishermen from Doolin, Fanore, Gleninagh and from further down the coast were fishing in this rich stretch of water between the coast and the three islands of Aran. Somehow or other, they had understood what was going on. They would have heard the cannon, seen the English ships in pursuit, perhaps followed the path of the arrows, and now saw one of their own was

being hunted. Setanta was an O'Connor, one of the main clans
in Doolin; the man and his boat would have been known to
all of them.

And then all of these men left their lucrative fishing grounds
and, rowing lightly and strongly, turned their prows towards
the harbour. For a moment Mara could not understand what
was happening. But then, as she looked, she could see that
they were joining each other. Joining together so that the boats
stretched in a long line, forming a frail barrier between the
fast-moving fourth ship and the wounded *pucán* being towed
by the little curragh.

'My God, Mara, do you see that!' shouted Turlough.

'I do indeed, my lord,' she called back. 'Your people love
you and they will not allow traitors to betray you.'

With a glow of satisfaction which warmed her frozen body,
she saw how O'Brien of Arra's face had fallen with dismay at
the sight of the fishermen's blockade. Donán seemed to be
sunk in lethargy, his face the hue of an overcooked yolk of
egg.

But would it do any good? Presumably the fast-moving
fourth ship was filled with men armed with bows and arrows.
When they came near to the line of little curraghs would they
not shoot? It would be easy to pick off the fishermen one by
one and if they missed the bodies they could shoot the little
boats. These skin-covered curraghs could be easily pierced and
would sink just as easily.

And then came her answer. From the island came a loud
single note – the sound of a horn, one of those huge, old-
fashioned bronze horns. It sounded once, and then again. It
must have been some sort of signal because Mara could see a
sail being lowered from the dangerously nearby ship, and then
another. Bit by bit, as happens with sailing craft, the ship wheeled
around and set off back to the island, making its way in series
of long diagonal swoops where it appeared to be making little
progress but which, step by step, brought it nearer to the island.

'Going back!' Turlough was at her side in an instant, gazing
back out to sea. 'Why do you think they went back? They
could easily have fired on these unfortunate fishermen. My
heart was in my mouth for the poor fellows.'

'I think your cousin on Aran, Brian the Spaniard, recognized that the game was up,' said Mara, in those clear tones which she knew would carry above the sound of wind and water. 'He guessed that we would have these two traitors in our hands and that a terrible punishment would await them. By withdrawing now, he can always plead that he knew nothing of this plot and he can claim that the evidence these two will probably try to give against him is false and that he is your majesty's most faithful and most loyal servant.'

Turlough gave her an uncertain glance and hastened to go back to watch Setanta's progress. Mara bestowed a keen, appraising look at Donán, the son-in-law, and at O'Brien of Arra. Donán had buried his face in his hands and O'Brien was staring ahead with a grim look on his face. She was glad that he had overheard the proof that his cousin and foster-brother on Aran had deserted him and left him to the king's mercy.

It was probably the sight of all the fishermen uniting in support of Turlough that had determined the man on Aran that, not only had the plot failed, but there would be no support for it. Someone who lives on an island is dependent on the people who live on the coast – dependent not just for fuel for his fires, but also for linen for his clothing and goods for his house as well as for a market for his fish.

'Not long more,' shouted Turlough exultantly as they neared the shore. 'By God, this man here is a great rower. How can he do it in water like this? He's pouring sweat, poor fellow.'

The faces of the men-at-arms at the harbour wall, and of Ulick Burke amongst them, could now be seen very clearly. There were crowds behind them. It looked as though all of the people of the village and from the countryside around had come out of their houses to welcome their king. The other fishermen did not go back to the sea and to their fishing. Several threw ropes on to the deck of the *pucán* and they helped with the towing. Mara hung on to the tiller – it had been her part in the rescue and she was reluctant to give it up to anyone.

Before they landed she had to come to a decision about the man from Connaught who owned the boat. In theory, he had

no rights if he was in a kingdom other than his own, except
by invitation. But in fact, his offence was committed on the
sea and, in any case, Doolin was in the kingdom of Corcomroe
where another Brehon had charge of legal matters. The easiest
and probably the wisest decision was to take no action. He
was a very small fish, compared to the two big fish that had
been captured.

Mara beckoned to the king who came back to her. 'Shall
we let the boatman go free?' she queried. 'No doubt both men
from Connaught have been heavily bribed to do this, but they
have been punished. Neither man has a seaworthy boat; nor
will they find the people of Doolin anxious to help them in
any way.'

'Yes, yes, we won't trouble our heads about them,' said
Turlough hurriedly. He looked at her hesitantly, but she did
not meet his eyes. She knew his gentle, forgiving nature well,
but she did not feel in the least forgiving. Too much harm
had been done. Turlough would like to excuse Donán and
O'Brien of Arra as well; let them get away with their crimes,
but that was something she was determined was not going to
happen. In her mind she was already setting the scene and
deciding on strategy. She beckoned to the bodyguard.

'Let the boat owner go as soon as we disembark,' she said to
him. Although she spoke quietly there was a sudden lull in the
wind and she saw O'Brien of Arra look at her with some hope
in his eyes. Perhaps he thought that he would be released also.

As the fishermen's boats neared the harbour wall, several
fishermen plunged into the water, walking out until they were
waist high in it, untied the ropes leading to the *pucán* and
carefully dragged it to its berth. Mara released her hold on the
tiller and walked forward to where the bodyguard was untying
the ropes around the boat's owner.

'The king's mercy is releasing you,' she told him curtly. 'But
never let me see your face again, or you may find yourself
with a heavy fine. Get back to where you came from as soon
as your boat is mended and you can pass that message on to
your companion as well. Now stay here on your boat until
the king's party has ridden away, or I won't be responsible for
what might happen to you at the hands of his men-at-arms.'

Then she left him without a backward glance. The threat of violence from the men-at-arms was a more potent one than a court of law, she thought, but she did not repent her words. If this affair was to have a good conclusion she would have to be very tough.

The cheering when Turlough walked safe and well from the boat was loud enough to be heard in the next kingdom and it did not diminish when Mara followed him. The men-at-arms, looking guilty and worried, surrounded their king as if determined that, even in the face of a command, they would not leave him again. Everyone had a story to tell; how the cannon was heard, how they had seen the English ships, how they had guessed that these were up to no good . . .

Mara turned a deaf ear to several plans for exacting ransom from the English ships that she could hear going on around her. If the poor fishing people of Doolin wished to get some silver in return for dragging the ships off the rocks, she was not going to prevent them. Brian the Spaniard, Brian of Aran, would, she guessed, lie low for quite some time. Little could be proved against him and Turlough would probably be happy to overlook the possible part he had played in this plot.

Mara turned to nod an acknowledgement to Ulick Burke, who had exhausted his exclamations of horror to Turlough and was now addressing her. 'What an adventure, my dear Brehon. Who would have thought it?'

'Who, indeed,' said Mara looking around to see whether the innkeeper had brought out her horse yet.

'There was I, innocent as a babe unborn, commiserating with this fellow about the hole in his boat, offering to be the one who stayed behind since my lord's son-in-law and cousin were so very anxious to accompany him on the first boat.' Ulick gave Mara a keen look and she gazed back blandly. Let him keep guessing, she thought. She was not certain whether he was guilty or not, but she would find out soon. His eyes were now on the bound figures of Donán and O'Brien of Arra and he did not look surprised. Neither, however, did he look particularly worried.

'What—' he began but she interrupted him quickly saying that she had to get back to the castle at once.

Turlough's men, she noticed with amusement, had borrowed Setanta's cart and placed the bound bodies of Donán and O'Brien of Arra in it beside the net full of shining fish for the castle. Neither said anything, but their faces were full of disgust. To be thrown into a fish-smelling donkey cart was the depths of ignominy for two close relatives of the king.

'Won't do them a bit of harm,' she said decisively to Turlough when he whispered a protest. 'After all, they say the son of God rode on a donkey!' She was pleased with herself for this piece of biblical knowledge. It silenced Turlough, who looked taken aback, and it amused Setanta who was climbing up to the driver's seat.

Anyway, they're probably not as wet and cold as I am, she thought as she stiffly mounted her horse. Quickly she clapped her heels to the animal's sides and Brig, her beloved mare, responded by flying along the road as fleet as any deer.

A hot bath, hair wash and clean dry clothes, she thought as she galloped past the hedgerows, which were white with the snowy purity of the blackthorn blossom. Deliberately, she kept her mind from what had passed today and what would have to happen this afternoon. She needed to be fresh and she needed to have her wits about her. She would not rush the interrogation of the two guilty men. She had given orders to the king's bodyguards that the men were to be kept under close surveillance in the cellar of the Ballinalacken. The dungeon, she had called it within in their earshot. Her first priority was to be clean, warm and dry. Then would come the action.

There would be two trials, she planned. The formal and legal one would be held at Poulnabrone, the place of justice where all the clans of the Burren could come and stand around the ancient tomb of their ancestors to hear and see justice being administered.

But the first hearing would take place today at Ballinalacken Castle in the presence of king and Brehon.

Twenty

Oirechta
(The Courts of Law)

There are five courts in Irish law:
1. *In the background of all courts is the court of the king, the bishop and those who are master of laws. This is there in case of dispute.*
2. *Also in the background is the side court where historians, who have knowledge of past events, help with deciding the payment of sureties and hostage sureties and matters of lineage.*
3. *The waiting court where the guilty and the innocent await judgement while the judges ponder their verdict.*
4. *The court apart where witnesses must wait with clear minds and in seclusion. These witnesses must not be interfered with lest their evidence be falsified.*
5. *The courts themselves where the judges of the kingdoms go to give their verdicts. These must be held in an open place where all may attend and see that justice is done.*

It was almost evening before Mara decided to send for the prisoners. She dressed carefully in a black gown, woven from the finest wool, over a creamy-white, lace-edged *léine*, and around her neck she knotted a red silk scarf. Her dark-brown hair was shining after its wash and she coiled it at the back of her neck and then spent a couple of minutes studying her reflection in the looking-glass of the bedroom. She looked good, she thought, judicial and a little stern.

Then she woke Turlough.

'Leave the talking to me,' she warned. 'I know you. You will be telling them that you understand completely; that we'll forget the whole business and *why don't we all have a cup of wine together.*'

Turlough grinned awkwardly. 'Well, he's a bit of a poor fellow, Donán,' he began but she cut off him off abruptly.

'Not at all as poor a fellow as the young man, Eamon, a man with a promising future, who is lying dead in a grave at Noughaval church,' she said curtly. 'You're not forgetting that this affair led to a murder, are you?'

Turlough looked subdued and a little confused. 'I don't understand how—' he began, but once again she cut him off.

'Wear this gown and that doublet,' she said, fishing out the objects from the wooden press by the window. 'I want you in royal purple and saffron. You are a king of three kingdoms and your safety has to be of paramount importance to your subjects of whom I am one. Now you get dressed and come down to the Great Hall. I have some orders to give, but I will await you there.'

And then she left him and went in search of Ulick Burke, the Lord of Clanrickard. He was sitting on the seat by the window sipping some wine with a bored expression.

'Come in, Brehon, come in, you find me all alone; me, a man who likes the society of his friends. Now tell me all about the exciting events of today. Start at the beginning and go right to the end.'

His tone was cordial but his eyes were wary as they studied her.

'From the beginning?' queried Mara, lifting her black eyebrows delicately. 'I would have thought that you knew the beginning, my Lord of Clanrickard.'

Ulick's face altered subtly and she knew that he had understood her. She pressed home her advantage. 'I would have thought that a man like you who knows all the gossip would have heard a few rumours,' she said innocently.

He studied her face. 'Perhaps a few,' he murmured, 'but you know this country, Brehon. There are always rumours.'

'Rumours about what?' she enquired.

'Well, you know, I always felt that Turlough was right not wholly to trust O'Brien of Arra, but you will have to ask him about that,' he said sounding more confident.

He was slippery as a fish, she thought and was probably a match for her in wits. She would find out more from Donán and O'Brien of Arra, but in the meantime, since he was her husband's oldest and best friend and the godfather of her son, she would not quarrel unnecessarily with him. It would do him no harm, though, to be aware that she had her eye on him. She smiled at him.

'I can assure you that I have many sources of information and that I will do everything in my power to ensure the safety of our king,' she said softly.

'My dear Brehon, we all rely on your wisdom and your sharp wits,' he returned.

'And now, since you cannot help me with any new information, I wonder could I ask you to occupy yourself elsewhere for the moment? Supper will be in a couple of hours' time, but before that my lord and I need the hall for a judicial affair.' Mara spoke sharply and decisively, deliberately making no response to his compliment. She scanned his face closely, but could read no hint of discomfiture in his expression. Perhaps he was not directly involved; it would be like him to sit on the fence and see which way the wind blew, she thought, with a sudden vivid picture of the small, neat figure perched up high and holding a wet finger aloft to check the direction of the air currents before committing himself to any action.

'I shall take some of this excellent wine up to my bedroom and repose before the meal.' Ulick picked up a ewer of wine and walked towards the door, carrying his silver cup in his other hand.

'While you slept a message came for you,' he said over his shoulder. 'One of your scholars came with it. It was from Nuala to say that Muiris – is that the name? The farmer who was so badly injured outside the flax garden – that he had come to his senses and that he did not remember what had happened to him. So disappointing for you, dear Brehon,' he went on with a false air of sympathy.

'Well, the truth may be hidden, but a wise judge has many ways of finding it,' she said in oracular manner and then turned her back on him. Let him worry if he has anything on his conscience, she thought. She herself was not completely sure about the criminal who attempted to murder Muiris. It could be one of two people, she thought, and hoped that she could surprise the truth out of the guilty person. She waited until the sound of Ulick's footsteps on the stone stairs had died away and then rang a bell to summon a servant.

'Tell the guardsmen to bring up the prisoners,' she said when a man appeared. Before Turlough arrived she would have time for a few sharp questions. And, more importantly, she would have time to set the scene.

She dragged over two tall, ornate chairs and placed them with their backs to the window, putting two small, humble stools in front of them. The guilty pair would have the light from the western sun directly shining into their faces.

'Come in,' she called at the knock on the door. 'Place the prisoners in front of me,' she ordered, 'and both of you stand on guard behind them.'

Once they had shuffled in, heavily chained, and were seated, she delayed for a moment, studying both faces. 'I understand everything,' she said rapidly after she had allowed a long minute to elapse, 'so don't attempt to lie to me.'

They both looked away; Donán buried his head in his hands and groaned. The sound seemed to give courage to O'Brien and he looked contemptuously at the young man and then turned to Mara. 'I don't know why you persist in including me, Brehon. I presume that you are investigating the death of the lawyer, Eamon. I could have had nothing to do with this. I was on the other side of the river Shannon, in a different kingdom, when this happened and I can bring forty witnesses to prove that I never left the castle at Arra on that Saturday.'

At that moment the door opened and Turlough came in. Mara jumped to her feet, welcomed him and escorted him to the chair by the window. Only when he was seated did she take her place beside him. As Brehon of one of his kingdoms, it was now her responsibility to lay the facts of the case before him.

'My lord,' she said formally. 'This is a very painful matter. It touches the security of your person, the security of the realm, involves the murder of a young lawyer and the attempted murder of a farmer.' She stopped and waited to marshal her thoughts. Now she no longer looked at the two men but inwardly to where she seemed to see, neatly arranged and tabulated on that slab of rock, all of the complications and the puzzles of this strange affair. She took her time, and did not speak until she was ready.

'It's a story of two legal documents, two deeds of law, each having been signed by a lawyer and witnessed in accordance with the law,' she began, her eyes fixed on O'Brien's arrogant face. 'The one was straightforward. It was the deed of lease for the profitable flax garden; this deed was signed and witnessed by me personally and it is only important because it gave the lawyer, Eamon, the opportunity to conduct his secret mission.'

Mara turned slightly so that she appeared to be addressing the king, but she was very aware of the two men in front of her. Fachtnan's liberty and perhaps his life hung on a knife edge. All depended now on her skill with words.

'The other document was different. I have never seen this deed. I presume that it is now at the castle of the O'Kelly in Ui Maine. Unless of course it has already been sent to Kildare for the perusal of the Great Earl.' Quickly, with a slight gesture of one hand, she checked Turlough's start when he heard the detested name of the Earl of Kildare.

'However,' she resumed, 'I think that this second deed was also drawn up at my law school at Cahermacnaghten. Eamon, as a visiting young lawyer, here ostensibly to learn about the workings of such schools, had access to my books, my writing materials, and . . .' Mara fumbled in her pouch and took out the two small circles of pink, still tied in a bow. 'These linen tapes were found above the flax garden on the Aillwee Mountain. I know this tape well and I believe it to be unique. When I was a very young child I persuaded my father to have it dyed pink rather than left white and by an accident a huge quantity was done and Cahermacnaghten law school still uses that pink tape to bind its legal documents.' Perhaps by the time the tape came to an end, she thought, little Cormac would be starting work in his mother's school and then he could choose the colour.

'So, Eamon drew up the second deed. But what deed?' Turlough sounded puzzled and Mara was glad of the interruption which brought her thoughts back to the immediate business. She had expected exclamations or denials but O'Brien of Arra seemed grimly determined to say nothing for the moment and he sat with mouth compressed and arms folded. Donán still had not lifted his head and he sat as one who had been turned to stone.

'It was a deed of contract, my lord,' explained Mara. 'Certain of your allies were willing to be bribed to go over to the side of the Great Earl and conspire to seize you and imprison you; probably deliver you to the King of England, perhaps to your death. That was their side of the contract and no doubt the earl or his minion offered some titles or lands as reward. Am I not correct?' She addressed herself to O'Brien and was glad to see him flinch.

'No, no,' he protested. 'It was not like that at all.' He stopped, made a slight grimace, seemed to realize that he had betrayed himself and then continued eagerly, addressing Turlough.

'There was no thought of personal harm to you, my lord.' O'Brien strove to make his voice sound earnest and sincere. 'The plan was to take you by ship from Aran to Dublin Castle. Once you were there, the Earl of Kildare would try to persuade you that the future for Ireland lay in England; that King Henry VIII had plans to make Ireland a prosperous place where ancient, outmoded ways of life would be changed and . . .'

'You say you meant me no harm, but you plotted to take my kingdom from me,' roared Turlough.

'Not so, my lord; you would no longer be king, of course, but you would have the revenues from almost all of your present lands and you would be made earl by the king himself, King Henry VIII.'

'Traitor!' Turlough hurled the word at his cousin as if it were a cannon ball and O'Brien flinched.

'It was not my plan, originally,' he said with dignity.

'No, you don't have the brains,' said Turlough cruelly. 'I can guess whose plan it was, who organized these ships, who was going to be the one that would load me with the best of food and give me too much to drink and then send me like a package around to Dublin Castle to wait for the earl to have his will with me.'

O'Brien was silent, but Mara knew that Turlough had guessed correctly.

Through the open shutters, from the ground outside, a

high-pitched shriek of fury rose up. For some time she had been aware that the two little boys, Art and Cormac, were running around on the greensward in front of the castle. Setanta was kicking a soft leather ball towards them while Bran the wolfhound patrolled the far wall to make sure that neither child escaped. Cormac had fallen and lay wailing on the ground. Art began to run for the ball and then changed his mind and toddled back to where his foster-brother lay and stood over him, plucking at the short woollen jacket that Cormac wore over his *léine* until the king's little son was on his feet again.

Closer than brothers, thought Mara.

'Brian the Spaniard of Aran, as you have guessed, my lord, made the plan,' she said crisply, still addressing Turlough and ignoring the other two men. 'He got word to your cousin here, his foster-brother, O'Brien of Arra, and asked for his cooperation. He could arrange everything from Aran; could engage the two treacherous boatmen, could make sure that plenty of English ships were standing by to convey his king into the hands of his enemies. He could do all that, but he needed someone to be here at Ballinalacken to persuade you to make a visit to Aran and to see that your men-at-arms and your bodyguards were left behind. He recruited Eamon the lawyer, bribed him heavily no doubt. Eamon spoke to my scholar, Fiona, about a bagful of silver. His task was to go from *taoiseach* to *taoiseach* and to engage their loyalty so that there would be enough recruited to counter any uprising once it was known that their beloved king had been captured.'

Turlough gave a violent snort at that but Mara ignored him. This matter had to be wound up as soon as possible.

'I'm not sure when you, Donán,' she went on rapidly, 'were recruited to the conspiracy. Whether it was at your own place, or whether it was here under my eyes. I fear the latter.'

Donán lifted his head, as if to reply and deny the charge, but then dropped it again. His face was deadly white, but Mara felt no mercy for him. She placed no credence on O'Brien of Arra and his assertion that Turlough would not have been hurt and that it was purely a question of getting him to listen to the arguments. Anyone who knew Turlough should certainly have known that he would not have given up his kingdoms for any English bribe. He would probably have been killed. And then his kingdom would have been overrun.

Donán, though, with his permanent sense of grievance that no one had come to the rescue when his home was lost – well, that was a different matter. He would have been open to any persuasion.

'I suppose they offered you your family heritage, they told you that you would have the castle of Nenagh and your lands and the rich market there returned to you, isn't that correct?' Mara's voice was harsh. Donán was the weak link and she had to break him as soon as possible.

'You agreed to this. You played your part. You even managed to inveigle Ulick Burke into being the one to suggest you all went to Aran.' She paused for a moment to see whether either man would follow up on this, but neither said a word. They did not even glance at each other. So Ulick Burke, Lord of Clanrickard, was possibly still a loyal ally. For Turlough's sake, she hoped so.

'The plan was a clever one, my lord, but something went wrong. In the first place, Eamon was very much in love with my scholar Fiona and took her along. So I got to know about his journey and how he went north, instead of recrossing the Shannon at O'Briensbridge. And secondly, because he was in love, and because he was greedy for more silver to enable him to marry, he attempted to blackmail you when he met you on the Aillwee Mountain.'

'What was the lad Eamon doing there in the first place?' asked Turlough, looking puzzled.

'Just taking a shortcut back from Ui Maine,' said Mara casually and watched comprehension dawn on his face. One of his great enemies, O'Kelly of Ui Maine, had been tipped off that the three kingdoms would be in a state of disarray within a week. Mara nodded at him and then returned to Donán.

'The evening before you had been telling me about your sore throat and I sent you over to Nuala. I know Nuala and I know that she would have given you a medical lecture on every bone in the throat and would undoubtedly have told you how one could kill by squeezing the thyroid cartilage. You are a strong young man and you took Eamon by surprise, possibly first stunning him with your heavy stick and then murdering him by punching him in the base of the neck. You then tipped the body down the mountain to make it look as though it were an accident and went back to rejoin the hunting party. There was little fear that you would have been missed, because they were scattered all over the mountainside. The only question now in my mind is the same question that my lord asked you. Why did you do it? You had been given a castle which was as good as the one that had been taken away from you. What was so special about Nenagh?' Deliberately she introduced a note of enormous scorn into her voice and he responded immediately, looking at her with blazing eyes.

'Someone lacking the blood of the nobility, someone like yourself, could not possibly understand,' he sneered.

'Understand what? Understand why you joined in with the plans of Brian the Spaniard of Aran? Is that what you are saying?'

He hesitated for a moment and then, with an air of defiance, he nodded.

'And you have nothing else to say? No other word of excuse?'

Mara waited for a moment and then when he said nothing she spoke, with great formality, to Turlough.

'My lord, I am now assured of the guilt of these two prisoners and I think that we need to confer in private about their fate. Guards, take them outside the door and guard them well.'

They shuffled forward, the manacles and shackles clanking as they moved. Mara watched them carefully and then just as one of the guards had opened the door she turned to Turlough and said in a low tone, but one that she knew from experience would carry well, 'My lord, I would advise that we use English law in this case. The punishment for traitors under English law is that they be hanged, drawn and quartered.' She could see Turlough start to splutter indignantly so she drowned his voice immediately by giving a loud, clear explanation detailing all the gory details of strangulation, evisceration, disembowelment, and emasculation exactly in the order in which they would be perpetrated.

Once the door shut behind them she put her finger to her lips and he obediently kept quiet. Mara shut her eyes and forced herself to count slowly up to one hundred. The time would seem long to those outside, straining their ears to hear about their fate. When she opened her eyes Turlough had already opened his mouth and hastily Mara put her finger on to his lips.

And then before he could speak she went to the door and told the guards to bring the prisoners in and to stand them before her. Both were white-faced and shivering, O'Brien in hardly better shape than Donán. She watched them for a long moment, her face grave, her eyes intent upon their faces, before she spoke.

'Donán O'Kennedy and Brian Ruadh O'Brien of Arra, you have deliberately chosen to forsake the Irish way of life, to abandon the Irish law and to make yourselves subject to England and to the English king. Have you anything to say as to why the sentence under English law should not be passed upon you for your crimes?'

This prodded them into action. O'Brien had plenty to say though Donán contented himself with nodding vigorously at every point made by his fellow conspirator. Mara listened stony-faced and sighed when O'Brien had reached the end of his arguments.

'They that live by the sword, shall die by the sword,' she said, thinking that the words had a good sound about them though she was not sure where they came from. 'You, my lords, have chosen to live by the English way of life, so you shall die by the English way of law.' She allowed a long pause to elapse, watching with satisfaction how the two white faces before her began to glisten with sweat.

'Unless . . .' she said dubiously. She turned to face Turlough. 'But perhaps you might not wish to agree to this, my lord.'

Then she turned back to the two men again and spoke quickly before Turlough could assure her that he would agree to anything. So far he had only managed to nod in a bewildered way.

'My Lord of Arra,' she said to O'Brien. 'Your steward is here in the house. Send for him. Write to your ally O'Kelly of Ui Maine. Tell him to release my young scholar. No doubt it was about that very matter that your steward came here. Tell him that your life depends on this matter; that only if Fachtnan arrives back here, unharmed, will there be any chance of mercy for you where you will be tried under Irish law, not under English. What do you say, my Lord of Arra?'

He nodded sullenly and she commanded the guard to take off his manacles and bring him to a side table. She herself laid the writing material in front of him, smoothed out the vellum, sharpened the quill and checked the ink pot.

'Write at length, my lord,' she said. 'And when you tell O'Kelly that this is a matter of life and death, make sure that you take good care to spell out what sort of death awaits you if Fachtnan is not back at Cahermacnaghten by tomorrow.'

Epilogue

Caithréim Choirdhealbhaigh
(The Triumphs of Turlough)
Written in the year of Our Lord 1459
By Sean Mac Ruaidhrí Mac Craith

The government of Ireland being now in the year 1172 come into foreigners' hands, and regal dignity divorced from all and singular, the clans of Milesius the Spaniard's blood, Donough cairbreach mac Donall More O'Brien (whose spears were tough and his battalions numerous) became chief in his father's stead and assumed the power, renowned of old, to maintain and govern Thomond's fair and pleasant countries; the entirety of which dominion was this: from Cuchullin's far-famed Leap to the Boromean Tribute's ford; from the borders of Birra to Knockany in Cliu máil, and from the Eoghanacht of Cashel to the northernmost part of Burren, land of white stones.

So if Eamon was not murdered, the king would now be imprisoned or killed,' mused Shane with a twelve-year-old boy's happy lack of consciousness of the emotions of those around him.

'Tell us about O'Kelly, Fachtnan. What was he like?' said Moylan hurriedly, looking from the face of Fiona to the face of Mara and turning slightly pink with anxiety to avoid painful subjects.

'Well, he wasn't a bad fellow,' said Fachtnan judicially. 'I ate at his table and slept by his fire. He was very apologetic about '*detaining me*' as he put it and went to great pains to explain that I would be released unharmed in a week's time. He said that his own Brehon had a great respect for you,' he added, addressing Mara. 'It seems a pity that he is at loggerheads with King Turlough.'

'It all goes back to the battle of Knockdoe in Galway seven years ago,' said Mara with a sigh. 'It started as a private matter between O'Kelly and Ulick Burke, the Lord of Clanrickard, and each looked for allies. Clanrickard called on King Turlough for aid and he brought in the MacNamara from near Limerick, O'Carroll of Ely, O'Brien of Aran, O'Kennedy of Ormonde. And then O'Kelly got help from the Earl of Kildare, the Great Earl, as they call him, and O'Donnell of Tir Conaill and MacDermot of Connaught and there was a great battle which was won by both sides – depending on who tells the story,' she finished lightly.

'What was the private matter?' asked Shane curiously.

'Well, the Clanrickard, Ulick Burke, stole the O'Kelly's wife,' said Mara.

'Is that all?' said Shane with disgust. Nuala, who was sitting very close to Fachtnan, smiled a secret, womanly smile at Mara while the older boys looked amused.

'Let's talk about the murder, Brehon,' said Moylan smoothly. 'What first got you on the trail of Donán O'Kennedy?'

'I think it was Nuala who got me thinking,' said Mara honestly. 'She was the one that was very sure that Fachtnan had set out to investigate where Eamon had gone when he went north from O'Briensbridge. Perhaps, Fachtnan, you would tell us all about that now,' she ended. She would not betray Nuala's anguish to the others. Perhaps someday she might tell Fachtnan. She looked at him with a slight exasperation. He had greeted Nuala with brotherly affection, but blushed to the roots of his brown hair when faced with Fiona.

Now he gave Nuala a nice smile, but avoided looking at Fiona. 'I was quite lucky,' he began, 'because there were lots of farmers around when I was going along the road on the east side of the river. One of these had been up all night with a calving cow and he had seen a young man riding fast along the road. I described Eamon and the horse and he was quite sure.'

'Riding fast?' queried Moylan.

Fachtnan nodded approval at the interruption. 'That's right and that's what made me think that Eamon was going some-where, not just wasting time, or riding away in a temper, because . . .' Here, for the first time, he glanced at Fiona.

'Because he had had a row with me,' finished Fiona. 'I've told everyone about that, Fachtnan. You saw it, didn't you? And you followed me back to Ballinalacken, didn't you?'

'Get on with the story,' said Nuala tensely and Fiona gave her a surprised look.

'Yes,' intervened Mara. 'That's very interesting, Fachtnan, I think you made a very good deduction there. You seem to have had your wits about you more than I had. I found this case so confusing.'

'Well I picked up the trail again when I was a few miles from Ui Maine. I met a farmer who was taking his cows home for milking. I pulled my horse into a gate to allow them to pass. He thanked me and then he shouted over something about being glad that there were a few young men with manners left in the world. He was muttering something about the young fellow who nearly pushed a cow into the ditch at morning milking time, so I described Eamon and he said that was the man.'

'So then you knew you were on the right trail.' Shane nodded wisely.

'That's right.' Fachtnan gave a grin. 'It went to my head so much that I got stupid. By then I was pretty convinced that Eamon was on an errand to the O'Kelly; it was the only thing that made sense. I thought it might be O'Brien of Arra who sent him, but then I remembered that Eamon had been very full of himself all of that day and was doing something mysterious in the schoolhouse the night before. He had locked the door and when I looked in the window I could see him by the light of the candle and he looked as if he was writing some document or deed.'

'Anyway, what happened?' asked Aidan, more interested in the adventure than in the deduction.

'Well, a fellow came along on a horse, along the same road as I was travelling. He overtook me and I shouted out to him to know whether he had seen a young man on a horse with a black and white tail. He stopped immediately and turned back and said the young fellow was staying with a relation of his and he would bring me to him.' Fachtnan gave a shrug of embarrassment. 'Well, you know the rest,' he said. 'Now it's your turn, Brehon.'

'My excuse for not seeing the truth earlier is that the business of the flax garden distracted me,' said Mara. 'Once the burned contract was found just above it and also the pink tape, well, it almost seemed sure that the murder of Eamon had been committed, perhaps inadvertently, by either Cathal, Gobnait or Owney.'

Was Gobnait responsible for the attack on Muiris? she wondered. Donán had denied it, but Turlough had contemptuously said that the man was a liar and had always been a liar. Muiris had made an excellent recovery and had told Mara that he had finally made up his mind that the business of flax working was too complicated and that he had a conversation with Gobnait where he had hinted that he might not bid. Did she believe him, or did she decide to make sure that he would not be in a position to bid? Perhaps the matter would have to be left. Most people would blame Donán O'Kennedy; a man who had already committed one murder and who had tried to commit an act of treachery against his king, benefactor and father-in-law would be capable of anything. But was he guilty?

'And when did you start thinking that it might be a political murder?' asked Fiona, distracting Mara from her thoughts.

'Well, of course, you gave me quite a few hints without knowing it,' said Mara. 'You told me that O'Brien was furious at the sight of you and immediately shooed you out of the room. You told me that Eamon had talked of getting a bagful of silver and seemed to think that he would have enough to get married on. And you were the one that told us that Eamon had taken the northern route from O'Briensbridge, a route which, as you pointed out to him, would lead to Ui Maine and the land of the O'Kellys.'

'Girls!' exclaimed Aidan in disgust. 'Why didn't you put those things together, Fiona? You could have deduced the whole thing if you had. You were too busy thinking of your love life.'

'Shut up, birdbrain,' retorted Fiona. 'We haven't heard much of use from you, have we?'

'And then of course there were my own observations of Eamon,' continued Mara, ignoring this friendly exchange. 'I had noticed him doing a lot of chatting with all of Turlough's allies, probably probing their loyalties, trying to see whether he could recruit them to the rebellion planned by O'Brien of Arra. And this should have led me to remember that Eamon had been busy in the time that he was with us, going first over to Aran to see Brian the Spaniard and then going back to Arra, no doubt with details of the plan.'

'I remember that,' said Hugh. 'I thought that he wasn't doing much study of our law school and that he seemed to be going here and there all the time.'

'That's right,' agreed Mara. 'The evidence was there under our eyes. I feel so stupid. I remember Setanta commenting on the English ships out to sea near Aran and I took no notice. I also remember noticing that no seagulls followed them and so should have guessed that they were not fishing, just lying in wait.'

'And then there was the clue of the second loop of legal tape,' said Moylan nodding his head wisely.

'Showing that there had been another deed, either stolen from Eamon or burned,' said Aidan brightly.

'Or else delivered to O'Kelly,' said Fiona. 'Much more likely, don't you agree?'

'What was in that deed, do you think, Brehon?' asked Hugh.

'I imagine it was probably a list of names and an agreement as to lands or compensation that the rebels would receive if they joined in the conspiracy,' said Mara.

'But it hasn't been found, is that right?' asked Shane. 'Or even a copy of it?'

'Not yet,' said Mara briefly. She had done her best to search the belongings of the two prisoners, but had been hampered by Turlough who didn't really want to know any more.

'Let's make a fresh start and put all this behind us,' he had said firmly, and added that Ulick Burke had agreed with him that it was best not to know. In all probability, the deed was now with The Great Earl in County Kildare or perhaps even on its way over to England to Henry VIII himself.

'What about that neck cartilage, though?' asked Fiona suddenly. 'How did Donán know to kill Eamon by squeezing his throat at that spot? He had no medical knowledge or legal knowledge either.'

'I'm not sure but . . .' Mara directed a glance at Nuala who immediately flushed and said:

'Do you know, I think that I might have told him. You sent him over to me because he kept getting sore throats and I just wanted to explain the structure of the throat to him.'

'The trouble with you, Nuala, is that you think everyone wants to be a physician,' said Aidan in a friendly fashion. 'When I asked you for something for my spots you went on for about half an hour about the skin. You must have told me a million facts. I couldn't get away from you.'

'She's very clever,' said Fachtnan affectionately.

'So Donán had the knowledge, he had the opportunity. I remember the king lecturing about people straying away from each other on the mountainside.' Mara hesitated but these scholars of hers had to know the ins and outs of power in the land, so she spoke freely and honestly. 'I think that Donán was sick of living on his father-in-law's charity and he was offered the bribe of receiving back his own castle and lands at Nenagh in return for persuading the king to go to Aran. The murder of Eamon was not planned. I think that Eamon, after he had handed over the deed to O'Kelly, took a shortcut back from Ui Maine and was seen by Donán who came over to find out about his mission. Eamon, who wanted to get married, was not content with the silver that he had been promised. He probably threatened Donán, told him that he would inform the king about the whole business, and Donán hit him with his stick – probably just stunned him – and then decided to kill him by squeezing the neck cartilage. After that, he tipped the body down the mountainside and hoped that it would be counted as an accident.'

'They were both greedy, weren't they?' observed Hugh.

Mara nodded and then rose to her feet with a sigh. 'Now you must all go and see that you have everything ready for your journeys to your homes tomorrow,' she said. 'Nuala, will you wait for me? I'll be with you in about ten minutes, but first I must write up the events in my casebook.'

'The tale of dreadful deeds of murder, mayhem and of treachery, dark and vile,' said Shane, quoting from one of the ancient poets, and she allowed him to have the last word.

When they had all gone out noisily, joking and laughing, Mara went to the wooden press, took out the bound book of

vellum sheets, dipped her goose quill into the ink of bitter gall
and wrote:

I, Mara, Brehon of the Burren, and then she stopped. She still
felt rather shaky when she remembered how close she had
been to losing her husband by her failure to solve this murder
quickly. She stared out of the window. How could she have
been so stupid as to miss so many clues?

But spring was in the air, the first swallow of the year had
darted past the window, the apple trees budded, her baby son
was growing strong and tall and her husband, King Turlough,
was alive and well.

Mara picked up her pen again, smiling to herself as it moved
fluently along the pages until at the end she wrote with a
flourish:

Si finis bonus est, totum bonum erit.

All's well that ends well, she thought as she walked across
the law school enclosure to find Nuala and to tell her that her
master at Thomond, the great physician Donogh O'Hickey,
wanted his apprentice back so much that he was sending his
son, Donogh Oge O'Hickey, to collect her tomorrow morning.
Perhaps this might be the dawning of a new spring for the
girl who was as dear to her as her own daughter.

CPSIA information can be obtained at www.ICGtesting.com
Printed in the USA
BVOW071333020712

294167BV00002B/1/P